Knee-Deep in Wonder

METROPOLITAN BOOKS

Henry Holt and Company   New York

Knee-Deep in Wonder

· A NOVEL ·

APRIL REYNOLDS

Metropolitan Books
Henry Holt and Company, LLC
Publishers since 1866
115 West 18th Street
New York, New York 10011

Metropolitan Books™ is a registered
trademark of Henry Holt and Company, LLC.

Library of Congress Cataloging-in-Publication Data

Reynolds, April.
    Knee-deep in wonder / April Reynolds.
        p.   cm.
    ISBN 0-8050-7346-9
    1. Women—Arkansas—Fiction.   2. African American
women—Fiction.   3. African American families—Fiction.
4. Funeral rites and ceremonies—Fiction.   5. Arkansas—Fiction.
I. Title.

PS3618.E588R48 2003
813'.6—dc21   2003051180

Henry Holt books are available for special
promotions and premiums. For details contact:
Director, Special Markets.

Designed by Paula Russell Szafranski

Printed in the United States of America

1   3   5   7   9   10   8   6   4   2

To my father

Memory believes before knowing remembers.

—WILLIAM FAULKNER, *Light in August*

Knee-Deep in Wonder

1

AUTUMN IN ARKANSAS flaunts only its absence; a broken promise, it's the worst of summers called by another name. Sullen September heat causes yellow jasmines and bell-flowers to pant for mercy, the reek of their dying scent as loud as a scream. Buildings bulge with wet heat, and children turned out-of-doors by well-meaning mothers wilt in their front yards or search for shade beneath pecan trees. Even language melts on the tongue. Sentences slur, words gasp for breath in the mouth. Howdy takes days to say. Like death, the autumn heat is inescapable.

It crawled up the woman's skirt as she stepped out of the airplane at Pine Bluff. Her once crisply ironed green dress turned limp and clung to her thighs as she walked past the only baggage claim in the Pine Bluff airport toward the Greyhound ticket booth. And I pick corduroy, she thought, pulling at her sleeve. She felt her collar-length hair curling into a bird's nest from the humidity. Her crayon-brown legs taking long strides, she approached the bus depot directly outside the airport's double doors, licking at the sweat mustache sprouting on her upper lip. "Excuse me. When does the next bus leave for Stamps?" Her voice sounded strong despite the heat.

"That's a thirty-minute wait. But we got a little bench over to the side for folks to sit." The bus attendant pointed to a slab of shadow.

Her gaze followed his arm. "I don't see a bench."

He stepped away from the booth. "Over yonder," he said, a small smile on his lips. "Give me your name and I'll call you when the bus come on."

"Helene. Helene Strickland. And thank you." She turned away from the booth, her wooden sandals clicking lightly on the sidewalk. The metal awning that jutted away from the building would no more provide respite from the sun than a leaky bucket hold water. She stood in the shadow and because of the sudden darkness barely saw them—six or seven lean black men huddled just beyond the bench, wearing the uniform of mechanics: loose green shirts with matching pants. Two squatted on their haunches while the rest stood, each with one leg braced against the dark wall. They watched her approach, their eyes winking. Appreciative but restrained, their eyes drank in the swell of leg between her narrow ankles and dimpled knees.

She stopped for a moment, uncertain. They're just eating lunch, calm down, she thought, as she looked at the aluminum foil and apple cores strewn on the ground. Brown paper bags rolled down like stockings sat in a heap in front of them.

When she came near the bench, their low hissing swallowed her up. "Big-leg gal, come here. Come here. Come on, little bit. Baby girl." The two sitting down opened their legs suddenly and then barked laughter. "Juicy baby. Juicy." Their whispers, sweet and urgent, came from mouths that didn't seem to move at all. The toothpicks and Kool king cigarettes jutted from their lips, motionless; their faces so still Helene wondered if she was really hearing anything at all. Her doubt surged as she listened to the murmuring. "Big-legged gal. Come here, big-legged gal. Let me give you something." The voices seemed to escape from the wall behind them. She crept closer, her hands fluttering, smoothing her dress down around her thighs and knees, her collar no longer just wilted but wet with sweat. Damp air curled her pressed hair. She sat, coughed lightly, and fished in her purse for cigarettes. Helene ducked her head into her palm, out of habit, to shield the sputtering flame from nonexistent wind. As the cigarette came to life and Helene breathed in deeply, the whispers grew louder. "Where you going? Can I come with you? Come on, big-legged gal." But Helene ignored them and dove again into her purse, pulling out a letter. She plunged into its contents, into her mother's rambling words.

My girl,
Done cleaned this house bottom to roof. And I come
cross this little thing that only can belong to some baby,
when I was washing out the—

But she couldn't stay with the letter, since what had been whispers rose just shy of regular speech. Constant, beseeching, the voices looped around Helene's concentration, choking off her train of thought. She looked up from her lap, turned toward the young men, and did the unforgivable: she smiled. A woman's smile that conveyed *Thank you, but no thank you,* with a blast of teeth. The flattery that had accompanied her all the way to the bench abruptly stopped, leaving an ache of silence. The two men who sat on their heels stood and the taller one looked right at Helene. His inert face finally moved. Brown lips parted and Helene saw a white gleam. "Twat," he said softly and spat carefully, aiming at the bare spot between his feet.

She half stood, caught in a stumble, falling over her unsteady feet, hardly hearing the bus attendant. "Miss Helene," he called out. "Miss Helene?" Her wooden sandals tapped out her path as she turned back for one more look at the clutter of men, but already they had shuffled away. "Miss Helene, you back there?"

"Has the bus come?" She threw her burning cigarette on the ground.

"It's early today," the attendant said. Perhaps, if Helene hadn't tripped the way she had, out of sight of those brown lips lifting, sneering; perhaps if she hadn't still been chewing on the word *twat*, almost physically trying to rub away the sting, she would have seen it coming—the attendant's gummy smile laced with curiosity, the bus ticket held just out of her reach. But fresh back in the South, she fell head-long into the inevitable conversation, drowning in its words. "Knew some Stricklands in Georgia. You one of them?" The smile grew as the attendant, still holding her ticket, walked away to stand behind the ticket booth.

Helene followed him. "No, I don't know anyone in Georgia." She reached for her ticket but the man turned away, his hands dashing beneath the counter as if he were looking for something.

"Eastman, Georgia?"

"No."

"Barely sound like you from the South, girl. Where you from?" His hand surfaced from beneath the counter without her ticket.

"I live in Washington, D.C."

"Naw, baby. I mean, where your people?" She heard her own private ugliness wrapped in comfortable talk.

"Uh, listen. I'm in a bit of a rush. Could you give me my ticket? I can't board the bus without it. Thank you."

Again his hand darted under the counter, and he reluctantly handed over her pass. "Don't mind me. I just—"

"I won't," she muttered, yanking the ticket out from his fingers.

Helene got on the bus and the door closed behind her in a muted whoosh. "Hello there, little lady," the driver said, as she passed his wide grin. Not until she watched Fordyce's textile plants race alongside the bus did she reach inside her purse again. The conversation with the attendant and the confrontation with the men under the depot's awning still pinched. "Southern ugliness," Helene said quietly to the empty seat beside her. And that's not all that's ugly around here, she thought, as she looked out the window. Factories making transportation equipment rose from lakes of asphalt, meat processing and leather plants gave way to long stretches of forest that every now and then were interrupted by soybean and rice farms.

When the bus reached Camden, Helene's hand was still stroking the closed letter inside her purse. How did she know my address? Unlike the cache she kept in a trunk at her uncle's house, this letter, arriving at her apartment in Washington, was only two weeks old. Helene had opened it but hadn't read all through, afraid that old childhood desires would flare. Queen Ester, Helene's mother, had put her daughter out before she could hold her head up; never mind the story Helene had heard about her mother wanting her to live in a better place, that Queen Ester had left Helene in Aunt Annie b's arms and then crouched to the ground in a wash of tears as she cried out, "This mine, it's my baby girl!" Helene didn't believe any of it, because if that were true, she thought, as she strummed her fingers on the bus window, Mama wouldn't have turned me away so many times since then. Her mother was a hand held up before Helene—large, final, allowing nothing to pass. All she could see were the faint lines etched in the palm, complicated yet soothing.

So, no, she hadn't read more than the first two sentences of her mother's letter, not quite ready to lift the scab of a barely healed wound. But that changed when her uncle Ed called two days ago and told her Annie b had dropped to the floor and not gotten back up. She had fallen in the kitchen with a plate in her hand, sucking her teeth, Helene's uncle said, "Like she was trying to tell the floor to mind and it pulled her on down just for ugly's sake." Uncle Ed had come in from the yard and seen her folded under the sink. "You get on up, b. Just get on up," he'd said. Only then, after Ed's call, did she read the rest of her mother's letter, beating back old hurt when she saw the second page was a grocery list: bananas, peas (frozen), milk, bacon. And at the bottom, her mother's words marching on the paper: *You come, hear me?*

Now on the bus, as it entered Magnolia, she pulled the letter out, placing it on her lap. The pages fell open of their own accord. This time she didn't bother to read. Wasn't her father gone, her grandmother passed on soon after, and her mother . . . well, shit, who knew? She didn't need a letter to tell her all that. She fingered the paper's edge, looking out the window again. Now there was just her uncle, fading right before her eyes, although she wouldn't actually see this until he opened his front door. For now, she watched the Arkansas wilderness fly past, and like the letter in her lap, memory fell open, like a sleeping mouth.

Helene had spent her life swirling around the edges of Lafayette County, Queen Ester's county. Taken to Dallas and then to Heber Springs, Arkansas, Helene, by the age of four, knew that all the front doors she walked through were never home. Aunt Annie b, Uncle Ed, and Helene stayed in places just long enough for Annie b to plant maple trees in front yards, put basil, thyme, and rosebushes into the ground out of season, forever limp and wilting despite all her coaxing and cursing. The constant moving Ed put them through was marked by the trail of unfinished gardens Annie b left in her wake.

Edward Taylor was an insurance salesman, peddling home and health policies for twenty-three dollars a year. Parceled and divided, payments were not even two dollars a month, "And for that, that child of yours can get to a hospital and get well if she ever get sick," Uncle Ed would say over the dinner table, recounting what he told potential customers. "And what they say? What they say, my baby girl?" he asked, looking up at Helene from his plate, and at six years old she could mock a voice full of tired sass: "Just give me the burial policy, anything else just a curse." Ada, Oklahoma; Colby, Kansas; Monroe, Louisiana; places that were on the brink,

as Uncle Ed said, close enough to prosperity that the towns-
people could hold out their tongues to feel glasses of instant
lemonade and lawn chairs coming their way. McCool, Mississippi; Best, Texas; Floyd, New Mexico. But despite new post
offices and the opening of a second bank, there was never a
chicken in every pot. Finally, by the age of thirteen, Helene
realized that they weren't moving to towns on the edge of
affluence (Ed was thirty-forty years late without knowing it),
but to places that had just peaked. By the time Helene's family arrived on the four-lane interstate highway, the citizens
of any given town had grown tired of hoping for better and
were wary of anyone giving guarantees.

So it was little wonder that Ed's insurance company never
really got off the ground. His pledge—that if anything went
awry there'd be money to cover it—seemed too good to be
true. People's suspicious natures affected both Ed's business
and Helene's young life. She was the child whose dresses had
been bought from the sickness and death of others, and
though her presence never stirred up real hatred—no hair of
hers was stolen and burnt in the flame of red candles, no one
spat over his shoulder when she walked by—Helene was
treated with careful negligence. Children avoided her because,
plucked and placed every six months, she gave off the heady
smell of a dying flower, too bright and colorful to belong to
third grade. Children were wary of her too-generous offers:
"You can take all my sandwich, I ate before I left the house."
Loud laughter that should have been only a small snicker
made them doubt their sharp wit. Their rejection didn't really
matter, since Helene was never in one place long enough to
stop being a stranger. Instead, she moved, always just beyond
Lafayette County. Helene's life took on the shape of a clock.
Uncle Ed would set them down in the middle of the short

hand and then take them to the tip of the long hand, and Queen Ester was always the little knob at the center.

At eighteen, Helene tried to leave the clock behind, flinging herself into Spelman College, where she learned to press her hair and talk on the phone with confidence about the late work of Jackson Pollock. Following graduation she grabbed a bus to Seattle and hitched a ride to Palo Alto, trying hard not to stare at the white girls with short skirts and no panties who could talk and smoke cigarettes at the same time, each floating word visible in the air. But Helene knew that she was still sitting somewhere on time's long hand, that the face of the clock in which she lived had no perimeter.

Off and on she would come back to Uncle Ed and Aunt Annie b, to Stamps, Arkansas, where they had retired. She trickled into their lives with letters from Little Rock, where she was a nurse's aide, then with a handful of phone calls from Jonesboro and later Washington, D.C., until, finally, Helene in full landed in a heap at their doorstep, stiff from a four-hour bus ride. She readied a soft smile with just a bit of teeth to show grief, sympathy, and love all at the same time. But her smile failed when Uncle Ed opened the door. Annie b's death had chipped away at the traces of youth; a shock of gray now crowned her uncle's head. In the fall of 1976, Helene realized she was surrounded by the old, the dead, and the dying.

2

SWOLLEN AND BROODING, a mother-to-be spent nights dreaming of the palest brown baby boys skipping through trees, their hair bouncing free of tangles. She knew the destiny of mulatto children: to sing "Them Golden Slippers" with James Bland or learn how to play slide banjo for The South Before the War minstrels. She coveted that life. And she thought these things because she believed in the Bible, coaxed along by ignorance and her grandmother's interpretations. Negroes were damned, descendants of Cain, not to be mistaken for the chosen ones, the Israelites. Notwithstanding all their oppression, the Israelites had legions upon legions of philosophers and poets. Or perhaps the Negro was not even the descendant of Cain but simply the mark, the smudge—God's smearing of Cain's forehead or cheek—

since Cain, cursed or not, was not only destined to build cities but had been touched by God of His own volition. So Negroes couldn't even claim Cain as their ancestor; the cities did not belong to them. Maybe they were the descendants of Esau, who'd sold his birthright to Jacob for a bowl of soup and then God and Jacob laughed. Yes, the Negro was the truly damned, without a glimmer of respite or hope. So she prayed that the seed in her belly was light, because a black one . . . She shuddered at the dark thought.

Two months later, with her knees pulled up, the woman held the tiny baby. She sat up slightly to pass the newborn back into the arms of a midwife, who then laid the child slightly above the mother's crotch. The midwife, who had grasped and pulled the tiny woolly head, spoke softly to the new mother, "Look more like you, wouldn't you say?" She smiled at the woman, whose lifted knees shaded part of her face.

"No, wouldn't say; that thing look nothing like me," the woman whispered back, angry not only because in the end she had made exactly what she was, but because all her plotting had been for naught—months of lemons and fish oil, the calculated submission to cravings, eating out-of-season melon dipped in salt. You turn out too black to belong to me spite all I did, she thought, while panting out the afterbirth. As her belly had grown, she'd envisioned the creamy blend she was sure she'd produced. It would have been a new beginning, a life marked with questions like, "Where y'all get that baby from?" while she would smile demurely and reply, "Oh, he's mine." She wanted a child that would lift her and her husband out of their poverty with his beauty; scores of back doors would open for them, and inside minstrel shows would wait. Their child could have played the ragtime drums with

Buddy Bolden in New Orleans or sung with Willie "The Lion" Smith.

Raising her arm, she ran her hand over her own features—the wide full lips, the splayed nose—and sighed. She stared at her baby's face. Deep dark-brown eyes held a sadness the woman believed only she alone possessed. Naw, she thought, you ain't seen the down, down part of sorrow. That got my name on it.

A soft rap sounded at the door. The young woman, her hair damp and knotted around her head, moved her knee and saw the midwife's mouth stir, chewing words, but she couldn't hear what was being said, her panting eclipsing any other sound. Outside the door was her husband, panting too, his sweat pouring into his stiff collar because he heard nothing inside the small bedroom. He knocked again. "I told you, that's your man," the midwife said, pointing behind her.

"What?"

"The door, gal. You hear?"

"I hear it."

"Well?"

"What?"

"You want me to get it or don't you?"

"Get it."

"I asked you that before and then you go off and act like you don't hear me say what I just got through saying."

The man prepared to knock at the door a third time, but then he heard the soft even voice of the midwife and his wife's light reply followed by laughter chasing their quick-spoken words, as if they were sitting around a worn deck of cards and not a newborn child. He let his hand drop as he heard a delicate rustling. The door creaked open.

"Well?" he said.

"A baby girl," said the midwife.

"Oh."

"Black as tar." Her lips opened wide then. Toothless. He saw nothing but her brown gums. What he'd heard before hadn't been laughter but harsh cackling. "And she like to kill it, too, going still like she did when I told her she got to push." The husband nodded. "You know what the first thing she told me?" the midwife continued. "First thing out of her mouth?" She stuck her pinkie in her ear, pulled it out, and cleaned the wax refuse with her thumbnail. " 'I didn't want no gal, neither.' Ain't that something?" Both the midwife and the husband looked at the young woman in the bed.

The wife stared back at her husband and said to the midwife, "You get on out that door and get it off me."

"Why come? It's yours."

"You heard me, get out the door and get it off." The midwife, leaving the door ajar, shuffled back to the bed and scooped the child in her arms.

"Now what?"

"Take it, and you and him get on out." The woman turned away from them, lifting her knees higher still, trying to move away from the afterbirth that grew cold between her legs. "And you pay her with what we got." She contemplated the wall while she spoke to her husband.

The midwife stooped and picked up the basket she had brought with her. "I guess you can clean yourself up?" she asked, but the woman said nothing. "Sally in Our Alley" played its tune in her head while she fixed her eyes on the banjo case that sat in the corner. She heard the bedroom door bang shut and the slow onset of murmured voices in the front room. In the midst of the husband's bargaining (No, planting seed during cotton season is too much, he said, how about putting sheet metal on the hole on your roof?) came the old woman's swift glare surveying the small house, the uneven table, the bottom broke out of chairs (No, I don't think you can manage my roof). Absorbed in the wife's unhappiness (no minstrel show awaited them, the child was too dark for black-face; no one would ever ask where they got the girl because the answer was obvious), they forgot to name her. When husband and wife remembered three weeks later, the wife thought long and said finally, "Just don't name her at all."

But the man didn't take her at her word and gave his wife names to ponder: Mary Beth, Ruth Ann. He looked for some-thing to light up her face, watching for something to dawn in her and say, Yes, that's right, I like that. Eve just went to the well; Ester went to boss for seed; You better get Abigail some kind of dress. The child thought her flux of names was due to the growth of her feet and the surge of her height until her father told her different, and then she too watched and waited.

Neither of them had to wait for long. Perhaps they should have known, if not the child then at least the father, who woke in the night to hear his wife muttering, "Two dollars for the seed—yes, Lord—two dollars for that seed and boss man charge us five and a quarter; then to rent out them supplies is well nigh ten dollars a year, and Lord know we could hitch out to Athens and get it used for half that." He must have noticed and wondered at the new attention his wife gave to hemming, how she went out of her way to take in extra work. Yes, he must have known, since when she finally told him in the middle of the night, her hand clawed around his shoulder shaking him fiercely awake, he didn't seem surprised at all, just concerned. I can see what she fixing to say fore she do. Now here she come, lying to me like I been blind all these weeks and can't see a thing. Still, she shook him while she whispered hoarsely, "Hey, man, get on up. I got to talk. You hear? I got to talk."

He rose to his knees and caught her about the waist. "What is it now?"

She began, not realizing that she spoke as if they had been talking all along. Her voice was stripped of all charm; she was desperate, even though she didn't have to be since the husband had already been wondering where she kept that bag of tightly hemmed camisoles, unlaced bloomers, and the only pair of shoes they owned. "I been thinking. We gone to owe boss man fifty-two dollars at the end of this season, and I know that tween the two of us we only gone make forty-six. That's if I take in some sewing and all that."

"You woke me on up to tell me how much we owe boss man?"

"You listen. I reckon we been at this for damn near ten years." She paused, breathing heavily. "Well?"

"Well, what?"

"Ain't that right? Ain't we been here nigh ten years?"

"I reckon so."

"I know it. I know it." Her eyes lit, as if she had caught him admitting something he shouldn't have. "And fore then, your people had this same shake of land and boss man passed on to you all they owed him."

"You think I don't know that?"

"I know you do. You just listen." She shook him again, hard, on the arm. "With all that past money and the money we owe boss man too—well, that's well nigh one hundred and thirteen dollars. You know that, man?"

"Well, I reckon; I ain't thought on it that much, but that seem bout right."

"Now, how is we suppose to get out from under that kind of money?" She pulled back from him, her eyes triumphant, since they both knew that one hundred thirteen dollars might as well have been three thousand. They never could pay off boss man. Her hand moved from his arm to his lap. Both remembered that their daughter lay in the front room, unaware that her mother dreamed of numbers that smelled like money.

For a moment they said nothing, each waiting for the other to bare grievous teeth. But then he whispered, "I never wanted no baby in the first place."

"Well, you got your way, cause she sho ain't no baby no more."

"Still—"

"You shut it." She stood up abruptly. "I can't take it like this no more." She stopped again as if an idea had come upon her mid-flight, but the husband knew better. He saw a staged pause. "New Orleans or San Francisco. Get to see Billy Birch and Mr. Cotton, you know. Maybe . . . we could start there, and get a boat to some island. You think on it. If it's a no, I'll leave you too." He almost smiled, since this was what he'd expected as soon as she woke him.

"You can't leave me. Where you gone go without me?"

"What you trying to say? You ain't coming?"

"We got a baby girl."

"You done looked at her? She ain't no baby, bout as tall as me." She walked away from her husband, her bare feet soundless as she paced, though he heard the soft whisk of her dress. He realized she might as well be talking about a shirt she owned, too frayed for wear and now useless.

"And?"

"And what? This all you want? Living like this, with

grease brown paper for windows? This all you want? That's all?"

"You know it ain't."

"Well, that's all she can give us. Can't crawl from up under the debt we's in cause the boss man done fixed the books. That's all she give us." She stopped in front of her husband.

"I don't want no black tar-baby girl. Didn't even want no girl, and look what I got. I wanted a son to play banjo for the shows in Missouri. Why I got to take with me something I didn't want in the first place?" Both the husband and wife had raised their voices, and their daughter, tall but slight on the thin pallet in the front room, had shivered awake and trembled when she heard her mother. "I'm telling you now. First space I see, I'm gone."

And she was. Vanished in the middle of the night through the front door, that bag he knew all along was stuffed with camisoles and their only pair of shoes clutched at her side. Soon the husband left too. Except before he disappeared he tried to explain his upcoming absence. In the same way the wife was gripped with the thought of ever-rising debt, the husband was blinded by his own explanations. The week before his departure, he spoke to his daughter with words knotted up in question marks, rubbing her shoulders and head gently. In the middle of telling her that he had to go find her mother, his child peppered in, "When y'all coming back?" and "Why can't I come?" although she had heard her mother's whispering that not only was she too black, she wasn't even the right sex. The father nodded mindlessly at his daughter's fear, dreaming all the while of black men carrying parasols to shade themselves from the sun, their hands sticky and sweet from overripe cantaloupe. The girl saw her father's faraway gaze as he spoke to her, so when he crept though the window a week later she knew he wasn't coming back either.

Orphaned, she went from tenant to tenant on the farm, tall enough to see the way old Negro women held their mouths when they spoke about her mother. Though they did not realize it, they hated her, this child who helped gather cabbage and tomatoes in their small gardens and ran errands and gossip from house to house. They watched her suspiciously as she stooped to pick up stray things, noting the way her long legs gaped wide despite the fact she wore a dress. "Trouble just waiting on her," they murmured, watching her too-easy laughter, her draping arms as she caressed their children. "Look at her taking my baby and kissing her up under the neck. Don't tell me I'm living to see it."

Anyone that carefree after not only the mother but also the father left her was a child that trouble would snatch up as soon as it stopped by. All the women thought it was just a matter of time before the mother's haughty slyness would visit the child. But they let her stay in their homes for two years, her name changing as she moved from house to house. She was bestowed with the names of dead daughters and sons, lost husbands, cherished wives who had died in childbirth, till finally, despite her age, they put her out of their homes and their lives, for fear that, when the habits of the mother showed themselves in the child, their own children would become infected by proximity. So she became a roaming hand for picking cotton, until she turned seventeen and Sweets found her.

He was a drifter, a twenty-year-old man with no luggage or steady job. By 1914, he had traveled from Tennessee to as far as Oklahoma and Arizona, claiming to anyone within arm's reach that he had taught the great Bill Pickett every-thing he knew. "Bulldogging? Who you think taught Dusky Demon that little trick? I let him take credit. Myself, I didn't want to be bothered." Every grandmother within throwing distance knew he was no good. But with no people of her own, who could have told that to a seventeen-year-old girl?

She heard him first, whistling lightly in the full-grown corn; the sound, practiced and swift, pricked her ear and she stood up, spreading her arms through the tall stalks to get a better look. Then she saw him, walking slowly toward her, his jacket tucked under his arm, and the corn seemed to move out of his way: some idle, callous, free black man. With no one's apron to hide behind, no low whisper full of caution, she liked his soft laughter and easy way. And Sweets did what none of them had ever thought to do—he asked her name. He strolled closer and she dropped the basket she carried, swaying at his nearness. When he stood only a pace away, the jacket still under his arm, he sang her hello. Her laughter made him bolder and he took her hand, rubbing her thumb. "Who is you?"

She thought and thought, unsure of what to say, waiting for him to see the blank space of her dilemma and put in the name of an old lover.

"Girl, you hear me? What's your name?"

She looked past his shoulder, almost panting, *Lord, Lord, Lord*, waiting for an answer that would not break her heart or her back. Then she heard it. Like a ripe peach ready to drop, the name fell into her lap, beautiful and free of soft spots. The sound of her name almost made her knees buckle. "Liberty, my name Liberty."

They left the tenant farm soon after. Liberty didn't belong to anyone, so there was no one to ask whether he could take

20

her away; those old black mothers and grandmothers were glad to see her go, knowing that trouble had finally caught up with her. And that name (she told everyone in one day— every house, every field hand knew her name), the name that mocked them all and their predicament, was too much to bear. "She gone tell the wrong fella that name and get knocked out." But Liberty didn't hear their worry or their scorn, already in love with her Sweets, her honeyed man. Those old women were right about trouble catching up with her but wrong about the timing. It would take more than two decades to arrive, creeping up on her so softly she wouldn't notice it at all.

Eleven years after she had left Georgia with Sweets, Liberty stood in the open doorway of her house trying to step around her anger. She explained to her six-year-old daughter, last night's fight with Sweets had really begun as they journeyed to Lafayette County. "I reckon we was deep in wander fore I know Sweets ain't got no place in particular we had to get to. Sometime I think I never should of left with him in the first place, cause Lord know I can do bad enough by myself. Yes, well, I reckon I don't need no help with that. We was traveling in a circle of twenty tents, and every day we move to a different place. No old mamas with they set mouths looking at how I stoop to catch something. There we was moving long with the railroad, all them men hacking down anything in they way. We move from town to town— Augusta, Montgomery, Jackson, Beaumont—following the rails we make. Your daddy level the roadbed in front of the rails, working the job from sun up till sun dark; then he get at gambling his whole week pay with dice.

"Your mama now ain't like your mama then. I wasn't no mama at all, then. Two years pass, and I didn't say a word, cause that son-of-a-bitch daddy——" She winced slightly. "Well, I reckon I still was loving that low laugh of his and them soft hands. And maybe we could of stayed that way—you know, chasing the railroad."

She stopped for a moment and caught her breath. Images floated in front of her, of eating cold beans out of tin pails hunched and aching over their food. Liberty swallowed hard at the memory. She remembered learning how to cook, how to take care of the ailing, and how to read in those five years. One of the wives, Sue Ann Johnson—the only one who still took her hospitality toward the end, despite Sweets stealing away her husband's weekly pay—spent every free moment spoon-feeding Liberty the New Testament: *The kingdom of heaven is like unto leaven which a woman took, and hid in three measures of meal, till the whole was leavened.* And when Liberty asked why three, why put a number into anything like a measure of meal, Sue Ann snorted at her ignorance and replied, "Cause everything bout three. We live in threes: Mama, Daddy, babies. Even Jesus live in three: God, Son, Holy Ghost. You see? Might get passed over two times, but third time you might have a shot at whatever you hankering after. That ain't no mistake either, cause three is a blessed number, blessed by God. Three blessed, charmed, and whole. See? You can't even talk about three without giving three words to it." Liberty had let that advice settle on her, suddenly envious that Sue Ann had both husband and baby boy. Sue Ann resumed the lesson, but Liberty only half listened, now worried about the twoness of her and Sweets. Just one more and we'd be whole.

Liberty resumed her story. "Five years sweep on by and, well, I didn't even know it, cause in a way we was always in the same place. All them men working on one thing, stirring up everything within a hand's reach. Like we move in a cloud, and we go into town, and folk whispering they knew we was coming cause they saw the cloud miles off. I spose I was might proud that we was the ones caused all that commotion. See, your daddy...well, I loved your daddy for as long as anybody could of loved him, buying ribbons and tying them on anything I thought his eyes would get a notion to fall on. But love like that bound to wear out, and sure nough it did.

"Sweets was gambling, but I didn't know how much, cause your mama was innocent back then. Just like you is now, but I didn't have no mama like me to set me right. Any mama worth they salt would of seen Sweets coming through that corn and told him to get on. But I didn't have no mama like you got. Then Sweets was doing that dice, and I didn't see a thing—too busy trying to keep house and tying ribbons on anything I laid my hands on. Yes, Lord, I sure was innocent. Didn't see nothing till it was right up on me. All them men stop looking me in the face, wouldn't take my hospitality. I thought it was the other womens put them up to it. But it wasn't. It was Sweets. He was whopping all of them so bad they took it out on me. Sweets got so he was climbing out of the tent at night, gathering them all up and making them play.

"We was just out of Texas and I wanted to settle down, and here I was trying to slide up soft to Sweets and make him stay where we was. Well, he must of seen me coming, cause I only had to ask him one time. I didn't even get half way into what I was saying fore he say yes. There I was trying to push at him." Liberty suddenly mimicked her younger self. " 'What's gone happen when these here tracks run out? You think they gone hand you some kind of job just cause you kept with them since Georgia?'

"I spose we got off that rail just in time. All that money swollen in Sweets's pocket and them men looking at him, knowing they got goosed. Only so long you can get away with that. I was having you then, and we jumped off the rail and bought this land with all that money Sweets got off them men."

She paused again and lifted her hand to her forehead. "I spose even then I was innocent. Cause when I look back, it's a wonder I didn't know. All that money like a rock in his pants, and it never went down. We was buying everything I could think of. Here I was, making sure we got all the windows the way I want and the floor laid down just so and I never wondered where Sweets got all that money from. Like he had it in a trunk somewhere I didn't know about. Cause after we left the rail, I never did see him do no more gambling. He went off to get supplies and come back drunk and singing, but I didn't mind, cause he always come back with them supplies."

She laughed then, a mirthless sound that escaped from her mouth and tumbled into her next words. "Seem like every piece of clapboard we put up was a fight. And it ain't like Sweets had a notion of what he wanted, he just know he don't want it my way. Somebody should of told me how mean a little man can be. Then just when the house bout done you come, and by then I know it was just a matter of time. Cause Sweets was prowling, looking for a fight. I can't make biscuit worth a damn, far as he concerned. I spose Sweets was thinking I was the one keeping him from his money. With the house all done ain't no need for him to go off for supplies like he been saying."

Liberty pressed her strong hand on her daughter's head. "There you was, and Sweets act like he didn't want to be bothered with me nohow. The more I be with you, the more mad he get. Telling me how to be mama. I told him right then, 'You be the daddy and I be the mama.' "

She kept talking, her words only mindless chatter to the small child at her side. Her daughter moved slightly, curious to see her mother's face as she spoke. Only Liberty's heavy hand forced her daughter's eyes to the floor. Nevertheless, Queen Ester heard it, almost saw it: her mother's fumbling. "He was the one, not me." Liberty's voice tilted upward, trying to lay blame for their last fight on Sweets, the fight that made him tumble out their front door in the middle of the night, leaving it ajar.

He had snuck up behind her while she was dressing Queen Ester. "That child gone be your undoing." Liberty didn't hear a word he said, her lips pressed firmly against her child's belly. "Liberty, you hear me?" She turned her head then, a small smile on her lips. "You can't keep kissing on her like that."

"Why come? Ain't she mine?"

"She damn near seven years old."

"She still a baby." Liberty dipped her head to kiss Queen Ester's naked stomach.

Sweets caught her chin, stopping her. "You quit on that, you hear?"

She had been sitting, but now with her chin caught in his

hand she rose, throwing a tall shadow over her husband. "You let loose, Sweets." She said her words calmly, as if she were telling a dog to sit. "Just let loose."

"Ain't nothing of mine gone talk to me like that." His hand whirled back, only to be caught by Liberty's own fast hand.

"I ain't nothing of yours. Who told you that?" She laughed, an unexpected sound to both their ears, her laughter swollen with anger.

"You hush up now."

"Ain't." Her hand let go of his, quickly pulling back to push him.

"You ain't big enough for that," Sweets said, struggling under the blunt push of her hand.

"But ain't I though? Ain't I?" She laughed again and kicked him, striking his left knee. "Who ain't big enough for what round here? Telling me what to do with my own baby." Her foot rose again, striking the empty air. Sweets, hurt but quick, had scrambled to the open bedroom door and stood inside its frame. He looked at his wife and her gaping laughing mouth. She had grown four inches since he had known her.

"Now I ain't gone get tore up in my own house."

"You just keep on out of my way. Or the next time you take ahold of my chin, I ain't gone let you get away." He heard the menace in her voice and said nothing. But later, in the middle of the night, he left, not taking anything with him except the bulge in his pocket. In his haste, Sweets left the front door open. Now, Liberty stood before the door, knowing that her husband was not coming back. That make three of them, she thought: Mama, Daddy, and Sweets. Two out the door and one out the window. Well, don't that beat all.

———

Liberty swallowed a knot of hurt. "Niggers got to live they life in threes, I know that much. So I spose leaving and Liberty is through. Cause ain't nothing of mine gone ever get left by me." Although she had not paused, her voice had stopped fumbling. Queen Ester lifted her head, watching her mother's face. "You gone stay with me forever and ever. No child of mine gone have to kiss some baby only to get slapped away."

Close the door, close it, the small child thought, looking at the anger in her mother's face, not knowing that she too felt something, a displaced fury that should have landed on Sweets. But with his absence she aimed it at the door, which seemed to look not only thrown open but mocking. At last, Queen Ester pulled away from her mother's hand and said slowly, "Ain't we ought to close the door?"

Liberty smiled at her daughter's full-grown voice. Mama and baby both, she thought, reaching for the knob.

"There goes your son-of-a-bitch daddy," she said, as she locked the door.

3

FOR THREE DAYS, Helene and Uncle Ed searched for addresses, found lost insurance policies, and put names to faces. Uncle Ed's house ballooned, full of murmuring church ladies who hissed softly between their teeth because there was no plastic on the couch or doilies on the coffee table. They skirted round freestanding tables with their thumbs pushed out, testing for dust. "A man's house," they whispered, as the daughter who was not the daughter put iced tea in their hands and received mountains of potato salad and tuna casserole. Helpless, Helene searched their faces, looking for the blank spots in which to place a smile.

She made sure to stay close to Uncle Ed. Together, their hands reached for Annie b's basil seeds and old shoes, since they wanted to clutch at more than their sorrow. They tried not to observe themselves as they nodded with grace and composure at women Aunt Annie b had hated. Twelve hundred dollars later, she lay in her open coffin, on view so her close friends and sisters could gasp and see the ill-chosen lipstick she wore and the new dress Ed and Helene had had to buy because Annie b owned only Levi's. Everyone stared at the stitches showing through the bright pink lipstick, there to hold her lips together; the coroner had had to break her jaw because she had died with her mouth open.

"I think the funeral home really outdid itself," Helene said, leaving the viewing.

"You right about that." As he spoke, Uncle Ed smoothed down his rumpled tie. "Been so busy with Annie b, ain't had time to ask how you been."

"Oh, you know me. Same as always."

"You still working at that nursing home?"

"Yup."

"Been there—what, three years?"

"Going on four."

"Time sho can get behind you if you let it." They stood together in the parking lot. "Here come Ms. Tilly." An old woman walked toward them.

"Ed, Ms. Annie looked just beautiful."

"Thank you, Ms. Tilly, thank you."

"And I thought her dress was just lovely."

"Thank you, Ms. Tilly." Ed turned to Helene. "You remember my niece, Ms. Tilly?"

"Is that Helene?"

"Yes, ma'am," Helene said.

"Girl, you done got so big. Last time I seen you, you couldn't of been taller than my knee. You turned into a good-looking girl."

"Thank you, Ms. Tilly."

"Don't thank me, baby, thank your mama." Mrs. Tilly laughed into her hand, and Ed watched Helene's face darken.

"I don't want to keep you, Ms. Tilly," Ed said, as he moved farther into the parking lot toward his car.

"Oh, I ain't got to be nowhere. So what you doing now with yourself, Helene?"

"Just the same-old same-old. I work at a nursing home in D.C."

"You got family there?"

"No, just me."

"You ain't married yet?"

"No, no, not yet."

"I got a daughter bout you age. Husband work for the post office. I got three little grandchildren." Ms. Tilly dug into her purse and pulled out a bundle of photos. "That there's Reginald, Tyron, and LaShay. Last year's Christmas."

"Excuse me for cutting you, Ms. Tilly, but we still got some things to tend to back at the house." Ed grabbed Helene's elbow and steered her away. "I'll see you at the funeral, Ms. Tilly," he called out.

Helene and Ed got into the car in silence, though Ed tried to jump-start the conversation. "We got a movie house down the block there. Saw *Shaft* with Annie b couple years back. Remember me telling you about that catfish place, Tin Tin? Right there on your left." But Helene's responses were half-hearted. Ed searched his niece's face as he drove and saw her longing. She wanted mother love, deep and dark as a carpet. Sitting in the car, she was shivering with desire, an open throbbing stretch empty of everything but yearning. Her mother was the pause right before the shudder. Helene wanted her mama. Maybe even her daddy too.

When they pulled into the driveway, Helene said, "Do you still know the way down there?"

Ed slid the car into park and sighed. "Helene."

"Just draw me a map, okay? That's all I'm asking." Before he could answer, Helene hopped out of the car to water the wilting flowers in the yard. She had hummed with purpose since reading Queen Ester's letter and, unlike her previous trips to her mother's house, now she'd had time to plan. While Uncle Ed went inside to collect Aunt Annie b's clothes for the church donation, Helene kicked at the tires of her aunt's 1967 Chevy Impala, checking their air pressure. She got in, cleaned out the passenger seat, and then went through the glove compartment; she even thought of giving the Chevy a coat of Turtle Wax but changed her mind when she reached the back porch and found Annie b's old trunk.

Its groan welcomed her as she opened the lid. She crouched low to collect forgotten evidence: old letters, still in their worn envelopes, that she hadn't read since she was fourteen; a faded photo of her mother and grandmother surrounded by friends in front of their house; a torn page from the Lafayette telephone book that held neither her mother's name nor her grandmother's but the number of the abandoned sawmill where her father, Duck, had worked until he died. She slid them into her pocketbook, these slices of her family's past without her.

Entering the house, Helene hounded her uncle to draw the map to her mother's house, not letting up even though he had shriveled since her aunt's death. The skin of his cheeks and hands was now drawn tightly against pronounced bones, and his stomach, which had once looked like muscle that didn't know when to stop growing, lay slack inside his shirt.

Uncle Ed sat down and etched out a map on a piece of

cardboard, showing his niece how to jump through time and not get lost on the way. "South of Lafayette, east of Canfield, and a ways from the lake they got and you there—there's your mama. Waiting for you, in a manner of speaking.

"There's a walking bridge over Bacaw's Creek. Fore you get there, the road breaks in two. Now, you just take FM493 and you should be there in no time at all." Uncle Ed stared at the sheet of cardboard. "Watch out for FM493, cause you just get that one sign; there ain't gone be nothing else to show you the way." He shook his head. "Just stubborn, you. Anybody else with the kind of want you got in your teeth would of dropped it by now."

"I know it," she said. "I know it." And she grabbed the map from his hand.

Ed accompanied his niece out to the driveway. "You check the tires?" He patted the top of Annie b's Chevy. The car looked shabby. Both fenders were painted with primer and Ed had yet to put on the new muffler he had bought from the mechanic. "Don't get your heart set on your mama."

"I'm not."

"Ain't that what you always said? You know I done always wanted nothing but right for you."

"She's my mother. How could she be anything but right for me?" After hearing the fear in his voice, Helene's next words were smooth and beseeching. "Don't worry, you've got all those ladies to look after you while I'm gone."

"I'm just trying to tell you—"

"This time is different. I'm an adult now." Both remembered the trip he and Helene had made to Queen Ester's ten years ago. Helene had convinced Uncle Ed to drive her out to the house. From the passenger seat, she had watched the shimmer of trees passing and heard Uncle Ed's anxious voice. "You just smile if she don't come out. It take two to make ugly, and I done brought you up better than that." But her mother had let her into the living room, winking, calling Helene names that rang in her ears like ghosts. A Mable in a blue dress, a Morning whom her mother scolded for staying away so long. The past flickered before them, different colors, until Helene reminded her mother she was her daughter and then Queen Ester put her out.

Between the name-calling, Queen Ester had stuck a glass of water in her daughter's hand and Helene told her the things she thought a mother should know, her voice high and wavering while she tried to strike the note that would make Queen Ester give her tea or let her stay for dinner. Uncle Ed had stayed in the car, its purring engine drowning out the country silence. What Helene had to tell took no time, just a quick breath, a short exhale; everything important was said by the time her mother sat in the chair, except Helene wasn't sure she had been heard. Queen Ester had stared at her, waiting till Helene had to catch her breath. In the snippet of soundless air, the mother spat out, "I know something of mine is burning on that stove by now. You just get on." But this time, not only did Helene have Annie b's death but also the letter, its ripe invitation dangling at the end of the page.

"Helene?" Uncle Ed folded his hands over his stomach, his irritation breaking through her memory.

"Yes?"

"Your mama—"

"Those other times ..." she interrupted, then dwindled to

a close. Those other times, she thought, I didn't look so good, my shoes were run over with grass. "Mama's not like that all the time. Don't you remember when——"

"I remember. But your mama turn off and on like a switch."

"Uncle Ed, I know. I've been there." She looked at him over the rim of the open car door. A soft hush settled on them that she quickly broke. "Thank you."

"I just don't want you coming back here looking like a broke heart. Now you got all that old hurt stuffed in your purse. What good is all that gone do?"

"This time she asked for me."

"That come-on could mean just bout anything, coming from your mama. And that don't count for why you want to haul them letters with you."

"I just want to show her I've got them. Every time I go down there I forget."

"You thinking both y'all gone lean over them and make it right?" His voice curled with concern. "She ain't a bad woman, but you got to learn when to leave well enough alone."

"Uncle Ed, it's just this one time more. I just want to know. I want to know it all." Despite herself, she had become angry.

"All of what?" Shame crept into his face.

"All of everything."

"And what good is that gone do you?"

"Where was your father born?"

"Girl, you know all that." Ed looked tired, older than his age, but Helene pushed on.

"Tell me anyway."

"Virginia. Galax, Virginia."

"And your mother?"

"Texas."

"Were they good people?"

"Stop it, girl."

"Were they?"

"You know it."

"That's all I want to know, Uncle Ed. Where my daddy was from and was he among good people."

"I can tell you that."

"I want to know all the things in the middle, too. Can you tell me that?"

"Baby girl." He paused, sweeping his hand over his face. "And when you know all that, what you gone do then?"

She laughed. "Well, I guess I'll get married then." Uncle Ed thought, How somebody can be so grown and not grown at the same time just don't figure to reason. All those memories peeking from her purse, pretending to be salvation.

The morning school bell suddenly rang, hallowed, wailing. Ed watched his niece. Her face turned, trained and alert, her eyes on the children who had just appeared at the end of the block, covered in bright yellow and green jackets. Helene took in a quick breath as the clatter of shoes grew nearer. They peeled past Uncle Ed and Helene—a sea of arrogant children, satchels clapping against their knees. She watched on, helpless, angry, remembering the tight ring of third-grade children singing with brutal mouths, "Ain't got no mama, ain't got no daddy, you twice as ugly, and you hair is nappy."

"Children is a blessing," Uncle Ed said, looking at Helene's lonely face.

"Yeah."

"Bout your mama. Ain't gone be nothing but heartache."

"Yes, well. Let's see how she likes a dose," she said, envisioning Queen Ester's reaction to the news of Annie b's death. Helene slid into the car, wresting the door closed.

She meant her last words to Ed. How would her mother like to live a life satisfied with secrets and bits of stories? Helene remembered once when she tamely searched for her family's history, turning shiny when a couple who visited Uncle Ed claimed to come from Lafayette County and carelessly recalled having a meal at her grandmother's café. The aged and muddied southern voices rose to her memory. "Liberty, you say? Liberty Strickland? Oh, you know Liberty Strickland, Minyas. Died in 'fifty-nine, remember? Taller than a tree, your grandmama was. Oh, come on, Minyas. We went to sermon with the woman for damn near three years. Put the pie down, Minyas. Had that baby girl that was..." And then an uneasy trail into silence. "Your mama was so sweet and kind—Minyas, put that pie down—never did... Well, look at us wearing out the welcome. Come on, Minyas."

Their embarrassed getaway checked Helene's efforts but hadn't stopped her from looking for a nappy head at her college graduation, knowing if she found one she would have called, "Where have you been?" But the only head she saw was Aunt Annie b's—her aunt's hair shaved as short as Uncle Ed's.

The way to Lafayette was crooked and full of treachery. Places in town felt like objects snatched out of a sack and thrown down randomly. Barren churches and convenience stores sat at the dead end of farm market roads. No bank or gas station—the nearest bank in Bradley, the gas station in McKamie—just two general stores built side by side. Roads that seemed to know their way suddenly plunged into trees, only to reappear as backyards full of dead cars: a 1962 Plymouth without the fenders, a '59 Ford Edsel with the trunk folded in on itself like a sheet. Ed's map led Helene to shotgun houses empty of everything except decayed wood planks, a half-eaten tin roof, and a table in the backyard with a cloth held down with cinder blocks. What should have been a one-hour trip was doubled because of the lack of street signs. Helene didn't think it took that long because she lost her way but because Uncle Ed had drawn a map that took her to her mother's house the familiar route, as if she should know Lafayette County by touch, like the lining of her pants pockets.

Twelve backyards later, Helene thought perhaps her uncle had drawn the map the way he himself had stumbled upon her mother's house: as an errand gone awry. His way—tinged and overcome with the urge to have a meal, to look civil, and then go to the bathroom—was what had led him to Queen Ester's, for as far as Helene could tell, not a single house of the eleven she saw was home to a toilet.

And while she herself fought the urge to pee, Helene thought about how she could not ask Queen Ester why they had never fought over having her ears pierced, or over the boy when she was thirteen who was too short, too ugly, just too-too, because the time was gone. And the one question that Helene could ask—Just where were you, Mama?—she could answer herself, and to hear her mother say it would have knocked her down. As a child she had circled around Aunt Annie b, riddling her with questions. "But if she just gone, why don't she come back and take me with her?" Her eight-year-old logic reasoned: I'm so small she wouldn't even know I'm with her. Finally, in desperation, Annie b told her niece the truth: her mother was not traveling the world looking for a place to settle, she was always in the same place, but Helene had to stay with her aunt and uncle just the same. Then Helene had turned to praying, nightly chants that Annie b tried to scour away with chores, but Helene was single-minded. She murmured, knees creaking on the wooden floor, full of eight-year-old desire, I want my mama.

And so she began to talk to God. Soft and sweet, she told him that she too wanted to be sky. Once, Helene had heard a rattling at the curtain, and, mid-conversation she had stopped to see who was there. Helene thought it might be God or, better still, her mother. She went to the window and knelt in front of the glass, putting her hands up to meet her mother's; they would have been touching were it not for the pane. Helene whispered, "Mama is you you? Mama?" But Queen Ester couldn't hear her daughter.

Helene thought her mother must have seen her lips move, because Queen Ester raised her voice and pressed her face tightly against the glass. The distortion frightened Helene so much she took off down the hall and ran crying to her aunt that there was a monster outside her window. Sucking her teeth and looking down at the floor, Annie b said to Helene, "Naw, that's your mama."

Eighteen years ago, but Helene still remembered shaking. Aunt Annie b kissed Helene on the ear and said, "Gone to bed now," but she was licking her eye tooth, so Helene knew Annie b was mad and waited for the howling to start. When Aunt Annie b opened the door, Helene saw her mother standing on tiptoe trying to see beyond her aunt's shoulder. Helene heard her mother mumbling, although now she could hear the embarrassment as well. "How you been, b? Look like you done moved again."

Annie b grabbed Queen Ester by the coat collar to whisper something that was intended to slice her in half. "Can't you be decent?"

And it did. Queen Ester fell back from the porch, kicking up dust, pulling on her hair, and in a scream filled with question marks, she repeated Annie b's last word: "Decent? Decent? Decent?" She ran a curve around the house and Helene fled back to her room. Once inside, she saw Queen Ester galloping past the window, her mother's ratty coat waving good-bye as she rushed into the night air.

Helene's car stopped at the tip of her mother's wilderness, and what she saw first was as she remembered: a whisper of a path trying to forget itself through tall grass. Frayed rope barely held back bushes on the verge of becoming trees. The trail circled and turned, cutting a route in the trees that beckoned as a resting spot, only to push through and spill out into a swept yard. Whatever her mother did to make money didn't show itself in the front yard—no chickens or pig pen, no sizable garden filled with tomatoes or cabbage. Helene panted as she saw the peeking white of her mother's house, which seemed to stand sweet and alone in the middle of nothing, its arms thrown up in disrepair because its bricked bottom had cracked in several places and the foundations had given way. Faded white clapboard peeled away from the decaying wood underneath, and a railed wooden porch ran the length of the front. All the windows looked misplaced. The whole structure leaned to the left.

Helene didn't mind the leaning, which caused her to tilt her head; it was the door that gave her a bad feeling. Big and rounded at the top, it seemed swollen and almost bulged out of its frame. She stepped into the yard. Clumps of grass grew wild and tangled in unexpected places. Her uncle had warned her about the grass; mean as a miser and ugly, thorns rose from the ground and attacked her open toes. Trying to sneak up to the house was in vain, because the grass was predatory.

Helene tried to find a path where the thorns grew into soft grass as she approached the porch. She saw a screen door through the railing. Helene stooped to remove the remaining thorns from between her toes, and though her head was down she could see the curtain shivering. Just don't put me out before I can make you tell me everything, Helene thought, aching for her mother's voice, and I want it from the beginning. But before she could knock at the door, her mother stood there with the unused smile you give to strangers.

"Hello there," Queen Ester said, as if she couldn't fathom where she had previously seen her daughter. And before Helene said anything, she thought, Yes, yes, we were once like this, Mama standing in her half-open door, wearing the same housedress, only then the hair was free. And just as before, her mother's physicality made her ill at ease. Neither tall nor short, fat nor thin, light nor dark, Queen Ester seemed beyond description.

When Helene was thirteen, she had bought a bus ticket to Stamps, hitchhiked a ride all the way to her mother's house, and stumbled onto the porch, begging her mother to come out and see her, take care of her, because she couldn't go on living with Annie b. But Queen Ester wouldn't. She'd stood in the doorway, not with the bemused look she wore now but full of rage. She had banged the door closed and called Annie b to pick Helene up, yelling out to the porch, "Annie b is on her way." They waited together for Annie b, Queen Ester's face appearing and disappearing from her many windows, watching her daughter pace the length of the porch until Aunt Annie b drove up, wrapped a coat around Helene, and walked her to the car.

But this time her mother said hello as if she meant it. Her voice was coated with rust, her hair was pulled back and trapped underneath a green scarf—a mundane sight Helene needed to encourage her to walk through the door. "Yes?" Queen Ester said.

"Mama?"

"Look like you got news, girl." Her mother sounded hesitant, as if she spoke to someone behind Helene, out of her daughter's sight.

"Mama, I do. I do." Just get inside, Helene thought, stepping firmly on the wooden saddle between the porch and the door.

"You look good," her mama said, and Helene walked through in a whoosh, still expecting Queen Ester to blink and know Helene was her daughter and put her out.

Instead she grabbed Helene's hand, stroking her thumbnail. "Well," Queen Ester mumbled, but her eyes rested somewhere by her daughter's left temple. Helene looked down and saw brown toes exactly like her own. The pinkie toenail was shaped like a wood shaving, just sitting on top of the toe, all of them even and brown with no darkness around the joints. Just like me, Helene thought.

"Mama, I'm sorry I just showed up like this." She heard her mother's soft wet breathing. Queen Ester untangled her fingers from Helene's and placed her thumb in her mouth. Her next words came out pushed together.

"No problem t'all. Coulda sent word, though. Been nice if I could of met you in something more than my housedress."

She backed farther into the hallway, lifting her housedress to show its frayed hem. Helene had seen it before—green, with orange and blue flowers.

It was dark inside the house; the shades and blinds had been pulled closed. Groping along a wall for a moment, Queen Ester switched a light on and walked into the living room. She shook her head, then turned to Helene. "Yes, yes." And while Queen Ester was deciding where to put her sudden guest, just where Helene would fit among familiar things, her daughter tried to shake the feeling that something was awry. Getting into her mother's house shouldn't be so easy.

Turning on every light along the way, Queen Ester took her under the arm and ran her around that crooked house. As if aware she had denied Helene for so long, Queen Ester had a page's worth of explanation for every lamp and carpet. "We got this in Texarkana, and me and Mama sat up most of the night to sew a fringe on it. Feel that, girl. Don't make a lampshade like that no more." Helene's head swam with all the attention. "You know Mama put up this house damn near by herself. Course she never told me, but when folks come by, they make mention of it." Everything said was sprinkled with a touch of love. "Girl, you done grown. B sho did take care of you. Tell you that much."

Queen Ester's house was full of dead-end hallways and closets she introduced as rooms with no windows. They went upstairs first. Seven doors, but six rooms, on either side of the hallway, since the last door at the end of the hall opened to nothing, Queen Ester said. "Mama had a mind to put a balcony back here but never did get around to it. For the best, I suppose." The room Queen Ester said was for guests had no furniture, just a large green carpet and one rectangular window that hung so low on the wall it almost sat on the floor. Grandmother's office, as her mother called it, had no desk, only an upright wooden chair that stood alone in the middle of the room. On one wall you could look out of six windows the size of picture frames. Queen Ester's bedroom had a welcome mat in front of the door, but the door itself was boarded up.

"How do you get inside your bedroom?" Helene asked.

"I go through Mama's room. Got a door that lets me in the side way." Queen Ester folded her arms and cupped her elbows as they both stood on the welcoming mat; Helene looked at her mother, waiting for an explanation.

"Why is the door boarded?"

"Fell down one day. Just one day it was fine, and then the next it had a hole in it. And what's the use of a door with a hole in it?" Queen Ester stopped and licked her lips. "Let's go through Mama's way." In her room there was a twin bed, a chair at the foot of the bed, and an open gray train trunk. The small ironing board attached to the trunk was down and a pair of khaki pants were flung over it. Queen Ester led Helene back into the hallway, and they stood next to another door her mother wouldn't (couldn't) open.

"Cobwebs and Lord knows what all," Queen Ester said, as she pulled Helene past this closed-up room, down the corridor, which swayed like rolling hills. Queen Ester's mutterings— got this wallpaper in 'thirty-two, and me and Mama put it up real nice—dwindled to nothing as Helene gave only half a mind to her mother's voice. The other half had stalled in front of the closed door. Didn't I hear creaking? she thought, suspecting her mother's too-easy manner. You just don't go from nothing to all this. Fearful that her mother had coaxed her inside only to deny her what she needed to know most, Helene stumbled slightly on an imaginary nail, making her mother pause while she gained a balance she hadn't lost.

It seemed to be the only door that didn't look thrown and askew inside its frame; the knob was polished and gleamed from care. But Queen Ester shuffled down the stair and Helene followed. "I got coffee and tea," Queen Ester mumbled, pulling her daughter into the kitchen.

Watching the licking flame beneath the kettle, her mama said, "You look good," but she had said that before, so Helene knew that her mother was waiting for her to speak.

"Annie b died last Tuesday."

"Say what, now?"

Helene lifted her voice. "Aunt Annie died."

"You don't say." Something akin to pleasure marked her face, a sudden glee around the mouth. It was as if Queen Ester had woken. Her eyes looked ready to hold anything, like a jar waiting to be filled.

"Mama?"

"Yes, yes. I hear. Dead?" She swallowed several times and then asked, "What of, baby?"

"Heart attack."

"Well, if that ain't quick, I don't know what is." Helene almost said, No, that's not quite right; she struggled till the end, but she didn't. Her mother's joyous eyes stopped her.

"So, how y'all gone take care of it?" Queen Ester stepped back from the stove with the kettle and tumbled hot water into the cups.

"Well"—nervous laughter bubbled to her daughter's lips—"well, Aunt Annie b belonged to Union Baptist, so—uh, there's a group of church ladies helping Uncle Ed with the particulars. I think Uncle Ed had in mind a small quiet service. Annie b would have wanted it that way."

Confusion slipped back over Queen Ester's face. Soft, with just a trace of tear, she said, "Well, I'll be." That was all. They wouldn't fall to the ground together, there would be no tangling of arms.

Helene felt uncertain of what to say next. "The funeral is Wednesday."

"Never understood why the dead get a show in the middle of the week," Queen Ester said, dipping her tea bag in and out of her cup. Her voice had sharpened. The promise that had been there when they ran around the house had vanished.

"Are you coming? Uncle Ed says hello."

"Ed? Ain't seen him in—well, since before my mama passed . . . Back in 'fifty, I think. Is he still big as the sky?" And she paused. "Awful, ain't it, the way folks only think to get out when somebody dead."

"Are you coming?"

Queen Ester squinted when Helene asked again. "No, can't say I am—going, that is. Miss Annie b and me didn't get along when she was living, and I don't suppose I should act like I like her now that she dead." Queen Ester gulped down barely steeped tea, and Helene watched as her mother's mouth disappeared from her view. "No, no, I'm not going nowhere."

Helene thought that if there were two mamas, this one would have tried to show her the door. Helene remembered Uncle Ed's worry and his question: "Can't you leave well enough alone?" Except now he sounded full of mocking.

"She's dead," Helene pleaded. "I want you to be there; she would want you there too."

"See, now that's a lie, plain and simple. What am I going to go for? So folks can stare at me and lie and say how good I look, when I know I look like I fell down? So I can hear people lying about how much they miss her and then hear myself lie about how much I miss her too? No. No, I don't need that kind of mess. How many funerals you been to? Can't be more than I have. I know Annie b dead. What am I going to go to Stamps for, to make sure?"

The rust was off her mother's voice. Queen Ester's tongue flapped like a runaway. She had turned the faucet on, letting the water run, and suds toppled over the sink and onto the floor, but she didn't notice. Lord, Helene thought, maybe Uncle Ed was right. Maybe I should have stayed at home.

"You listening?"

"Yes, Mama, I'm listening," Helene said.

"Cause it sho don't look like it."

"Just because I'm not looking you directly in the eye doesn't mean I'm not attentive."

"Oh, there you go," said Queen Ester.

Her mother was quick; she knew back talk when she heard it. And the first thing to fly out of my mouth shouldn't have been Annie b's funeral, Helene thought. I should have told Mama how I missed her and how I thought she looked like me. How I don't hold it against her for sending me away like something she didn't want. I could tell her that her toes are like mine, so she'd know I won't lead her to anything bad and unknown. Nice and easy, I should have talked to her, like a stroll that takes you nowhere. But now her skin was up and Helene not only had to smooth her down but also had to get her in the car.

"Mama, listen, let's talk about Annie b later. I mean, I didn't just come down here to get you to go to the funeral. Stamps is real nice, you know..." Helene's voice dwindled, but she coughed and began again. "Mama, remember the window? You and me at the window? I have your letters." Gently, she groped in her purse, forgetting she had left them in the car. "I know you probably don't... such a long time ago. I wanted to ask you—"

"What you want to know about that room anyway?" Queen Ester interrupted.

Helene swallowed her words.

Changing her mind, Queen Ester began mid-sentence as if they were picking up on an old conversation. "Short thing, too. Couldn't be no more than five seven. Short and looked like toast made just right—brown and brown over. And pretty, which don't ever look right on a man, but I guess that's why Mama let him stay. Friends with your daddy, Duck, if I remember it right. Guess he was a friend of mine too."

There was a slight pause in her voice, but then she said his name in a slow and concentrated moan. His name came out of her mouth like a hard, labored birth. "Ah... Chess. He didn't never listen to Mama—"

"Grandma knew him?" As Helene questioned, her mother's eyebrows set down.

"Yeah, she did. You know how your grandma was. Took in every stray cat, dog, and raccoon in Lafayette. Guess she didn't know the difference when Chess came sliding up on the porch."

"I guess she wouldn't have," Helene said. Even Annie b softened when she spoke of Liberty.

Queen Ester continued. "Your grandma took in anything and everything. When she was living, this house was filled with things other folks would of turned out the door." She moved out of her puddle and then grinned. "Got myself some kind of wet." She pulled opened a drawer and took out a kitchen towel. After patting herself dry, she put it back in its place and continued. "You know, we had this chicken that wouldn't lay eggs worth nothing. Shoulda killed it. All that bird was good for was a cooking pot. But Mama said, 'Naw, it ain't right to kill a body just cause it don't act the way you expect it to.'

"Then we had this cow that looked like rain and only thought about giving us milk on Saturday nights. I kept telling Mama: Steak, steak. But she wouldn't listen. Had that cow for the longest time. Folks was always stopping by to tip they hat or tip a cup or get a slice of pie or talk when they wives swept them out of the door."

Without prompting, Queen Ester was filling in the blank spaces of her daughter's memory and Helene loved her for it. She could see black women in thin cotton dresses, draped on bar stools, laughter in their mouths, while they waited for her grandmother to fill their plates.

"Yes, yes, them piano fingers of his." Queen Ester's voice broke into Helene's thoughts, and suddenly she remembered: tapered hands holding a caramel Mary Jane between two fingers. Yes, I'm sure that was Chess. All I needed to start remembering were these things around me. Mama's troubled hands holding her empty cup, her rumbling voice, and the fistful of letters on the car seat. His hands were attached to the candy placed in my mouth, the fleeting taste of a Mary Jane suddenly snatched away, its sweetness turned bitter on the tongue. Where was this? Yes, right in front of the house, this house, my house, and then Helene wondered if it were her uncle's knowing she thought of now or her own.

Why my house? And then she remembered: someone had told her—Uncle Ed?—some deep rolling voice saying, "Yeah, this your house, baby girl, more yours than anybody, cause here, right inside the door, right upstairs you was born." Rolling laughter. "You the only one born in this house. Now what about that? Ain't that something? Not many folks can say they was born in a house with a blanket waiting on them when they come out." Did something turn sour in the voice? Whatever it was, it smelled bad, since Helene or someone else wrinkled their nose.

"But Chess couldn't play for nothing and couldn't read to boot. Best he could do was write his name. He should have been listening when Mama was trying to teach him what a group of letters say."

In the space that opened up while Queen Ester caught her breath, Helene asked about her father. "But Mama, what about Daddy?" she whispered softly, her voice studied, casual. "What was Daddy like?"

"Oh, your daddy was real nice, real nice man." Queen Ester picked up a dishrag folded on the kitchen sink, playing with its ragged edges. "Real nice." She spun her finger around a loose thread and pulled. Hard. "Yes, sir. Nice as pie."

"There's got to be more than that, Mama. Uncle Ed said he worked at a place called Mr. Carthers's sawmill."

"Yeah, that's right." But Queen Ester didn't look up as she spoke; her eyes held fast to the unraveling dishrag. Loop after loop, its stitches opened as Queen Ester plucked at the thread. "I made this myself. With that sewing machine you saw upstairs. Chain-stitch machine is what I got. Tug a bit on a loose thread, and whatever you make is liable to fall apart.

Just like this here." She tugged at the string. "I always wanted one of them lockstitch machines they got out there now. Pedaling ain't so hard."

Helene waited for her mother to pick up her story and spin a life out for her father the way she had for Chess and her grandmother. According to Aunt Annie he was good, boring. He never stole anyone's wife, beat a child, or drank himself into a stupor. No one talked about him, a vanished thing whose name (Helene only knew his nickname; Ed had thought and thought and come up with nothing else) she had heard twice, foolish and poor sounding—Duck. The name of a boy of twelve. That was her father. He died right before Helene was born, cut to pieces in a sawmill accident. Filling two sacks they put into a coffin, along with bloodstained wood shavings, he was the parent gone by childbirth, a mother accident that chose the father instead.

Queen Ester's silence had crept between them and spread. "Yes, well, that's nice. We should try to get you one." Helene smiled at her mother, but Queen Ester didn't look up from her hands. A nest of thread sat in her palm. "About Daddy. How long did he work at the sawmill? What did he do there? Where is it?" Helene piled questions atop of questions. "How old was he when he died?"

"Good Lord," Queen Ester said. "Well, let's see then. All them questions in a row, just lined on up, you got them. I don't know. That sawmill was over yonder."

Helene tried to disguise her disappointment. "Why don't you know?"

Queen Ester put the rag down at the edge of the sink. "Well, baby"—she picked at the unraveled string, her fingers gnawing at the thread—"your daddy come and gone so quick, ain't like nobody got to know him."

"But you said that Chess was a friend of Daddy's?"

"That's right, baby. Chess sho was a friend of Duck's."

"So where's Chess? Where is he now?"

Queen Ester pinched the edge of the dishrag and bit at the thread with her teeth. She looked satisfied. "Baby, Chess dead."

4

IN 1927, CHESTER Hubbert believed he was knee-deep in the life being lived by every Negro in the state of Mississippi: steeped in rising debt and back-crushing work. Even in the late twenties, cotton plantations still dotted the delta, mixed with sawmills. Land once covered with willow oaks and cottonwood trees was now laced, crisscross fashion, with acres of land worked and worked over by black hands. For the most part, Chester was right. His father sharecropped for the Sillers plantation, kissing debt so tenderly that for seven straight seasons he'd been clutching at the hope that he could crawl out from under the money he owed Mr. Sillers. But in other ways Chester was wrong: his mother sang, traveling in an arc that took her to places like Itta Bena and Cleveland, Mississippi, where she sat on high stools, her legs open while she bellowed melancholy songs about string beans and the Devil. White men wearing loosened plaid bow ties stared at the ever-darkening gap between her thighs. And on the days when she struggled home, smelling of male sweat and whiskey, Mrs. Hubbert would stay up all night with Chess, whispering stories about gleaming black men who fought in barns with knives and women who could save whole cities with their bare hands. For fourteen years, Chess lived almost like every other Negro in Mississippi: quietly, with despair within arm's reach. But then in late April 1927, with spring struggling to arrive, it began to rain.

When it came, without a rumble, sharecroppers and owners alike were thankful. With cotton cultivating only weeks away, they had been worried because a generally rainy winter had turned stingy in early November, cracking low-tide creeks and withering gardens. Backbreaking work had become even more so, and every farmer between Corinth and Pascagoula prayed for just three days of rain—the ceaseless rolling kind, so that by May the earth would fold up and over itself like cloth—and at the end of April their prayers were answered. Before a grandmother could clutch her knee with familiar pain, it started to rain in the early morning.

When one day turned into two, which flashed into three, something not too far from pride swelled inside the tenants of the Sillers plantation. Hadn't they prayed and He delivered? They began plotting how many days it would take to finish cultivating so many acres and planned visits to faraway relatives. Even when the rain stretched to four days and five, they refused to be troubled. "Didn't we ask for rain? Can't look God in the mouth now," they all murmured over late dinner. But by the end of the week, the rueful comments stuttered to a close. Even the old couldn't stamp out general concern with, "Ain't studying no rain. Week worth of rain ain't nothing." Mrs. Hubbert reined in her travels, only going as far as Oxford that weekend and then turning immediately back for home.

One week slid into two, and now when children tucked in their chins and raced to gather kindling out of the wood bins in the morning, topsoil greeted them at the front door. Dogwood blossoms and trumpet honeysuckle drowned on the vine. Without being told, the sharecroppers knew their prayers had turned into a curse. With almost a full month of rain, acres of land were too wet to cultivate, and even the stubborn—who thought, You want rain? Gone rain, then, and soaked themselves through while dropping cotton seed in the ground—had their efforts cleanly swept away.

A respite arrived in the middle of May. Sudden and harsh, the rain stopped. For five hours, nothing came down, and Mrs. Hubbert swept puddles of muddy water off her porch. But before her neighbors could complete their collective grateful sigh, intermingled with mutterings of, "That sho was close," the rain began again, drenching marigolds and daylilies, and if anything it rained harder. Two more full weeks of rain went by, and Mrs. Hubbert didn't leave the house at all, since rumors reached the Sillers plantation that farther north, everything with the misfortune of standing still was now covered with water. What they had thought was personal grief was in fact drowning everything near the Mississippi River. Cairo, Illinois, was on the verge of being swept away; the Ohio River had turned contrary and begun flowing upstream.

Now, instead of planning visits to faraway family, the Sillers tenants had conversations that stayed close to the strength of the nearest levees, man-made structures that kept the river in its place. Many thought they should gather what they could and travel as far east as possible but, deep into debt with Mr. Sillers, no one could travel even to Jackson. And worst of all, there was gossip that Mrs. Sillers and her children had left for New York weeks ago.

So they gathered. Dread licked at their feet at night and no one wanted to say aloud what passed in front of their minds: that this was the one, the culmination of God's wrath that would wash away the sinners. If true, they were damned. Hadn't He said forty days and forty nights? A month had passed they were sure. Thirty-four days turned into thirty-seven, but there had been that five-hour break that stood between them and God's word. Mrs. Hubbert swore she had counted out the hours: from one to six o'clock. Others weren't so sure how long the lapse had lasted: wasn't it just as long as it took to get dinner ready? But Mrs. Hubbert held fast to her godless knowledge; five hours, no more, no less. Her certainty filled the Sillers tenants with fear, since to admit she was right was to concede that they were not destined; they were just unlucky.

They met, but not in the usual place, the church. With its weak roof, the church had stood in almost two feet of rain by the second week; now, at the beginning of June, the pews swam underwater. The tenants congregated instead at the Hubberts', safe from drowning since Mr. Hubbert tarred his roof each January. Desperate, neighbors crowded into the house; they spoke all at once. Maybe they should run, but where to? Texas too far away, flashed one woman's voice, silencing them for a moment. Despite themselves and their notions of self-sufficiency, they thought of getting help from Mr. Sillers, who hadn't said a word about the rain to any of his tenants. As far as they could tell, he still expected them to lay seed and chop cotton. But as quickly as they thought of him, they dismissed his phantom help. Wasn't it because of him they couldn't leave in the first place? Brooding produced a long stretch of silence, and in that space they pulled together the rumors they had heard from as far away as St. Louis. Murmuring turned to shouting. The old, feeling ignored, coughed sharply into their hands and banged the ground with weathered canes. Their hands rose as they assured people that just north of them the river had broken and stretched as long and calm as a dance floor.

Mrs. Hubbert moved into the middle of the room, trying to shoo away the small children running around the house. "Can't y'all go somewhere?" she said. Chess, who stood at her side, began tugging on her dress. "What, boy? Can't you see we taking care of grown folks' business?"

"Yes, ma'am."

"Round up these kids and put them somewhere."

"Can we go outside?"

"It's raining."

"I know it. But Mr. Paw said he gone make a raft. We can gone out and help."

"Well, Lord Jesus, what he think this is, God's flood?" His mother waited for laughter to scoop up her words but, the silence too long for her to bear, she added quickly, "Lord know he ain't no Noah," and then it came from every mouth, cautiously and without mirth. Mrs. Hubbert looked at the seven children standing at the front door. "Well, y'all gone and help Mr. Paw. Better than having you underfoot." The door swept open, then banged closed. Still in the middle of the room, Mrs. Hubbert thought, Well, at least them children gone. Might as well tell them what you heard, minus the ribbons you might add. She looked closely at the twelve men standing in the room, their hats still on. And they, in turn, watched Mrs. Hubbert, since sending children away always meant bad news.

Mr. Till plucked off his hat and spoke out. "Well, come on, Miz Hubbert. Say what you want."

"I been hearing how them levee men round up black folk and carry them off." Her words prompted a small rumble of voices.

Mr. Hubbert said softly, "We ain't that bad off."

"Fixing to be."

"Ain't you the one that started the laughing just now?"

"That was for them children's sakes. Mr. Paw ain't no fool; if he—"

"Girl, God ain't bout to send us no old-ass nigger for Noah."

"Who done said he's Noah? I ain't said that. I'm just saying Mr. Paw ain't no fool, is all."

"We right behind the government levee, girl."

"Don't I know it? But them levees just like this here house: man-made. If ain't no need to worry, why they been sweeping up the black folk?" She reached for her husband's hand. "We should hitch out and gone to the levee now. Tween all of us, we got three wagons. Let's get what we got—" Again she did not get to finish her thought. Angry, her husband interrupted.

"I ain't heading out to no levee. I seen Mr. Sillers on his own porch just yesterday, smoking his pipe. He ain't moved on no levee." Mr. Hubbert banged his hand on his table. But Mr. Till, who had coaxed Mrs. Hubbert into saying what was on her mind, spoke up.

"Well, now, that ain't quite right. My wife say he been packing; just real slow at it. She say he got a whole mess of trunks lined up in his parlor. I reckon he gone be gone by tomorrow." They all turned to Mrs. Till, who stood next to the window.

"He's right. I said just that, and I reckon it's true."

Mr. Hubbert refused to budge, refused to believe that even he with so little would be asked to leave it all. "I been in this house for more than fifteen years, tarred my roof every end of winter. It ever rain on you in this house? Well?"

"You know it ain't."

"That's what I'm saying. We don't need to take off to no levee. Right now we just as safe, safer than we would be standing under some white man." Mrs. Hubbert turned her back to her neighbors and cupped her husband under the chin.

"We can stay on here if you want. I ain't gone make us leave. But something's cooking if even Mr. Sillers packing."

Mr. Hubbert lowered his voice, laid his words coaxing and soft between them. "They really picking men to work the levee?"

"Done plucked Willy Boy's son right tween his mama's house and the church."

"Well, shit," Mr. Hubbert said, and his curse was quickly eclipsed by the fright that fell on his neighbors' faces. Mothers rubbed their hands over their chests in fear, and then they all began to plan to leave, since black and white alike knew that Willy Boy's son, whose mother liked to call him "my special little bit," weighed not even one hundred pounds, soaking wet. Though no one would say it aloud, Willy Boy's son was worthless. If they had swiped him up, something really bad lay afoot or else the people running the levee were desperate. Either way, everyone at the Hubberts' house knew it was time to go. The question was which levee. The Greenville levee was closest and strongest, but Mr. Till swore the white people there were mean as spit. The Helena, Mounds Landing, and Yazoo levees were all contemplated and dismissed. Finally the Sillers tenants decided on the Vicksburg levee. Though farther away than Greenville, it would be safest.

Chester spent the next three hours (along with everyone else), packing the good chairs, racing back and forth from his home to the wagon, stuffing between wooden planks nightgowns and Sunday shirts his mother could not bear to part with. Running with his arms full of things considered too worthy or too costly to leave, Chess thought—with the confidence of a fourteen-year-old mind crammed with his mother's nighttime stories of men lifting burning houses single-handedly to shake children gently out the front door— Yes, sir, this here is what I been waiting for all this time. The troubled faces of his neighbors didn't bother him, since to Chess that was how it was supposed to be—the look of flight, soaked clothes clinging to women and children. Chess watched them, their hope making them foolishly jam doors closed and nail to the floors items that were precious but unwieldy. The only thing missing as far as Chess could tell was singing—a choir of voices with baritones and sopranos, perhaps even a small child's voice trailing slightly behind a four/four beat.

More than seven hours had gone by since the tenants decided to flee for the levee when Chess, standing among them, was suddenly snatched up by his mother. Her hand tightened around his arm, dragging him to the wagon. Both mother and child landed inside it with a sharp hah. Mrs. Hubbert leaned toward her husband and said, "Let's get." And then Chess heard what his dreaming had previously drowned out: a loud plaintive moaning that seemed to come from everywhere.

"Hey, ma'am, what's that noise?"

His mother crouched low, her ear almost kissing her son's mouth. "What's that?"

"That's them cows, ain't it, ma'am? All that noise?"

Mrs. Hubbert pulled back from her son, her face tight. Just a child, a child, she thought, before she answered, "That's the water," and then she turned completely away from Chess, her body silently urging the mules to race faster than their sloshed clip-clip. And with both parents turned away, wildly spurred on by the roar of water, Chess dreamed again—his neighbors and their journey blinked away and, in their place, Lot fleeing with his two daughters and his wife, their arms thrown upward and bent at the elbow, the bangled wrists of the wicked waving with torture as angels fire down God's wrath. Yes, sir, this sho look like it, cept it's water this time. In the two wagons that seemed to float alongside his father's, rapt bemused faces were all fixed on one point: the levee that lay beyond their sight but stood there nonetheless, like hope lifting her dress to beckon.

Then something happened. The mules knew it first. Aware they were on the verge of being swept away, the mules quickened their pace, flanks taut. They neighed, bucking in their harnesses, shaking their bristled manes, frustrated by short haunches that could not meet their need. Their hooves felt the gash growing miles away. And Mrs. Hubbert, who saw their muscles gathering and tightening beneath their darkening gray hides, let out the breath she had been holding, believing that the mules were now bending to her will.

Chess heard it next, or rather his dreaming heard before

him—a long gathering and rolling that caused him to look away from his neighbors and stare back to where they had come from, almost chanting, Well, here it come; yes, sir, it sho is coming. He did not warn his parents that he heard what he did not hear—galloping water that would crash and drown them all within moments. Finally the grown people heard what made the mules lift their heads and snort within their rigging. But then it was too late. The rising Mississippi broke a private levee sixty miles away, leaving a slash in the man-made structure. Everything was swept by water. Chess, his parents, and the neighbors in the wagon could only look on as the other two wagons traveling with them drowned. Everyone in Mr. Hubbert's wagon thought, This is the one. We just didn't see it until now, and Mr. Paw we threw away. Later, Chess would only recall the sound—*ahhh*—and then the noise sliced away, like a spigot turned off.

So in the end Mr. Paw didn't seem so foolish building that raft though, foolish or no, Mr. Paw was shot straight in the air, his raft torn to pieces from the force of the water, and that Greenville government levee everyone promised them would last broke first thing in the morning before breakfast. Afterward (this would be five months on) people closest to Natchez said they woke because of the sound, a deafening peal of thunder. The tenant farmers from the Sillers plantation would say they'd heard no such thing, just a long moan that couldn't seem to stop itself. Even then the Sillers tenants hoped. Weren't they close to the Vicksburg levee? No more than fifty miles, a hard day's ride. If they could make good time, they'd get there in a day and a half. But hope had been misplaced, measured and folded, tucked away beneath the hats of men who still cursed that they were on their way to the levee in the first place. The Sillers tenants hoped the precious items nailed down to the floors of their homes were still dry. Yes, they hoped. Hoped about the wrong things.

Three afternoons later, they made it to Vicksburg. Soaked through, less than half of them remained: four children, five men, six women, two chairs, a trunk's worth of clothes, and a potbelly stove were all they had left. What once was a wagon had turned into a raft, since the sides had been torn off for paddles. And this should have been the end: before them the levee loomed like a fortress, a city in itself. They saw large vats of steaming food and, farther, crowds of people being helped up. Well, it's all about done now, Mr. Hubbert thought, watching the white man who seemed to be in charge of it all come toward him.

"You'll just keep on coming, I reckon." He stooped low, yelling. "I got enough, niggers."

Mr. Hubbert spoke up. "We from Sillers."

"That right?" General Cray Withers laughed with falsetto mirth, the three bands of fat on his chest, stomach, and hips moving quite distinctly from one another. "Well, now. We went by Sillers, couple weeks back, looking for niggers to work." Withers watched their faces. "Know what? Sillers say he ain't got no working niggers." Squatting on his haunches, Withers spat casually into the dirt.

"I don't know nothing bout all that." Mr. Hubbert bowed his head, taking off his hat.

"Don't say?" The general looked up and asked the man next to him, "Mr. Simmons, didn't we ride past the Sillers place looking for niggers and Sillers say he ain't got none?"

.

"Sho did."

Withers put his fat hand on his knee, his voice half musing. "Well, now. Seem like me and Simmons got the same recollecting. You ain't saying Mr. Sillers is a lie, is you?"

"Naw, sir." Mr. Hubbert rubbed his head softly with his hand. His voice carried just a thread of pleading.

"Look like we got a problem. Both me and Simmons got the same recollect, and you and me both know Sillers ain't no lie. You sho you from the Sillers plantation? Maybe that's where the mistake is."

Mr. Hubbert looked at the general through lowered eyes, both he and the general aware that it was too late to take back what had been said. Mr. Hubbert mumbled, "We's from Sillers."

"Maybe you is from Sillers, but you ain't a bunch of niggers. Ya'll niggers?" Loud laughter tore out of Mr. Withers's mouth. Mr. Simmons picked it up and laughed too: throaty, deep. The noise attracted the attention of several men and they left their work, walking over to the Hubbert wagon, curious.

"Yes, sir. We niggers."

"Yes, well, we got a problem indeed. Sillers told me right off that he ain't got no working niggers. Maybe ya'll a different set?"

Watch out, white man, Mr. Hubbert thought, scared to jump into the opening Mr. Withers seemed to give them. Mr. Hubbert said nothing, waiting for Withers to finish his thought. But Mr. Withers had grown tired; sitting on his heels, his legs had fallen asleep. His last words were spoken without thought, merely sounds to fill up time while he thought of a tactful way to ask Mr. Simmons to help him up. He blinked slowly, almost yawning. Damn niggers got me crouched down here and I can't get up, should let them float out there for a while; whoever heard of a white man bending to a bunch of niggers anyhow? he thought. And then he remembered the last words he had spoken aloud. With new eyes, he saw how the Sillers tenants stood bundled together on the raft. The smaller children gathered in a tight knot in the center of the raft, almost leaning into the soft arms of their mothers. They all seemed to swing with want. Sweat and rain collecting behind his knees, General Withers suddenly felt they should sing; he deserved that sort of solace. "Maybe you a bunch of singing niggers?" Withers looked at Mr. Hubbert, who caught his breath. "You hear me? I said maybe you a bunch of singing niggers."

Come all this way and now this, Mrs. Hubbert thought. She looked away from the levee, holding both her arms. "You niggers gone and sing!" Withers's voice rang extraordinarily loud, booming over the roar of the water. The people standing, gently swaying before him, said nothing; a soft jostling passed through the group as they readjusted soaked blankets and the children in their arms. He took a fat hand and grabbed Mr. Simmons's thigh, hauling himself up. The movement caused the three bands of fat to shudder. "You hear what I said? Y'all sing. Something nice."

Those from the Sillers plantation chewed heavy air between their teeth and watched farther down the levee a child being swung lightly up and away from a boat into the waiting arms of a man in khakis. All this way, and then a white man trying to turn church on us. They waited, turning away from the baby's midair flight to safety, heads bowed as they contemplated the shape of their hands. Nothing was revealed in their faces, no despair, just a weariness that suddenly swept through them all. But Chess couldn't take his eyes from the child being thrown into waiting arms. A woman with a bonnet tied fast under her chin with a yellow string reached for the levee next. There was nothing to grab onto except the khaki man's hand, and as she reached for him, her dress lifted, revealing one stocking rolled right above her knee. She almost leapt into his arms. By the time the last man on the boat stuck out his arm to be rescued from the water, Chess couldn't bear it. What was the harm in singing if he got to get atop the levee? He'd seen the woman's mouth move (hadn't he?), saying, "Thank you, thank you," her voice musical and light. She took the child in her hands, tucking his head beneath her chin, cooing (wasn't she?) and the men surrounded her, smiling. Why, she's singing, Chess thought. Something low and sweet, and her child gurgled in her arms. Maybe ma'am should be shamed, cause here we is still in the water; she sing all the time, sometimes for no money, he thought, his mouth already opening, shaping sounds with his tongue. I got to get atop this levee, if for nothing else but to see that baby up close. Desire pushed itself before dignity and hunkered at the base of his throat. Before he could stop himself, Chess sang. A high crackled sound quickly followed by a warbled baritone.

"Look like your boy know what's what," Withers said, smiling. And then Chess saw every face around him clap shut. With his singing, Chess had slashed away their sense of decorum and decency. Don't get into grown folks' business; don't speak unless spoke to; don't be nasty; and, most importantly, don't mess with the white folks were rules that southern Negro parents drummed into their children from birth. Chess had forgotten all his home training. The general extended his plump soft hand to Chess's mother. "All right. We got to get you up here." Afterward, with cold cornmeal coffee in everyone's hand, Chess realized he had made a mistake. His neighbors' silence fell around him; Mrs. Hubbert didn't even slap away his gaping curiosity, and when he asked to go and find the pretty white lady who had stood cooing (singing?) with her child in her arms, no one took him by the chin and shook hard. Why bother? their closed faces said. If you don't know enough by now to keep quiet when some white man trying to disgrace you and yours, you won't ever know. Then he knew. His hum full of longing had shamed them all, a shame so sharp he could not be punished.

The bunch of singing niggers who except for one did not sing were quickly put to work. The women and children fed the surviving livestock and helped prepare food for more than fifty thousand people, the smell of steaming vats of porridge seeping into their dreams. Mr. Hubbert and the four men in the wagon with him drove pilings, filled sandbags, and loaded supplies. Sixteen hours of work a day made a dollar, and that money moved from the county government to the Red Cross, never touched by a black hand. For twenty nights, Mr. Hubbert whispered his complaints to his wife. "Never should of left Sillers from the get-go. Colored folks ain't been this bad off since Granny was alive. And Chess, he just don't seem to know nothing. Caught him twice looking right up in the mouth of some white man. Still asking me bout that baby we saw tossed up to the levee. Gone get killed. They got guns on us. You hear me? Guns. Heard they shot some boy up near the top of the levee cause he was trying to leave to get back to his ma'am." One humiliation after another, till Mrs. Hubbert hushed her husband with her hand, not telling him that, as sure as she was black, that house of theirs had washed away, leaving behind not a stick of kindling.

For twenty days, Mrs. Hubbert's calming hand over her

husband's mouth was enough. But then he saw the canned peaches. Coddled in their own syrup. The Red Cross delivered five hundred White Rose cans of peaches right before lunch. Guns slipped into holsters and rifles slid onto backs as people surrounded the shipment. Men brought out their pocket knives, spearing open the cans. White women licked their fingers, giddy from the pleasure. Standing next to Chess, Mr. Hubbert dropped the sandbag he was holding and walked over to where the men congregated, still wearing his hat. "A taste," he said, his voice low but not hesitant. A man nearby heard him and stepped a pace away from the crate full of fruit.

"Say what, now?" His face was pleasant, puzzled. Chess, farther away but close enough to see his father's clenched hands, knew the man who had stepped away from the crowd; he was the last man from the boat.

"I said, a taste."

"Of what?"

"Them peaches."

"These here peaches ain't for the colored." The man smiled, and then turned away, but Mr. Hubbert wasn't finished, his voice still quiet turned dogged.

"Colored or no, I want a taste." He noticed Mr. Hubbert's clenched fist and his smile slipped. Not vanished, just slipped.

"Like I said before, son, these here peaches just for us. They ain't for the colored." He spoke slowly, licking his lips after each word. "Hey, one of y'all hand me some of them peaches." A female hand slid out of the crowd, holding an opened can. "See here?" The man's smile pulled higher on one side of his face. "This here peach for me." He dipped a hand and held a shiny slice of peach between two fingers. "Not for you." The peach touched his lips and syrup smeared

the corner of his mouth and slid down his chin. The smile
tied itself back in place. Chess and Mr. Hubbert saw it rise,
gleaming with corn syrup. And perhaps, if he hadn't done
that, Mr. Hubbert would have walked away, still longing for
sweet, with his hat on his head. But the smile, and the syrup
of the peach dripping off the man's chin and catching itself
on his belt buckle—it was too much. Thinking, breathing,
not this one last thing, not this, Mr. Hubbert raised his
clenched fist, swiped his thumb across that pretty man's lips,
and stuck the sweet refuse in his mouth.

So they shot him. A poor man's cousin next to lynching.
But with the rain and mud, a hanging or the coaxing of fire
to burn Mr. Hubbert at the stake would have taken more
effort. They shot him, the barrel of a Colt revolver shoved
into Mr. Hubbert's chest like a fist. And Chess, who still felt
a child's love for the cooing white lady, watched her move
out of the crowd that had quickly gathered to spit carefully
into his father's dead face.

And now Chess galloped, dropping the sandbag he had
filled. He slowed to a trot and then halted altogether, stopped
and questioned twice on the way to his mother. "Where you
running to, son?" He nodded dumbly, watching their mouths
ask the same question—"Where you off to, boy?"—unsure
of his answer, since his mind was elsewhere as he wiggled
out of their hands through a maze of lean-tos and cloth sack
tents. They wasn't man and wife, like I was thinking. They
family. Brother and sister. He recalled the woman's face as
she puckered, aiming. Her caution was undermined by her
lack of strength and her spittle caught on her bottom lip, a
string that she wiped away with the back of her hand. And
then she smiled, the same tight grin Chess had seen on the
man who taunted his father with the can of peaches. And

behind the memory of the sister's puckered mouth was his desire, unnamed and bubbling; he couldn't dwell on it until he was well away from the Vicksburg levee; an instinct of self-preservation had kicked in and wouldn't allow him to know what he desired most of all. He reached his mother, breathing harshly between his teeth, watching Mrs. Hubbert's face as she wrung a long unwieldy cloth in her hands.

"They done kilt him." Their exchange, filled with grief and anger, sat between them.

"What they done?"

"Kilt him. Wit a gun, two times. That woman spit in his face."

"No . . ."

"Yes, ma'am."

"That woman you was loving?"

"That same one."

"Then what?"

"They throw him in the river. The old ma'ams say that the river was spreading like a floor. But that ain't right. The river got a mouth. And the water open his mouth and swallow my daddy."

"Niggers and water ain't never mixed. That's a fact."

Chess went on running. Past his mother, their life, and off the levee. Yazoo City, Bastrop, Minden, then Magnolia, flying through small towns, pausing only long enough to buy two-cent root beer, wincing as the soda burned his throat, cajoling people for the treat, since now though sixteen years old his child's face and height made old childless women dig into their purses for loose change. His legs and thinking chanted together—Go, go, go—despite the fact that he was always offered a home—women with three children and no food to spare pleaded with him to take what they did not have—he felt forever destined to slip out of beds and hay-ticked pallets in the middle of the night (or early morning) to run again. Every overburdened woman fell prey to what they saw as innocence; Chess's slouch and speech seemed to say that on his own he could very well be killed by a rabbit snare laid in the woods. But what they thought was guilelessness was fear, tight and tangible, and not fear of being hauled back to the levee. Chess feared his own wanting. Two small towns away, he was overwhelmed by the knowledge of what he felt when he saw his father's thumb caress that white man's lips, and now he was pursued by his own desire. Night after night, Chess dreamed of his father being swallowed by a Mississippi that, with the help of a fevered imagination, had become a watery tongue the color of a dirty tide. But behind that dream stood his want, shaped with envy—to know beneath his hand the touch of those small pink lips. As much as he wanted the touch, he also wanted the look that went with it: shame marked with longing. A tender smear across the lips that felt so familiar the recipient couldn't conceal the desire that flared—never mind that the thumb belonged to a Negro, a man. That a lover's touch could erupt such hurt, shame, and love all at once scared him into running, because he knew that if he stayed within arm's reach of a white man's mouth, he would do it—take his boyish thumb and rub it across a pair of raging red lips, lynching be damned.

He fled for eleven years, trying to outrun a desire that would get him killed. Vidalia, Winnfield, Monroe—towns that only saw the billow of his jacket as he crossed their uneven main streets. And when he landed in Lafayette County, ready to cling to something firm, something other than a last conversation with his mother and the memory of his father's thumb, he thought, Lay it down, lay it down, for it kill you and me both. You ain't come all this way just to get dead.

For days he searched for work already taken, but then he saw the path—a whisper of feet and bushy undergrowth tied back with rope—and followed the steady stream of people who entered that wilderness. When he stood outside the swept yard he felt desire (different—quiet, almost tame) as he looked at the house that sat there. In 1938 it seemed almost brand new; white clapboard free of dust, the wings of the house stood open, beckoning. And for a moment (a moment stretched wide, allowing Chess to move through the yard and up the stairs of the porch) he felt an urge to walk into that house and rest, to drop this want that tasted like loathing. He stood on the doorstep of Liberty's house and suddenly felt ready to lay down this want, this hunger he could not satisfy. Liberty, finding his face at the back of her café, let him stay. Only minutes of conversation had flowed between them when Liberty fell prey to his innocence, scared because she and Queen Ester had been two for so long. So he stayed. One month turned into six and crawled into a year. Only then did Chess trick himself into unwanting what he craved, his legs folded softly away, head resting on the small high breasts of Liberty. She rubbed his back as he told her his mother's last words and of the desire he had tried to snap off. It took an entire night, but at the end Liberty thought she had swept away the last of Chess's weeping, speaking, weeping, weeping.

5

"WHY DOES HE have to be dead too?" Helene said, almost inconsolable. "Why? As if there isn't enough—"

Queen Ester interrupted her with that accent: nouns and verbs lopped off, extra sounds between words, vowels added. "Yes, ma'am. Keep swallowing that water like he run a mile shore to shore."

Helene pulled herself forward, straining to sort through her mother's cadences. What she really wanted were stories of Duck, her father, perhaps the way he knotted his tie (over then under, with the right hand doing most of the work), or how he liked his eggs (soft scrambled, lots of pepper, no salt), or even who his best friend was (Cecil Collard, a waiter at Lady Lady's in Little Rock, who died in 1974 of testicular cancer).

Queen Ester didn't know those things and didn't speak of them. "Chess, he got this girlfriend, Morning, and from my way of thinking can't be nobody but her that get him to go there in the first place. Pulling on him and whatnot. Like a lot of women are wont to do. The way I figure, Morning get him to do things his own wife never could. He's real queer about water. If you let him, he walk you clean away in another direction from where the spot of water be. Look like he can't stand more than a tub's worth. Mama say he act like that cause water that come up to most men's chest come up to Chess's neck. And short mens always nervous round high water. Never took no stock in what Mama said, though, cause when she said it don't look like she mean it. Not to say Mama lie, now. Your granny ain't no liar."

There was an implied past in her mother's words, knowledge just behind the language. The way Queen Ester spoke— in the present tense—admitted no past; there were no dead. Helene, tangled up in her mother's no-*then*-only-*now* telling, knew her mother had tricked her into thinking that what she wanted could be gotten easily, but nothing was further from the truth, because she had to plow through language that didn't want her there.

"But that side the point. Like I was saying before, about Chess and that water. Mama like to die when they tell her they found him the way they did. All big, floating just an arm away from the shallow end of the lake. Just drown." Queen Ester's lips started to quiver, shaking out a cry that her eyes refused to give.

"Just drown" was a new sorrow, freshly told, that Helene had to brush away lest her mother faint away in a heap of grief. Helene was almost tempted to reach into her purse and pull out a Kleenex, but in the sudden hush, she saw him:

Chess, a man so small, so thin, people would have thought he was ancient. His hand first, soft and curled with a caramel Mary Jane held between two fingers, the forefinger and thumb dainty, the nails clean, and the cuticles pushed back. Not like a woman's—no black woman in 1955 had the leisure to clean her nails. Maybe for church, but not in the middle of the week. Spotless clear nails, with a bit of shine, the way a harlot's nails were cloudless, as Annie b would say. Yes, a harlot. Someone who had that amount of time and felt no guilt. Helene saw those fragile fingers before her five-year-old face. She looked cunning as she closed her eyes and waited with her hands behind her back for his soft fingers to reach her lips with the sweet candy.

"Here, baby." A gentle cooing rolled in his throat, coaxing Helene closer, her eyes still shut, smiling an open baby-toothed smile. "Here, baby." Helene moved closer until her short dress brushed against Chess's khaki pants. Both Helenes shivered. She stood crotch-high, her face almost smothered against his thigh. "Here now, baby," he cooed, though now there was pity and longing in his voice that the girl didn't hear. Her child's desire was aware only that the Mary Jane hovered a tongue away.

"Open your eyes. I got to see your eyes fore you get some candy." She opened them, blinking furiously. "What my name?" he asked. In response, her voice croaked heavy as if she had been asleep. No words, just a noise, a sound gurgling in her throat. "Now, why you gone take candy from a man you don't know?" Frightened, Helene remembered her Aunt Annie b's words; they stung her face: nasty children with they tongue out, they hand out. No home training, none at all. Shamed, Helene stepped away from Chess and laughed.

"I don't want the candy."

"Yes you do. You just got to know my name fore you get it." But wary now, she was scared that she was on the verge of being whipped for being nasty; just out-and-out nasty. A childish smile held back tears. "Come on, now. I ain't gone get you," he said. She lifted her face, watched him through lashes. "That's right. Don't cry now." He breathed deeply, wiping his empty hand on his pant leg. "You ready?" Helene nodded. "My name Chess. Chester Hubbert. You like that name?" He crouched suddenly, knees folded in half like paper. "You hear? You like that name?" Helene nodded again. "You gone have to speak up, I can't hear. You saying yeah or no?"

"Yes."

"I bet you, you get this piece of sweet and forget all about me," he said sadly. "Little children forget, just like that." The thumb and middle finger of his other hand snapped loudly. "Tell some little bit to stay out of someplace, and the next day they done forgot all about what you said. You ain't like that, is you?" Helene shook her head. "Say what again?"

"No."

"So what's my name?"

"Chess."

"Chess what?"

"Chess Hubter."

"Almost right. You smart." He brought his hand to her mouth and, still firmly holding the Mary Jane, let her lick the caramel and his thumb. "I got one more thing to tell you. But I don't know. You might forget."

"Ain't."

"Well, I don't know. You might. Being a baby and all."

"Uh-uh."

"Well, what if I tell you and you call me a lie?" Helene's

face grew serious: no child ever called a grown-up a liar. "Well, I tell you what. I tell you this and you promise you ain't gone forget it?"

"No."

Chess grabbed her shoulder and pulled her close. "Where your daddy at?"

An image of Uncle Ed came to mind, his small stomach, tight shiny skin, an eagerness in the knees. "I don't know."

"You don't know where your own daddy at?"

She thought and said, "He at the house."

"No, he ain't." Chess smiled. "Have some more candy." He put the Mary Jane and his forefinger in her mouth. She sucked softly, and a begging noise came out when he took his hand away. "Your daddy ain't at your house. He right here." Helene looked past his shoulder; her eyes skimmed the yard and the porch.

"No, he ain't."

"Yes, he is. Cause I'm your daddy." He caressed her cheek. "Me. I'm your daddy." Helene's five-year-old face turned joyful. She and Chess opened their lips and let out boundless laughter. Then there was no sound from Chess's moving mouth. Memory blinked. Chess was no longer crouched in front of her and the caramel flew, covered with broken grass and dirt.

Like a picture show closing, the perfect image went dark. Helene was suspicious of her own thoughts. This was just too easy. House, table, chair, a dash of crazy mama, and ta-da! a father revealed. Helene wanted him so badly she had thought up a time and place that existed before her imagination. An acute case of wishful thinking, that's what she had. Memory that big doesn't just fall into your lap. If Helene was right, everything she loved had lied to her for as long as she could remember, and forgiveness could only be stretched so far. "Mama?" Helene spoke into the stillness of the kitchen.

Queen Ester shook herself, a sly embarrassment in the movement of her shoulders. "Quiet gets kind of long when folks try to collect theyselves," she finally said. Helene could have choked her. Just squeezed and squeezed until her mother doubled over, limp in her hands. Didn't her mother know she lived in hand-me-down memories that hung about her like a rich cousin's dress? Your mama told me to tell you she loves you very much; the barber's son, fore he died, told me to tell you that your granny said a hard head makes a soft ass. Every message came by word of mouth; no one had a phone, and the post office was considered a luxury, only to be checked once a month; every message contained a legion of unknown people: your uncle's cousin's sister's mama just had a baby.

Queen Ester did it too. "That boy was trying to scream his way out of a drowning, but by the time it reached Chess's ears the scream had turned to laughing." Helene looked puzzled. "Oh, I didn't tell you? There's a boy in that water. Some somebody. I ain't never see him. At least not living. Bout the time they fish him out, his own mama could of walk past him and not know it was hers. Maybe Mama see him before, in town. Used to be you walk into town and always bump into something brand new. Folks always throwing up some new something. We never got a bank, but that beauty shop got built in 'thirty-one. Just went to waste, though, since we all got rollers. Still, it got built. Me and Mama walk by and look on in, trying to see what's what. All them new men, walking round looking lost till some job or woman find them.

Train bring them in with the wood. But not now. Folks can't take no more of whatever they took for so long and float on down to Texas. Not to say we was ever bustling. We ain't never been that kind of place, but used to be that every now and again we get a hand worths of new faces.

"That boy who drowned with Chess was new like that. On the road through here without a mama to hold his hand. It ain't like that now. Coming up, I go to town with Mama and a whole passel of boys is running errands and whatnot for the grown folks. I ask Mama where they family, at least the mama, you know?" Queen Ester didn't notice Helene's rising anger. "And Mama say, calm as grass, 'They ain't got nobody. Ain't got no ma'am or no mister, either.' I was just a little bit then, and if you think I stay close to Mama before, well . . ." She paused, filling the kitchen with a laugh. "She could of sewed me into her pants pocket and it would of been right fine by me. Lord, where the mind go if you let it. That boy can't be more than twelve. Getting in some kind of mess. Cookie in the woods when it happen, and she say she hear him laughing. Sound just like Chess's dead wife, Halle. Ain't that something, gal, trying to save somebody and they sound just like your dead wife?"

Even with all her age and reason, Helene's mouth dropped open. She didn't want to know all this, not this. She could, perhaps, understand that her father was not who everybody said he was (if her memory hadn't fooled her). She could even tell herself that someone somewhere had gotten an important fact confused, and that the mistake had grown of its own will and couldn't be stopped. But Helene didn't want to hear as well that death was just a curtain and people could poke their heads around it to say hello.

She rose from her chair, looking to see if her purse was

nearby. Her start was halfhearted, her knees stiff with sitting. Her chair skipped lightly on the tiled floor, but Queen Ester went on talking, receding further into the brightly colored past.

Helene sank back into the chair. Despite herself, she was entranced by the sound of her mother's voice. Queen Ester moved from the counter and took a seat across from her daughter, her housedress pulled up slightly. She grunted softly as she rested her elbows on the table and went on speaking about death as she would a pancake recipe. Helene knew that the dead are dead. But she stayed anyway, because outside that kitchen, that house, there was nothing. Just a bunch of Southerners who took up her time and shamed her with their questions: Where you from, girl? Who are your people? She had no idea, no story with which to awe anyone. My great-grandfather helped start a town, built a house, saved a child. Queen Ester knew—she could tell her. Just no more voices of dead wives who lure grown men to their drowning, she thought. The pleasantness masking her face was still there but slipping, being replaced by doubt and resistance she couldn't hide.

Queen Ester stood up from the chair with her legs apart, as if bracing for a blow. "Chess in that water moaning, yelling, 'Halle! Halle!'" she howled, a noise that hovered between a laugh and a scream. "I ain't the one that see Chess drowning, but what happen come from so many mouths, everybody say how Cookie hear the laughing, and how Chess just a mama's hug away from the safe side of the water. Morning get him out there, then Halle was calling to him and making him go in that lake. No other way make any sense. Not when you take Chess and his queerness with the water. Ain't nothing but the sound of his dead wife that make him get out there. Cause Halle was the color of Land O' Lakes and her hair soft as the cotton Mama bought at Mr. Jameson's store.

"You know the store when you come on here? Been closed for years, but in my time anything you can dream of was somewhere in that store. Whole tin of sardines for thirty cents, buy two tins and Mr. Jameson liable to throw in some crackers for free. Had shoes and bolts of nice pretty cloth, canned peas and homemade pickles and eggs that sit right on the counter next to the checkout. Mama saving up all that money to get combed cotton from Mr. Jameson don't make no sense, considering that Mama got a cotton field right in our own backyard. Sweet Jesus, gal, you should've seen Halle's hair. Couldn't sing worth a lick, but that girl's hair—Lord's redemption." Queen Ester smoothed down the lapels of her housedress with her hands.

"And I tell you another thing. It's strange that Halle's name slid out of Chess's mouth. Them two was married, but that didn't stop Chess. I hear he keep Morning and Halle at the same time. Running from house to house, extra set of pants hanging in Morning's closet. Ain't no kind of woman gone stand for that. Got so bad, he take Morning down to Bo Web's, like ain't nobody gone tell Halle about it. If that ain't enough, he didn't have the sense to keep his mouth closed. The Lord made him talk about it in his sleep."

Helene couldn't help but smile. Queen Ester grinned back.

"I can never figure out why people down this way say Chess loved Halle like nobody's business. Helene, girl, don't you believe that mess for one minute. Seem like all you got to do to make folks forget your sins is try to save some nappy-headed drowning boy and damn well make sure you drown too." Her voice trailed off; she pressed down with her hands against the table as if to push herself away.

"Where are you going?" Helene asked.

"Chess make me tired, always did," her mother answered. "It's a nap for me. Don't go nowhere. You ain't thinking of leaving, is you?" A worried look crossed Queen Ester's face.

"No."

"All right then. I'll see you in an hour." Queen Ester stood in the doorway. "Oh, and about Annie b? I still ain't going." She left, and Helene heard the stairs groaning in response to her feet. A moment more, and Helene was sure Queen Ester would have laughed at her only child for rushing down here to try and throw her in a black dress and claim her as her own.

So why aren't I worried? she thought. Why didn't I tackle her and say she can't run away until I hear what I want to know and in the right order, like a broken stick pieced back together? Why didn't I do that? Why didn't I walk away when she said the dead spoke to Chess and he heard and followed, till he went into the lake, breathed in water like air, holding some young boy he mistook for his wife, who he didn't love or cheated on even if he did? Because it could really happen in this house—the dead poking their heads out from closets could really happen right here. Helene noticed the stillness, the absence of her mother. Longing smashed against her chest, and then fast on that followed anger and bravado. Liar, she thought. Why won't you tell me? Maybe because you won't share him. Maybe because you've got that big patchwork quilt of history that you want to give me bit by bit, but never all the pieces I need to make me whole.

He said it, I know he did. Lies birth lies, like English ivy, tangled greenery that goes on leaping long after it's forgotten its purpose, that only wants to climb the wall to show you it can. Before I leave, if I leave—no, when I leave—you'll tell me just how it happened that this man was mine all along and no one told me different. How it happened that everyone—Helene stopped. She suddenly realized that everyone meant just that: everyone.

Uncle Ed. Perhaps he didn't know. Perhaps he's just like me; he heard what they told him and didn't check their faces. Uncle Ed didn't lie, surely. Maybe Aunt Annie b, because she could be that mean, that spiteful, but not Uncle Ed. He didn't know. A hurtful thought formed and Helene's logic could not sweep it away. He's a smart man, isn't he? Of course he is. Well, no one can be that blind for that long. He knew; he just didn't tell. It's not the kind of secret a bunch of women can hold together. He knew and he never said a word, not a word. Must be nice to be a man in the South. Right or wrong, you're always right. Able to dodge responsibility like a boxer. Yes, that must be nice.

6

BY 1930, LIBERTY had been living in Lafayette County without Sweets for five years. Five years without someone to sass her and tell her to quit on that every time she wanted to kiss her baby girl under the chin. Five years without back talk, insults, and smirks. Without someone saying, "Who sings night-night songs to a baby that can carry her own tune?" After her husband's departure Liberty fell headlong in love. Suddenly everything about her daughter was charmed and precious. Who more than Liberty treasured the sound of Queen Ester's footsteps as she ran down the hall? Or the way her little baby girl chewed her lunch with her mouth open? Just beautiful.

It had begun simply enough. One night it occurred to Liberty that she didn't have to wait until morning to see Queen Ester. Nothing stood in her way, certainly not Sweets, she thought, as she got up from her bed and tiptoed to Queen Ester's room. As she opened her daughter's door, she called out softly in the dark, "Baby, you come get in bed with me if you like. I'll sing you one more song fore bed." Liberty was enchanted with the look of wonder and pleasure that stole across her daughter's face when she woke up. She don't want to wait till morning either, Liberty thought, watching her girl fling off her covers. If what make her that happy make me happy, what's the harm? She waited a month to do it again, thrilled with Queen Ester's delight and surprise.

Slowly, once in a while became night after night. After tucking Queen Ester into bed, Liberty would appear again in her daughter's doorway to ask breathlessly, as if the thought had just crossed her mind, "You can come sleep with me, Queenie. I sing you one more song fore bed." And Queen Ester, who hadn't fallen asleep at all, put aside her pretending to stumble into her mother's arms. She had been waiting on her mother's arrival, listening for Liberty's pacing, since her excitement sprang not from the suspense of whether her mother would come but when. Sometimes Liberty would hold back for just minutes; other nights she would wait for as long as two hours to suddenly step out of the dark. Queen Ester cherished the moment when her mother walked into her room, wearing a mischievous smile, ready to feed her songs that felt like secrets.

> *Bye-bye blues, bells ring, birds sing,*
> *sun is shining, no more pining.*
> *Just we two, smiling through,*
> *don't sigh, don't cry, bye-bye blues.*
> *Bye-bye to all your blues and sorrows,*
> *bye-bye cause they'll be gone tomorrow.*

The song alone was worth spending an hour and some-times two, clawing the sleep away, struggling against her body's warmth. Liberty would sing the lead and Queen Ester would sing its counterpoint:

Bye-bye blues, bells will ring and birds all sing.
Stop your moping, keep on hoping.
The two of us together, just me and you,
will keep smiling, smiling through.
So don't you sigh and don't you cry.
Bye-bye blues.

Liberty knew very few songs from beginning to end. So what if the song Queen Ester loved best contained the words "just we two"?

They would live three more years alone, eight years alto-gether without husband, friend, or neighbor, and all the while Liberty treated their love like something covert, though there was no one watching. She knew Sweets had left, but to admit he was gone for good meant they were now two, a breakable number. So she treated Queen Ester as if someone lurked around the corner to snatch her. Strangely enough, it felt like the best way to be with her daughter—at once playful and imperiled. Whether they were two or three, love didn't mean a thing until someone threatened to pull it away.

By the time Sweets walked out, Liberty had skimmed five thousand three hundred sixty-eight dollars. Sweets had to sleep, and Liberty had taken as much as twenty dollars from his money clip at any one time. Sweets hadn't noticed. And if he had, so what? She was the wife. Now church shoes were worn all through the week. Liberty dressed Queen Ester in the same outfit, ordered in three different colors. At forty-two cents a pound, Liberty fed them round steak every third month. Like her love, the money seemed endless. They lived high for almost eight years: ice cream on Sundays, rose-scented soap for washing up, hour-long baths till Queen Ester stepped out from the tub gleaming. Liberty had no friend to shove reality down her throat, no one to say, "Sweets been gone for how long? Girl, he ain't coming back. You better hold on to that money you took off him." Liberty treated her husband's disappearance like an extended vacation. Man get that mad, got to walk it off. And that takes a spell. No need to cut corners; Sweets would be back to fill her pockets any day now. Never mind that any day stretched into eight years.

But in 1933, the five thousand three hundred sixty-eight dollars Liberty had thought would last as long as Sweets was gone had dwindled down to two. And without Sweets's ever-full money clip, things fell down at Liberty's house. Lemon cakes and rhubarb pies made just because became a habit of the past. The generator in the backyard broke and Liberty didn't have the money to fix it. Now she and Queen Ester had dinners lit by kerosene lamps and candles. Queen Ester turned ragged. Quickly she outgrew the dresses specially ordered, and Liberty's night songs turned to clever explanations. "I was gone buy you a new dress, baby. But you look so sweet in them old ones. Like the little bit you was when everything was just right. And they ain't too tight, is they?"

"No, ma'am." Queen Ester snuggled deeper into her arms.

"You ain't just saying that, is you?" Liberty pulled back slightly to get a better look at her child's face. Winter air rushed between them and bit hard into Queen Ester's bare stomach.

"No, ma'am, I ain't just saying that," Queen Ester said, hoping that Liberty would pull her close again.

"All right. All right then. You know, when I was your age, I was damn near six feet."

"You wasn't."

"Oh, yes, ma'am, I was." Liberty could feel beneath her chin her daughter's lips jut out with pouting. "Naw, I was just teasing. I was a little bit just like you. But then I grow right on up." The cold had vanished, and creeping warmth now made it impossible to fight sleep. Queen Ester yawned. "Like I'm gone grow on up, Mama?"

"Not while I'm watching. You can be a little bit for as long as we want. You ain't got to make a way. That's for me to do."

But those two dollars wouldn't go very far and she knew it. Worse, Sweets's money had spoiled Liberty, made her proud. Despite having lived in Lafayette County for eleven years, Liberty and Queen Ester were almost strangers. Ignorant of her neighbors' intricate trading system, Liberty didn't know she could get two baskets of tomatoes from Carol Lee for a bolt of fabric. Poo-Poo fixed generators and anything else slightly electrical if you agreed to take in his laundry for a month. She could have gotten her roof retarred by Minyas and his boys if she gave them rhubarb pies anytime they asked.

Liberty was just as ignorant of Lafayette's history. A hundred years had passed before the people of Lafayette County realized they had forgotten to lay down sidewalks. The calm stitching of cement and stone that meant a place had really decided to settle never came to Lafayette, and the county's lapse gave it the air of being an accident. There were things in its favor. It had the wanting. Any man who could walk ten miles without falling down wanted enough to get a car. (Disgusted with himself for loving the Model T—by 1933, the unbreakable metal owned by every farmer and sawmill boss was on its way out—a man would also dream of a Chadwick, which was rumored to run at 110 miles per hour.) But he still couldn't figure out—or, rather, no one told him—how to get electricity or a toilet into his house.

The county also had the strength. Hacking and hacking away under the yoke of the sawmills (which took seventy-three years to get to Lafayette and then the companies just upped and went, taking the money and all that went with it), the people prayed for post offices and courthouses, doorknobs and curtains, all of which never came. Still, they chopped at the oaks and the pines and watched the trains leave with logs and broken men.

Liberty didn't know that in 1901 there had been more folks congregating at the sawmill quarters than at the churches. Years later, when the goldenseals refused to grow anywhere but the cemeteries and the violets sprang stupefied between the railroad tracks, the newly arrived, looking creased in their store-bought khakis, asked themselves if this was all there was: the ripe smell of dying dogtooth violets and the sawmills that at a distance had the awful air of a plantation that ran on wood instead of cotton. But no one was there to answer, because by then the old had vanished, fleeing to Texas or returning whence they came.

Had Liberty known all this, Lafayette's history and thus its wounded pride, perhaps she wouldn't have carried herself the way she did: head up so high people wondered how she managed to get where she was going, and constantly picking at that child of hers. Plucking away imaginary lint, smoothing Queen Ester's eyebrows, and the like. To the town she seemed haughty. No "How you?" or concern that Carol Lee's baby had just died of tuberculosis. "Lady too big for her britches," they said. Collectively they turned their backs on her, keeping secret the way they got by on grim kindness. And Liberty failed to notice their upturned noses because she was so busy creating explanations for Queen Ester that all came to the same thing: "We can't afford it." And just as she overlooked Lafayette County's history and its trade-and-barter system, she never registered that there was no line when she went to the general store for supplies and that the manager had begun to wait on her as if she were a white woman. She could spend thirty minutes wandering the aisles if she liked, not realizing that she paid for the "Yes, ma'ams" and "Thank yous" along with the cans of sardines and steak. Mr. Jameson, the owner, was the only adult she traded more than three words with, the only adult to ask her how her day was going. If she said she was tired or mad, he'd cluck out his commiseration. He'd help her find work, now that she had run out of Sweets's money. Liberty was sure of it.

She arrived at the general store just as it opened. "Morning, Miss Liberty," Mr. Jameson said, when she walked through the door. He stood behind the counter, tall, slim, with a full head of black hair, putting on his work apron.

"Morning."

"What you in the mood for today?" Mr. Jameson asked. Liberty heard herself respond to the familiar exchange, but wished it would hurry and end.

She spoke abruptly. "You got work?"

He paused, taking in his steady customer as she stated the obvious.

"I'm big and strong. Know how to sew and cook. I keep a clean house. Ain't got no bad habits. And I ain't one for talking bout other folks' business. And I don't need much either. Just enough to see bout me and mine."

"How many mine?" His voice was suddenly brisk. Not mean, just hurried, as if something had wildly burnt behind the door and needed his attention quickly.

"Just one. I got a little girl."

"Well, now——" Mr. Jameson began.

"It don't look like it, but I can keep out of folks' ways till they need me and lend a hand real quick."

"Miss Liberty——"

"I know how to can fruit and such . . ."

"Miss Liberty——"

"I can launder . . ."

"Miss Liberty——"

"Excuse me for cutting you, but I know how to——"

"Miss Liberty, I ain't got enough work around here to keep me busy most the day. Depression done snatched away most of my customers. Fact of the matter is, you was the only one left that come by regular." He pursed his lips together in thought and moved his hands over the length of the register table. "Maybe Mr. Carthers got work for you out at his place."

She snorted. "My place damn near big as his."

"Sure it is. But then, he ain't come in here asking me for work." She pushed back from the counter and Mr. Jameson saw her sudden repugnance.

"I ain't never coming back in here."

Liberty raced toward the door, her face still showing her disgust. She wasn't angry, just appalled, and not at Mr. Jameson but at herself for being so unsuspecting. Old doubts resurfaced. Thought I ran past being this innocent. Told Queen Ester so year ago. But he was being so nice and I made nice with him. Just when I think I know what's around the corner, he push his lips out at me, like I just threw something dead on the counter. Maybe I ain't innocent no more, just stupid.

Her arm flew out ready to yank the doorknob, but the door slid open of its own accord. She stumbled, tripping over the door saddle into a tiny woman who caught Liberty around the waist. For a moment she held Liberty's entire weight in her arms, belying her own short stature. "You all right there?" She set Liberty on her feet.

"Almost had a real spill," Liberty panted out, straightening her clothes back into place. She looked at the woman for the first time. Dark chocolate, without a scar in sight, she was better than pretty, to Liberty she was beautiful. "Thank you for catching me up like that."

"Any time." The woman smiled, revealing dimples.

"Well. Morning," Liberty said, moving away, but the woman grabbed her wrist.

"You looking for work?"

Liberty stiffened at the question. "Who told you that?"

"Heard you asking in the store." She still held Liberty's wrist, though she felt her grow rigid.

"You listening in?"

"Well, you wasn't talking like it was some kind of secret." Then she let go before Liberty could decide whether or not to wrench her wrist free. "I'm Mable. Mable Pickett."

"Liberty Strickland." She couldn't think what else to say. Despite her anger, Liberty laughed, suddenly charmed by Mable's boldness, strength, and dimples. Her laughter rose for a moment more and then subsided into a soft chuckle. Now she was giggling at her own stupidity. "And yeah, I need work."

⸻

They became friends. During the next few weeks, while she tried to think of work Liberty could do, Mable told the story of her entire life. About Curlene, her best girlfriend, who was also from Virginia, who knew Mable had to leave her house because her daddy thought she was too pretty, and when her mama finally found out she told Mable to "gone on." Curlene, who Mable had convinced to buy the same Sears catalog number 782 blue dress; Curlene, who Mable cried all the way onto the train with her. Once in Lafayette, Curlene took a husband for nine years until he was knifed up north in a dance hall near Little Rock, while Mable played house with her John-John till he decided to quit the sawmill and Mable all in one go. Then Curlene couldn't take it anymore and, before Mable could get to her, to remind her friend of the dress they shared, her friend was gone.

So then Mable had no Curlene and no John-John. Though it hurt that Curlene had left, the thought of John-John made Mable sick at the stomach. Not only did he quit her right after pulling her skirt over her head, but in two weeks every bill collector south of Stamps and north of Walker Creek was knocking at her door, and after the third visit the car, a Model T, the only promise John-John had ever kept, was gone too. Six months later with even the curtains taken, Mable decided she had learned her lesson with men. But then she met Downtown, and sooner than she could have imagined there she was behind Bo Web's café, her stockings tangled around her ankles.

She told Liberty about the whole naming business. How after he had his way with her, he wanted to know her name and she wouldn't hand it over, because she wasn't sure, despite sharing a basket of chicken in Bo Web's backyard, if she wanted to get that personal. What else was a person besides what they called themselves? she said. She laughed, telling Liberty all the stunts he had pulled and the carrying on he did for two months. Coming from the store where he worked to catch her washing dishes, doing a seam or hem, or hanging clothes on the line. He'd take her in his arms and breathe his one question into her collar. "You ready yet?" He waited on her to say what was simple, what most people said almost in passing: "My name is ..."

He tried. Casually walking behind her with his hands in his pockets, he followed her when she left the store where she did errands. On her rounds of folks making small talk, he'd turn to the people she'd spoken with and say, "That lady, yeah, the one in the yellow dress"—or green shirt or pink scarf—"what's her name?" But they all knew who he was. They had seen him walking out of Mable's house buckling his belt; they had heard about the chicken basket and the grass—Bo Web's wife didn't hang around the back of the house for nothing—so they thought his question was some lover's game. Loving a game or two themselves, they made fun with him when they had the time.

"That gal?"

"Yeah."

"Can't say I rightly know." Or, worse yet, they gave him names that weren't Mable's.

"That gal?"

"Yeah."

"She sho got a leaning toward them smart colors."

"Yeah."

"Well, sometimes she answer to Sweet Girl, then Pretty Girl, and I even seen a time or two when she turn around at

Baby Girl. I suppose any one of them can get you some-where."

After six months, he stopped asking, tired of hearing his question hover in the air and then drop, still loving the way she murmured "Downtown" after Bo Web's and fried chicken. Mable liked that he always said thank you when she put toast or coffee down in front of him, and how he listened to all the gossip and stories she brought to his house, some-thing John-John never did—when Mable tried to talk John-John would just spit in the sink and walk out the door. She didn't understand that about John-John, because Mable could tell a story or piece of gossip like nobody's business.

It was Mable who heard everything, the trivial and tri-umphant. So when Cookie wanted to know what Poo-Poo was doing with his spare time, she went to Mable and asked. Instead of telling Cookie that Poo-Poo was working off a debt to Mr. Carthers on account of Mr. Carthers got Poo-Poo's cousin out of jail, Mable just said, It's not what you think, and left it at that. When Banky told her he and his woman were thinking about having another baby, even though the first child, Banky Two, lived with Banky One's mother, Mable had the sense to tell everyone she could get her hands on and shame him into thinking of someone else besides himself.

"Yeah, well, not everybody got time to think about holding and telling gossip," Liberty said.

"Girl, don't tell me."

"Mable, what am I gone do?" They sat in the kitchen, drinking coffee.

"I heard the sawmill quarters need somebody to launder."

Liberty sipped her coffee and thought for a moment. "What I'm gone do with Queen Ester?"

"Cookie take in kids sometimes."

Liberty wrinkled her nose. "She can't be under nobody's care but mine, Mable."

You and that girl, Mable thought. Queen Ester napped upstairs while they had their afternoon coffee. Though her daughter was fourteen years old, Liberty still made the girl take a nap during the day.

"Maybe when Sweets get back—"

"Sweets ain't coming back," Mable said, cutting her off. She settled herself in her chair. "What we need to do is figure out what you good at."

"Cooking, cleaning, keeping house. Just like everybody else."

"Yeah . . ." Mable trailed off. Suddenly she smiled. "Cept you got this house."

"So?"

"So? So we can start an eating place. Folks can stop in for pie and such."

"Listen to you. Ain't nobody gone come way out here."

"Look who you talking to."

As good as her word, Mable somehow got tables, chairs, and customers within the first six months. And the work made Liberty practical. With cooking and cleaning up for as many as twenty people, who had time to kiss some child under the chin? No longer did she go through the effort of putting Queen Ester to bed only to wake her again with a good-night song. Now rhubarb and lemon pies were made for the flow of paying customers and extra money bought more supplies, not church shoes. To Queen Ester, Liberty's new responsibilities felt like negligence, so she spent more time than she should have thinking of ways to remind Liberty of their blissful years together. She couldn't remember the last time her mother called to her, "Down to eat, child," for her dinner. Too scared to throw a tantrum, she turned sullen, secretive, waiting to emerge out of dark corners, wanting her mother to wear again her eager playful smile. Liberty, strict, sometimes even mean, didn't help. "Girl, you come out of that dark. Hear me?"

"Just looking, Mama."

"Looking at what?"

"You."

"You ain't got to be in the dark to see me."

"Yes, ma'am." Queen Ester said nothing more, watching her mother through lowered lashes. But she continued to watch her mother from the crook of the hallways.

Except for Queen Ester's queer ways, which Liberty was too busy to think about, things at the house had turned around. When she went to buy supplies, people said hello as if they meant it. Over the next four years she made friends: Monroe, Wilde, and Mable. She spent nights now smoking cigarettes and playing cards on her porch. Thursdays, Monroe always managed to hustle up a pint of whiskey to pass around while they choked on adult laughter. Except for Queen Ester, and me and mine not being three, things are good now, Liberty would think. Too good.

Maybe they were, since soon after that, Monroe killed Wilde over a game of dominoes with a knife or a razor or something sharp enough to take a life. Mable made her way over to Liberty's to tell her. It was Thursday, and Liberty was expecting them all. Mable approached the path that Liberty's customers had worn from the road to the café. Mable smiled, thinking about that path, because of the worrying she and Liberty had done while they planned the café over how folks would find a house a wilderness away. She trotted down the footpath until she stood in the swept yard that enclosed the house, her feet marking and breaking the intricate pattern of circles made in the dust before dawn by Queen Ester. Mable set her hand on the doorknob and pushed open the door. "We don't have no eggs," Liberty said, and before Mable could remember what she came for she took up her part in a conversation they had had every week since the café opened.

"You say that every Thursday. How you expect somebody to eat hash without some eggs stirred up in them? Liberty, sometime you don't make no sense."

"Mable, I would still have some eggs left over if you wouldn't come in every day asking for eggs to go with your hash. You need to be thankful for what you receive the rest of the week."

"I be thankful if you get me some eggs on Thursday."

"Lord as my witness, you getting as bad as Wilde, coming in here asking for roast turkey like it's Thanksgiving every day."

Then Mable remembered and the light talk, which because of its Thursday-after-Thursday litany didn't even take up space in the mind, stopped. Breaking into Liberty's smile, Mable said, "Monroe done killed Wilde."

It was midday; she had been on her feet all morning, and Liberty was tired. But before she could think how to mourn and run the café at the same time, her customers flared up with the news of Wilde and Monroe, pressing her for information.

"What that Mable just say?"

"Mable say Monroe killed Wilde," Liberty said quietly.

"Probably over some woman. Ain't that the way it always is?" Porch said to Banky.

"Me myself, I make it my business never to get tied up with women and dominoes. Lord knows you die quick that way."

Liberty watched her customers weave together a tale. Their voices rose and grew sharp until, finally having a story that made sense, they smiled, nodded, and said Monroe had killed Wilde over a woman, more than likely that Annabelle who lived in Bradley, the one Wilde went to see every now and again. And somehow Monroe found out about it. Then he got jealous of Wilde or the other way around, but it didn't matter because the outcome was the same.

"Wilde's poor mama. She got to be in a bad way. Wilde was young."

"Wilde's mama? What about Wilde? You get a little piece of tail and see what happens, what I say," Banky said.

"I say shut it. All of you." Mable came through the door, food on a plate, steaming. She sat down in an empty chair, the plate balancing on her knee. Liberty pushed away from the bar, calmly lifted the plate from Mable's knee, and placed the hash in front of Porch. "So what the story on Monroe and Wilde?"

"Monroe, Monroe just up and killed him. They was off a ways from Josephine's house, just playing dominoes like always. Betting and all the money heaping up on Wilde side, and Monroe just losing worse and worse as the game run on—"

Mable stopped. "Liberty, ain't see none of this firsthand." Any answer that Liberty gave was swallowed up by the cacophony. The death of Wilde was now in the mouths and ears of the café, and because of the strangeness of death and dominoes, the men and women tore at its pieces, making it manageable and commonplace. Snatches of words—the problem with gambling between friends, Joe Louis's recent heavyweight title, and the price of catalog dresses—floated in the air.

They didn't see him because he didn't look like a long journey but rather a hard day's work. He had been in Lafayette for three days. Three days of searching for work at the sawmills, the stores, or as an extra hand for picking cotton, corn, or tobacco, and nothing came to fruition. The sawmills and stores had enough workers, and cotton and corn were out of season. From a casual stroll—the lazy bend and thrust of knee and foot that the newly arrived affect to look as if they've always been in town—to the hurried desperate pace of a traveler running out of what he brought with him, the man walked up and down Main Street, frightened of his idleness. He followed the slow trickle of people that entered the woods and came upon Liberty's café, beckoned by the house whose wings opened in a gesture of welcome.

He walked in mid-story, and it took him time to find the source. Opening the front door, he was faced with stairs, so he looked to the left and caught sight of five pine tables in a loose circle covered with what seemed like large dresses split open to protect the naked wood. Unnoticed, he heard the young woman tell a tale, sitting with her legs open and relaxed like a man drinking, but her mouth hasty and snarled as she spoke.

He took a chair at an empty table and waited, rubbing his palms against his knees. A woman who was taller than anything stood braced against a bar counter—there were no bottles, just clean empty glasses—and he wondered how she pulled off being that big without looking fat. He stared at them all, one by one, assuming that the men were there because they had no work and the women for the free talk.

The man needed food, a cup of coffee with sugar and no milk, maybe a piece of hoecake if there was any to be had. But he didn't realize Liberty ran the café as she would a dinner party; her customers were guests and like the best of hostesses she sensed their hunger without being told. It was not good that the man walked in not bothering with a hello and waited for a moment to catch her eye. It would never come, as there was no need for Liberty to look up and survey what there was.

While he waited, the conversation curled around back to the death; it couldn't help itself. The talk had started out innocent, a soft complaint from Carol Lee about a dress and her man.

"I told him I needs a new dress and he say, 'You needs a new job.' 'I tell you what,' I tell him. 'I gets a new dress or you get a new girl.' "

"I done seen you three times since Sunday, ain't a once in the same dress. That's all a man got to say," Porch offered his view.

"You cheap, Porch. Shit, you ain't got no woman now."

"Don't need no woman—cost too much."

"Man need his drink," Banky joined in.

"You look at that Wilde. He drink all day, put all his money down gambling and see?" Poo-Poo said. "God didn't even let his eyes close at the end."

"God good to make a man open his eyes at the end," Porch said. "Need to see all that ain't no more. God have me see a last bit of tail at the end, bless Him."

"Now see, Porch, I knowed you ain't had no tail in a year or more." Poo-Poo laughed.

"Get out my drawers, man."

"Shit, somebody got to get in them. They lonely."

"That's not what your mama was moaning last night," Porch said.

"Damn, man, how you pull that off? My mama dead." The room filled with the spill of laughter. Porch, doubled over in his chair, held his hands to his chest.

Unceasing, coasting, the laughter rode on, until the echo stopped and tears came unchecked and spread until everyone in the café was crying over pointless anguish. Even Queen Ester's eyes brimmed—she was listening behind the door to the kitchen. There was no shame, no reason for the women not to lift their dresses and hide their faces or for the men not to bury their heads in the crooks of their arms.

On it went until the man whom they had not seen, or maybe saw in a flicker but forgot, coughed. "I think I'm with the Porch man. Can't hate a man for wanting to see the last bit of tail." Although he spoke softly, his round Mississippi tones restful and quiet in the café, they thought they heard arrogance. With tears still damp on their faces, their hands limp and half open in surprise, they turned on him.

"Ain't nobody asked you. You think, just cause you got a bit of dirt on your pants, you one of us?" said Other. The café awoke as Other strung together more words than they ever heard him say before. It was common knowledge that if anyone was short a hand and needed a strong arm or a pair of legs to walk a mile, Other was the official stand-and-deliver man. What's next? they all thought, watching Other come out of the corner to stand in the middle of the room.

"Chester. From Clarksdale, Mississippi. Call me Chess."

"So? So? Like we——"

"Other, hush! Since when you start talking that way?" Liberty placed her words in the space Other meant to speak. "Ain't nobody brand new gone get cut up like that in my café. Nobody."

She grabbed a glass and filled it from the pitcher of water, revealing her teeth as she drank. "Well . . . I have to say that they make them fine in Clarksdale." Small teeth. He noticed that as she made a full smile. Small teeth for a big woman like that, Chess thought. As if the teeth of her childhood had stayed in her mouth for safety, just to be contrary, while the rest of her grew and grew. He looked at her teeth, at her mouth that wanted to be still a child's, and then at her breasts.

He wasn't the only one who noticed her smile and the slight swing of her high breasts beneath her workman's shirt. Her words carried weight; the women in the room looked again. But this time they conjured what ought to be there, so now his skin was not brown, it was light chocolate; his lips were wide and pink at the center. Under the spell of sudden charm, they gave him muscles hidden beneath his shirt; they imagined love resting in the crook of his arms.

Shifting in their seats, they leaned forward, uncomfortable and ready. They coiled their questions around him, anchoring him to the floor. "Now, where you from?"

"Mable, didn't you hear him the first time round? Clarksdale."

"Where bout in Clarksdale?"

"Near Moon Lake."

"Maybe we all need to hitch a ride to Clarksdale."

"I think I be satisfied with what we got right here." Each woman had nabbed a line, picking up where the other had left off, but suddenly they formed a choir; their mouths made one voice.

"What's your name?"

"Chess."

"What you doing away from home?"

"Where you gone go after here?"

"Sugar, tell me, where you going?"

"All right now." Liberty broke in. Again, she reached for the pitcher behind the bar and splashed water into another glass. She held it out to him. "Where you headed to?" said Liberty.

"Right here."

"Got kin in town?"

"Naw, ma'am."

"Then what you doing here?"

"Didn't know folks couldn't come and go as they please." He showed surprise when she took a cigarette and matches from her pocket. She tucked in her chin as she put the cigarette in her mouth, her lips soft as she mumbled through the strike of the match.

"Generally speaking, folks move around for a reason, and I just wondering bout yours."

"Too many good-looking men where I come from; needed to get out so I could be special." He tried to look casual as he leaned back in his chair, forcing himself to unclench his hands.

"Well, now that you special, where you gone live?"

"Ain't thought bout it."

"Better think."

"Yeah?"

"Yeah."

He thought of where his feet could take him. He had no family here, no mother. Hard and sweet he longed for a mama with thick thighs, soft breasts, a high swollen stomach that would always look as if she carried a child, a mama to hold his head between her worn hands and murmur with mother love, All right, all right now. He dropped his head into his hands as he thought of being lost in a mother's soft apron.

"What you do that for?"

Chess jumped. "What?"

She was small and lean, dressed or rather strangled in a thin cotton dress, as if someone (and not the girl—no girl would willingly wear a dress meant for a child), as if someone could not resign themselves to the obvious: the small high breasts, the touch of expanded hips. Least seventeen, he thought, regardless of the dress, and she needed a brassiere.

"What you do that for?" she said again.

"Needs to think."

"Bout what?"

"Bout where I gone stay." His words dismissed her question because of its simpleness with an apparent answer that stood between them like another person. Staring as she was staring, he looked at her smooth skin, envying the softness that hadn't yet flared to black on the elbows and knees. But about her eyes, in her hands he spied concern and knowing; the sort of burdened anxiety printed on the faces of grandmothers and dying uncles who push themselves up on their stale pillows and point their wizened fingers, as they take account of what they are leaving behind. He could have taken one or the other, but both—worry and wisdom—trapped inside this little girl who didn't even have the decency to wear wrinkles, was just much too much. She stared at him as if she knew about the whistling of his feet as he ran away from home, his journey so fast he didn't think of a jacket until shivering and drinking root beer in Jackson, Mississippi. Chess saw knowing and loving on this young thing, who had woman-ness thrown on her like a coat. But despite his fear, he remembered her age and answered, "You sure nosy."

"Ain't nosy. Just wondering. You not staying here."

"Like I told you, I'm thinking." His voice went high as he leaned in, tilting his chair toward her small figure, and thought now that she could maybe even be eighteen. She had fooled him because he had not seen her hands. What girl who should be licking the taste of flirtation could stand before a grown man and trick him into thinking she was six years old?

Liberty came over. "That's my girl, Queen Ester."

"Now how a girl get a name like that?"

"Like everybody else do, at birth. Don't she look like royalty to you?" Liberty put her hand on Queen Ester's head.

"Face too quiet."

"What?" Queen Ester and Liberty said at the same time.

"Her face. It's too quiet."

"Listen, if you gone stay here with me, you better know can't nothing get as mad as a mama when her child in question," Liberty said, switching the conversation as if Chess had asked, she had said yes, and she was rolling out the house rules.

He should have said thank you, but she didn't give him time. "My name Liberty." She spoke low, because he hadn't asked for her name either. He had hit something soft, and Liberty melted under his need. "You can stay here as long as you like. So go get a broom and sweep up that front porch, cause you can't just look good and sit round here. Queen Ester show you where everything is." He stood up from the table, and she watched him take steps toward the front of the house. "Say now," she called, and swooped over the bar table to grab a plate. "Eat that." And she slid cold hash on the table. "Ain't no eggs today."

He stayed, Queen Ester's wishes be damned. Fluttering around the house, he left chores half done or not done at all. Under his care, plates were stacked in the drying rack still coated with chicken or pork grease; garden rows were dug neither straight nor deep enough for seed to take root. Too clumsy to become Liberty's short-order cook, too sullen to make any long-lasting (or even short but bright-burning) friendships with the men who frequented the café and thus make a way to find outside paying work, Chess spent his mornings plucking chicken eggs from ornery fowl and sweeping (then re-sweeping) the downstairs floors. This one chore, which even Queen Ester grudgingly admitted Chess did well, was done over and over partly because customers brought the swept yard in with them through the front door—it took only three days for Chess to start cursing the yard—and partly because Queen Ester declared the second story off limits to any man, never mind if he lived in the same house as she did.

As for Liberty, too old to be lover to Chess (to be fair, she hadn't thought of it then), she quickly became his mother.

I'm big enough for two, she thought, so what if he ain't passed through me? A baby girl and a baby boy all for my own: behind that thought lay deep satisfaction. As she told her little girl, niggers live they lives in threes, and there he came, a third without prompting, making their lives a whole thing that couldn't be splintered. *Cleave unto me.* In the space of fourteen days, she turned soft, loving the shine of what she thought was his innocence. His sullenness toward other men, and sometimes other women, and sometimes toward her own child—she called his quiet ways. Her ease touched the women of her café, and they all began to love his mystery, the way he watched their mouths when they told him of their trivial days. *Looked up and the hemming was crooked as all get-out; scorched the rice; my cake came out just fine, thank you very much.*

Liberty didn't mind that he always seemed to take sick when church rolled around on Sunday. Or that she constantly found the print of his palm in the hoecake batter. They were three; they were three, and Liberty reveled in their completeness. So what if Queen Ester roamed the house, uncomfortable, anxious, marking her claim on every piece of movable furniture. From the outside (hadn't Mable and Buttermilk both said the same?) it looked as if Liberty fed Queen Ester and Chess from her long trough of mother love and the two had equal shares. And though Liberty served up enough love that for Queen Ester to ask for more would be sheer gluttony, the daughter looked at Chess spitefully, cursing that he shared in what was rightfully hers. Her mother had grown so patient. When did breaking a dish and sleeping most of the morning and sometimes well into the afternoon become not only things to tolerate but reason for gleeful burping laughter? Queen Ester watched Chess's laziness with disgust. They, Queen Ester and Chess, weren't brother and sister, they weren't even far-flung kin, just two strangers thrown in the same house and loved by the same woman. Queen Ester's stomach rolled as she heard of the rumors that reached the house as soon as it became known that some man—or perhaps child, as some declared; no grown person could be that short—lived in Liberty's house for free.

Perhaps they would have stayed that way—Queen Ester counting the slights and Chess basking in Liberty's mother love—but one night, after the café coughed out its last customer, Liberty, Queen Ester, and Chess sat at the kitchen table with leftovers heaped before them. Liberty slid that morning's biscuits onto their plates (Chess's first) and then warmed collard greens and cold ham.

For two weeks this had been the worst time of day for them all. Without the business of chores or hungry customers, they had nothing between them except the kitchen table. Conversation struggled, since everyone at the table understood that some questions could march through easy silence and cause pain. Before the meal was over, Queen Ester was overcome by curiosity tinged with meanness. She was sure that if Chess's story spilled out (maybe he done killed somebody by accident, she thought, and now he on the run), Liberty would have to choose between their safety and his, and he would have to go. Mind, Queen Ester didn't want Chess turned over to some white man in uniform; even she (young and younger still because Liberty pushed her daughter back to the cradle) knew no black man was safe in the hands of white police. No, she didn't want Chess handed over to anyone, she just wanted him to go back to his town, overripe with handsome men.

After the last helpings of collard greens were twice offered and refused, she asked, "How come you don't never tell us where you come from?"

"I told you, Mississippi. Clarksdale, Mississippi."

"You said, but who is your ma'am? And where your daddy at? Ain't you got no people?"

"Hush all that, Queenie." Liberty's voice cut between them, and Chess looked at her with relief. "If Chess don't want to say he ain't got to."

"We got a right to know, him living with us and all. What if his ma'am out there looking for him right now, and he over here living with us and his ma'am out there with her heart broke cause she ain't got a clue?" Queen Ester looked up at her mother. "What if you was that ma'am, walking and asking all over?"

"All right, all right. It's too late for this, Queenie. Tomorrow we gone take care of this very thing." But indecision shook Liberty's voice. Cleaning away the dishes, she thought about Queen Ester's accusation, some mother roaming, calling out for her only son (if he were the only son). Dinner and nighttime chores were done, and—ready for bed—Liberty again felt a hard slice of uncertainty. Perhaps they weren't three. Maybe Chess belonged to someone else. And then desire came to stand beside her doubt: well, Lord, I just want to know, not even cause he in my care. It's my right. I'm the one who feeds him and shakes him on up in the morning. Just about anybody would say it's my right to know, for my and my baby girl's care. We can't have just anybody living here. And if I said that very thing to somebody, they would amen me. I just want to know for the knowing's worth. Queenie (bless mine) made me want to know; and now here

I am, hurt to me and mine be damned. Even if he tell me something so mean we can't go back to these here days. I want to know what's what anyway. Though Liberty didn't (wouldn't) admit it, Chess had become a second chance, a Sweets for Liberty to try again with, the son her mother had wanted so badly, a man who because of his mystery she could fill with whatever she liked. She heaved a sigh and struggled into her robe, groping in the dark for the doorknob to her bedroom.

Chess was waiting for her. Still in his khakis and shirt, he was sitting on the bed, a drowsy smile on his lips, when she opened the door to his room.

"Hey, man."

"Hey, there."

"What you doing up this late?"

"Don't make me ask you the same."

"I won't," Liberty said, sitting down on the bed next to him. Her hand rose and settled on his knee.

Without prompting, he began. Out it came, full of careful evasions, sprinkled liberally with half-truths, more wishful than really lived. Liberty lapped it up. "God truth's ain't never seen so much water. I ain't gone say when it started, cause truth be told I don't know. I know ten years that's passed ain't so far away I can't recollect, but I wasn't grown then like I is now, and maybe I just had my mind on everything I shouldn't of. I remember asking my ma'am what was all that racket, and she couldn't hear so she bend in close and I ask her again, 'What's all that noise?' and she must of thought the running around must of curled my mind, cause she screamed back to me, 'That's the water!' And, well, that's about all I can recollect."

But Chess was lying. He remembered it all, the look on

his neighbors' faces, the sweep of the rising flood. He held that back from Liberty, afraid of what his voice would do. Liberty nodded, and he resumed. "Well, we made it to the levee." He paused again, slowing carefully. "You ever seen a baby midair? I mean just up in the middle of nothing with they feet out and all? We was all climbing up on the levee and I turned, I turned like this—" he stopped then, lifting his head up, and Liberty saw yearning crawl over his face— "and some white man down a ways threw his baby clean into the air. My heart liked to stop, cause who knows what could of been on the other side of that fall? I mean, the baby turned out to be all right and all, I don't want you to think different. But a whole mess of things could of gone on while that baby was up in the air with nothing to hold it. And I always try to figure what that man must of think right fore his kin left his arms. He could of throw her off too hard or too easy. Why, that baby liable to fly clean over waiting hands or drop in the river and not a nothing nobody could do.

"We got to the levee too, and none of us had to fly in the air to get on and that's the God's heaven's truth. We all got pulled up easy as pie. And boy, I tell you. Just about everything and everybody was on that levee, you hear me? We get up the morning and work the levee till dinner. Nary drop of food in between. I was hungry then, and my ma'am tell me, Bless be you alive. My ma'am was a singer, I tell you that? Go to the jook joints and belt it out. I ain't never went with her, but she tell me all about it soon as she get home."

He's just about there, Liberty thought, watching him through lowered lids; what's all that sidestepping with some flying baby? What was that? White baby, midair or no, always safe. She sighed gently as Chess continued.

"We worked that levee into the ground, with no sun to

show us through. Just the rain that light up sometimes and then it get so gray we can't see none and they tell us to lay off. I can't remember how long we do that for; feel like forever sometimes, and then again when I think on it feel like no time at all. Like all them days push together and one minute we getting on the levee and the next Daddy getting dead."

His eyes held trouble. "I got my own switch-mark tales," Liberty spoke softly. "Don't you go around thinking you the only somebody that got something to say that gone make these eyes roll."

"I ain't trying to make no such thing." But he was, Liberty heard it in his voice, and she cursed her child, angry that Queen Ester had provoked a curiosity that Liberty initially had not had. "They kill my daddy dead, and you go off and tell me—"

She reached for his hand. "I ain't mean it like I said it. Gone tell it." She tried to keep her voice calm. Chess's hand was now in her own, and she rubbed the inside of his palm for her own sake, because still she wanted to know. Not about the father, hadn't she heard it all? Some black man out of place or just where he should be was suddenly (and it was always suddenly; no one ever told a story where the dying knew they were on their way) knocked down or strung up. She just wanted to know about the mother, whether she should worry that some singing mama was on her way to snatch back what she had loved so well.

"We was working, just as hard as always. And some white man walked up to my daddy and kill him dead. I can't even recall what that white man thought was the matter. That man blow a hole clean on through my daddy, and then they throwed him in the river." Finally done, Chess settled into silence, waiting for Liberty if not to say amen then at least to murmur, Yes, well.

Liberty had almost worn a hole in his palm when she finally asked, "But where your ma'am at?"

"My ma'am ain't coming for me. She knew I was gone run and blessed it, and that a fact. 'Niggers and water ain't never mixed.' That's what she told me. She ain't coming." And Liberty let go of the breath she had been holding.

If Liberty had loved Chess before, well, knowing there was no mama around the corner made her close to careless. Everything was touched by charm, worthy of laughter. Who could watch a grown man that dearly and never tire? She chuckled at her customers' grumbling, somehow pleased by their complaints and worries. At night, her daughter and Chess would lie on her bed, talking about their day, and Liberty would let them fall asleep, one child tucked beneath her armpit, the other in the crook of her elbow. Didn't I say I could fit them both? she thought, listening to her daughter's heavy breathing. Knowing for sure that Chess was motherless, she paid more attention to everything. An extra kiss when he was tired, a second serving scraped from the bottom of empty pots. One month rolled into two, stretched into three. Not only were they family (even Queen Ester turned soft in the face of Liberty's inexhaustible tenderness), they were three.

But suddenly it stopped. Chess moved into an empty bedroom on the second floor, bluntly telling Liberty he wanted privacy. He kept it locked, but somehow every morning he found his clothes laid out at the foot of his bed. Chess grew disgusted that Liberty didn't wait for him to finish his plate before she filled it again, that she laughed at his jokes before he had told them. There were only so many times a grown man could stand to be kissed under the chin. His mother's

stories ran out on him, and still they—Liberty and Queen
Ester, though Queen Ester was the worse of the two—
prodded him for more. Three months' full of every sort of
kindness Liberty could think of crawled into four. And just
what lay behind Chess's disgust? Boredom. He looked around
the house, tired of the lopsided windows, of the same people
who came a wilderness away to share Liberty's company, of
Queen Ester, who by now didn't seem as crazy as he had first
thought, just sad. Finally, he was bored with Liberty. His
listlessness surprised him. He never thought he would grow
weary of looking at those small teeth or her high swinging
breasts with standing nipples.

Oftentimes mornings fell into afternoons, and Chess would
spend those hours asleep, not waking even to relieve himself
or eat the meal Liberty brought up to him on a tray. "He
take sick, Mama?" Queen Ester would ask, curious to know
why Chess stayed willingly in his bedroom for most of the day.

Her mother would reply sullenly, "I don't know, baby."

Queen Ester felt lonely, not for Chess but for the stories
he used to weave for them at night before she dropped off
to sleep, lonely because if she were right in thinking Chess
had become sick, perhaps her mother was beginning to fall
ill as well. They had come close to what they were before
Liberty opened the café. What had happened to her
mother's laughter that seemed forever tumbling free? Suddenly everything stopped being charmed. Chess's bedridden
state made everyone exhausted. Liberty dragged around the
house looking too tired to hold up her own head. Now
Queen Ester wouldn't dare do the things that used to earn
her a light kiss on the nose. Without realizing it, Chess had
given Queen Ester courage; without him around she became

secretive again, listening behind closed doors, standing where darkness gathered in corners, watching the happenings in the café without taking part. And just when Queen Ester thought things couldn't get any worse, they did. In the middle of the fourth month, Chess, without so much as a by-your-leave, left the house. And yes, he closed the door behind him.

Just as no one saw his arrival, no one saw him go, including Liberty. Three days—Thursday, Friday, Saturday—came and went, and without Chess the house turned sour. His leaving mocked them all. "Where he at?" Queen Ester asked.

"Well, he ain't in my pocket, that's for sure," Liberty grumbled.

"You think he liable to head back to Mississippi?"

"Queenie—"

"That's a far piece. I mean, you can't gone and get him if he heading that far away, can you?" Hearing slickness, Liberty turned furious.

"If you don't get on with all that, I'm gone lay a hand on you." Queen Ester leapt out of her mother's reach.

It wasn't that he'd left, or even that he'd vanished and without bothering to tell her, that made Liberty's anger flare. Sometimes a man needed to be let alone, she thought. But he had closed the door behind him, completing what Sweets had left unfinished, and worse yet, in his last harsh gesture he had tried to be polite, as if being mindful of the door meant that Liberty needed this sort of courtesy to soothe her. Not me, she thought. I didn't get a closed door the last time and I sure don't need it now.

Now everything thumped in Liberty's hands. Cups full of coffee crashed on the café tables, brooms banged while sweeping the floor, dishes clattered in the kitchen sink. Liberty made a racket with everything she laid her hands on, and no one had the courage to say, "Who's acting like the baby girl now? You should be shamed, carrying on the way you is." People in the café turned into ballet dancers, tiptoeing around Liberty and her anger.

She still loved Chess, she'd treated him better than her own, but she had pride, the flagrant storming sort of pride that was capable of smashing a water pitcher she had saved for over two summers or punching through a wall she had built with her very own hands. Yes, Liberty had pride. Who would be above feeling a prick of it, when she stepped into her café and heard that hush that silenced every mouth? Gossip sprinkled with spite hovered above the tables.

"Heard he playing house."

"So soon?"

"Some folks don't need much time."

"Amen."

"Who he with?"

"Some lemonade piece named Halle."

"Girl, no."

"And Liberty the one give him her house."

"Didn't even lift a finger while he was here."

"Well, who the fool now?"

"Say, say. Tsk, here she come——"

Liberty, stepping into that room bloated with silence, knew full well that she had created the situation, had willingly shamed herself and hers because Chess in those few months had scratched something soft in her and made compassion her weakness. She couldn't stand her customers' smiles laced with sympathy. The words "Oh, it's all right" came too easily when she spilt their coffee or overcooked their eggs. Even Mable fell prey. "Girl, you sit down, I'll get it," she'd say, as if Liberty hadn't almost been running the café by herself since it opened.

Those days without Chess mocked her and at night the reproaches—*I should of, I should of*—scrambled into the bed with her, snapping away her sleep, making her see her own foolishness. I should of slapped his face clean through when he talk the way he do with Queenie. That's what I should of done. I did it with Sweets. Telling me not to kiss my own baby girl. I just let him run wild, him and Sweets both. Never said boo, and now everybody and they mama want to hold my hand. Should of made him get a job. Even Sweets got a job. Lord knows what he did, but he got one all right. Who ever heard of a grown man not working for a living? He never mention getting work. Just happy as a pig in shit for me to make a way for us all. I should of knowed he was up to leaving like that from the way he walked in. Sneaky and all that. Slip on in like a sneeze and not say a word to nobody. I should of knowed better. And then he walk out. Open or close door don't make no difference . . . On and on she went until morning, till she grew tired of hearing the sound of her voice. Recriminations wouldn't change a thing. She heaved herself out of bed and slipped into her robe. Well, the most I can do is stop picking at it, she thought, as she went to wake Queen Ester. "Get on up now."

"Hmmm?"

"I said get on up."

Queen Ester rolled on her back and stretched. "He ain't coming back, is he?"

"Naw. And I don't want him back neither."

Sunday morning came brand new for mother and daughter. Almost better than new, since both Liberty and Queen Ester began the day not only wanting to start from scratch but also needing a sabbath to shake the somberness that clung to their manless house. Liberty suggested they close the café for the day. Why not? she asked herself, we can't fall down in one day; they'll be here tomorrow for sure. "We ain't gone open today," Liberty told Queen Ester, then hushed her whooping.

"What we gone do?" Queen Ester asked.

"Well." Liberty stuck out her tongue, thinking. "I guess we'll see." Their five o'clock breakfast turned festive before their eyes. Two eggs apiece, bacon, hominy grits with fried catfish stirred in and jack biscuits on the side—a meal they wouldn't have had except on Christmas. Full as ticks, they napped most of the morning in the empty café, waking up every now and again to yell out the window, "We closed! Come by tomorrow!" and then giggle themselves back to sleep. It was almost noon before they fully woke up. "Maybe we ought to take him on out of here for good," Liberty said, as she stood and stretched out the kinks in her back. "You know, clean the house and make a big racket while we at it." They carried buckets full of hot water and a touch of lye, dust rags, and the mop. Together they scoured every floor and wall, beat out the rugs, washed the windows. Where the stool was too low, Queen Ester climbed on Liberty's back and laughed herself almost sick from the height. Even the rooms Chess hadn't seen they aired out. Queen Ester made wings of the doors and swung the wood hard back and forth, creating a gust that blew Liberty's shirt open. They ran through the house and wiped away every smudge and footprint that belonged to Chess. All the while, they made plans.

Maybe we could even do a coat of whitewash? Ideas for the day grew into projects that would take a week to do right. Need more than a day for that, and we got to open tomorrow. Maybe we keep the place closed for the week. Well, at least a couple of days, pick the weeds out of the yard, maybe after we done walk around town. Heard they moved the sawmill north a few miles. You want to go see it? Make a day out of that for sure. Got to get that catalog from Mable and get us both some shoes, maybe even a dress or two. By dinner, Liberty and Queen Ester had exhausted both themselves and their plans. Dinner was over, the heap of cold beans cramped their stomachs, and they both ached from the work they had done, too tired to take their bodies upstairs and put them in bed. Liberty dozed, her head resting in the cup of her palm, but Queen Ester kept moving. Her finger scratched her chin, then her cheek. A whole hand ran over her face, then her neck. She watched her mother drowse, and just when it seemed as if Liberty would sink into deep sleep, Queen Ester coughed loudly or clattered an empty bowl on the table. Finally, she said, "Ma'am?"

"Yes, baby." Liberty yawned.

"Why you let him stay on in the first place?"

She woke then, sitting up in her chair. She saw her daughter's hands moving as if they couldn't stop. "Stop all that fidgeting."

"Yes, ma'am." Queen Ester's hands fell to her sides. "Why you let him stay? We don't need anybody."

"I know we don't." Liberty stared at her daughter. Such a little thing. "I guess I saw him and thought we could go back to what we had with your daddy. Maybe cause I'm older and ain't innocent, I could of fixed the wrong with me and Sweets."

"What was wrong with you and Daddy?"

"I don't know." They fell into silence, with only Queen Ester's moving hands slicing the quiet.

"Shhh."

"What?" Queen Ester stopped shifting in her chair and heard a soft knocking at the door.

"Tell them we ain't open. Just yell it through the door."

Queen Ester ran down the hallway and screamed at the closed door, "We ain't open!"

"It's Mable."

Queen Ester grimaced and cracked open the door far enough to fit her shoulders and head.

"Hey, Miss Mable."

"Hey, baby. Where your mama at?"

"Look like you got news."

"I do. Where your mama at?"

"We was at the table."

"This important." Queen Ester didn't step aside. "Well, girl. Let me through. I swear the older you get"—Mable looked at Queen Ester—"you don't step aside, and I'm liable to forget the map I brung you."

"You got another map for me?" Glee slipped into Queen Ester's face.

"Sure I do, but I ain't gone give it less you straighten up."

"Sorry, Miss Mable." Queen Ester allowed Mable to step through the door.

"I bet you are." She reached into her bag and pulled out a folded piece of paper. "This here is Tennessee."

"I still got Alabama."

"I hope you do."

"You know they got a Lafayette there?"

"You don't say?"

"Sure do. You think there folks just like us there?"

Mable looked at Queen Ester. Liberty ought to be shamed letting Queenie get so old and foolish. Lord knows what's being said about the both of them. I'm gone talk to Liberty about it. "Ester, I told you I got something important to tell your ma'am."

Mable stepped into the kitchen, looking windswept and a little mad. "Clean enough to lick the floor, girl," she said to Liberty.

"Well, I thought we close for today and tidy up a bit."

"Ummm-hmm." Mable said, and looked around.

"Well, what is it?"

"Chess." As Mable said his name, Liberty wiped her hand over her face. "Drunk as a river-bottom coon and making a mess at Bo Web's."

"Uh-huh."

"Heard he done picked a fight with somebody and got cut. The man pissed in Bo Web's yard. Right next to the house."

"Uh-huh."

"And Liberty." Mable let her voice drop. "I got told he slapped some woman in the mouth."

"Uh-huh."

While Liberty and Mable talked, Queen Ester whisked in and out of the kitchen, catching snatches—no, whole sentences—that seemed to boom and fade in her ear. Between their words, Queen Ester thought, We shouldn't of wiped everything clear, like he was never with us. Now fore things get dry she miss him. The shoulds that climbed into bed with Liberty had come to rest in Queen Ester: we should of left a bit of him behind so Mama could see the mess he make when he round us. If she could see it, she tell Mable to get on out of here and stop bothering us. Queen Ester whooshed back and forth between the kitchen and the hallway, taking in their conversation.

"Well, somebody got to gone and get him."

"He ain't mine, Mable, to fetch."

What kind of excuse is that? Queen Ester thought, and then another thought leapt atop her first one: it's cause she bending. Mable standing there laying out the worse and Mama can't help but to pick at it, cause that's her way.

"Liberty, he more yours than anybody else. And Bo Web's old lady fit to be tied. She want him out of there."

"I ain't gone to get him."

"Who the one that let him stay from the get-go? Maybe he would of left by now if you hadn't let him in. Bo Web's lady ain't blaming him for acting up, she looking at you."

"Well, shit, Mable."

Queen Ester appeared in the kitchen doorway. "Mama, you ain't gone to go nowhere, is you?"

"Shut it and get out of grown folks' business." Queen Ester chewed her lip and walked out of the kitchen. Liberty looked at Mable again. "What was I saying?"

"I think you said, 'Well, shit, Mable.' "

Liberty took a deep breath. "Well, shit, Mable."

"Mama?" Queen Ester rushed back into the kitchen, wearing her yellow dress, too light for cold weather, too small for her breasts and hips. I don't know who's the worse off, Mable thought, Liberty for liking her girl this way or Ester for going long with it. "I can come with you, can't I?"

The brand-new day Queen Ester and Liberty had started was lost. Liberty went with Mable to Bo Web's to get Chess

and Queen Ester walked a step behind them. They tramped
through the wilderness that separated them from the town,
while Mable (breathless, since every step Liberty took meant
three for her) worried about Queen Ester's yellow dress. She
watched Liberty's hand slap away tree branches and wondered about the wisdom of her actions. Lord knew Bo Web's
woman had seen it all and would have been able to get rid
of Chess in the end. But she had cornered Mable, asking her
to get Liberty. Now here they were the three of them, slash-
ing through country darkness on their way to carry a grown
man home who didn't even have the decency to be kin. But
that didn't bother Mable. How many times had she gone and
plucked some child or grown man away from trouble? Lafayette's business was her business; no one would contest that.

The woods lay behind them now, and all three walked
quickly down the main dirt road without a light from a house
(and there were only three) to show them the way. So what's
gnawing at you, girl? Mable asked herself. It's that dress, that
too-light yellow almost-see-through dress. Maybe Queen Ester
didn't know any better, but Liberty should. We're on our way
to Bo Web's of all places, and that girl wearing a dress so
tight and thin she might as well be naked. Queen Ester was
not a child, whatever Liberty thought. How many times had
Mable seen Queen Ester at the table with her legs wide open,
calmly scratching her crotch as if there wasn't a man in sight?
One day trouble would come and settle on them, because as
far as Mable could tell, Liberty's love couldn't move beyond
what she thought was small. She grabbed Liberty's wrist.

"Liberty?" Mable whispered.

"What now?"

"What you gone do bout Queen Ester?"

"Ain't nothing wrong with her."

Step around the dress, Mable warned herself. "I'm just saying she ought to be turning wild by now. And look at her. She act a fool if you ain't three steps away."

"And I ought to shame her cause she mind and love her ma'am? Mable." Both their voices, though low, turned hot and sticky.

"Come on, girl, this me telling you."

"What you trying to say?" Liberty slowed down.

"She grown, Liberty. What is she, eighteen? Nineteen? And you seem like the only one that ain't noticed."

"You telling me how to raise what's mine?"

"You know I ain't gone do no such a thing."

"Really? Cause that's what it sound like you trying to do."

"Liberty."

"What?"

"They done opened a shop in town. One of them beauty parlors. Maybe Ester can work there."

"She got plenty to do round the house."

Mable looked at her old friend. "She grown, woman. You got her something so small, it's a wonder she can wipe her own ass."

"Shut your mouth."

"You ain't big enough to tell me to shut my mouth." Angry, both women quickened their steps. "You too busy playing patty-cake with Ester to hear all that's being said bout you."

"And what, you ain't busy enough?" Liberty pulled her wrist away from Mable's hand. "First you tell me I got to go fetch Chess, and here I am out in the middle of night when I should be at home. Now you telling me how to raise what's mine. You got no right, Mable. You got no right."

They traveled the rest of the way in silence. If Liberty hadn't been so angry, she would have walked into Bo Web's with her dignity wrapped about her, pulled Chess out by his ear, and walked out without a problem. No one would have contested her; she stood taller than them all. But with Mable's censure caught in her throat, she stumbled over the noise that greeted her at the door—two men playing harmonica and guitar in a corner while a third man roared about losing his house. Couples were swaying in the middle of the room, and a single tin flask passed from hand to hand.

Like I can find him in all this mess, Liberty thought, watching the tumble of bodies. "Where you think he at?" she asked Mable.

"I ain't seen him yet." Mable stood close to Liberty's shoulder, trying on tiptoe to look over the crowd of heads. "But here come Bo Web's woman." She saw Liberty standing in the door and struggled toward her.

"This yours? Get him on out of here. You hear that? Pissed on my floor last night. I can't have that kind of shit."

"I can't even see him."

"There he is." She pointed.

Drunk, Chess swayed in some woman's arms. Liberty gaped at him while he danced a slow two-step. One, two, slide-dip-slide. When he learn to dance like that? she thought.

"Well, gone and get him," Bo Web's wife barked.

All three women moved at once. Liberty in the front, Mable and Queen Ester close behind, they pushed through the crowd. Without having to share a nod, all three reached, arms out, hands extended, for Chess. Mable and Queen Ester stepped out from behind Liberty, forming a circle around Chess and the woman he danced with. A hand touched his thigh, the tail of his jacket, the collar of his shirt. Six hands but one pull, and, tangled in his partner's arms, Chess stumbled into the ring of women.

Just whose hand had reached him first? Liberty was sure it had been hers. Wasn't that Chess's small hand in her own? Sharp hahs were added to damns, and for a moment the five of them wobbled. In the midst of the confusion (where was Mable's hand? Is that Queen Ester or am I holding Chess?), they all, Halle too (caught up so fast in their embrace that *My name is* or *How do you do?* lay forgotten at their feet), glared at one another. Only when Mable coughed and said, "All right, get off my foot," did they unsnarl themselves. Liberty stepped back, looking at the woman Chess still held.

Waste of yella is what she is, Liberty thought, waste of yella and too much hair. One of those pretty-if-you-squint girls. Without being told, each woman knew her role: Liberty had come to take back what had been borrowed and Halle was there to remind Liberty that, for now at least, Chess was hers.

"Chess, now, you need to come on."

"Ain't going nowhere." He held Halle closer.

"Mama, he ain't coming."

"Didn't I tell you to stay at the house?"

"That your mama or something, Chess?" Halle looked up at Liberty and gave her a sly smile. And passing, too, if she can, Liberty thought, staring at Halle's hair, which, unbound, waved around them like another person.

"Naw, it ain't my mama." Chess spat out a humiliated chuckle.

"It's my mama," Queen Ester said.

Halle turned slightly, taking in Queen Ester's yellow dress and hard nipples. "Yeah, sure, baby."

"Look here, bitch. That's my girl. Chess, you need to come home."

"I ain't going nowhere. I'm a grown-ass man, I don't need to be fetched nowhere." His face turned nasty but he wore his beautiful smile, pink lips parted just so, even white teeth barely seen. "You gone, Liberty. Halle right; you ain't my ma'am." He stopped talking and burped. The ripe smell hovered. "Look like who needing who, now?"

Liberty pulled back from him and walked out of Bo Web's as if struck.

7

HELENE STOOD IN front of the living room's thick blue curtains, which were turning silver because of the unrelenting Lafayette sun, and felt it was not good for Queen Ester to stay alone in the house. Behind her the carpet had no tracks, no well-worn path to show the way Queen Ester moved around the living room.

Alone, in a room that felt empty, Helene wondered, Did her mother tuck her hands in the pit of her arms when it was cold in bed? Did her eyelids flutter in her sleep? Did she dream about how tall her daughter had grown, as she said in her letters? How could she have asked me whether I was middle-sized like her or bigger than a door like Grandmother, when I didn't know the height of the door? That's what I should have written, she thought. Instead of *I miss you* in three different crayon colors, Helene should have written, *How big is the door, Mama?*

The uncertain scrawl of her mother's handwriting was printed on pages of white paper, but appeared mostly inside used greeting cards with HAPPY VALENTINE'S DAY scratched out or the wings of cherubs torn off. By the time Helene learned to read, sixty-two stamped and sealed envelopes were resting in a brown paper bag waiting for her. (It was a moment she remembered well. Reading came to her suddenly—one day she couldn't read and the next day she could. The very first words she read to herself were on a banner, COME SEE OUR GRAND OPENING, and comprehension settled in her four-year-old mind without prompting. Aunt Annie b didn't believe Helene had read the words. "Lying little ass," she spat out, and Helene had smiled, trying to spell what Annie b had just said, getting slapped in the mouth in response.)

Queen Ester's letters found their way to Helene's house even when it wasn't Easter or Christmas or Thanksgiving or her birthday. The words *I love you* were stuck in the most unexpected places. Helene remembered reading the letters aloud—some of which contained only a sentence—as she thought Queen Ester would have done, but that was a child's fancy because she didn't know the sound of her mother's voice. So her Queen Ester cadence took on the note and pitch of her favorite Sunday school teacher or Annie b's most recent but least favorite visitor. She felt relief when she received letters written on white pages and not on mangled greeting cards.

When Helene was fourteen they stopped coming. The letters, arriving so surely that they found a place in Annie b's language—"Only things you can count on is death, taxes, and them letters you get from your mama"—were cut off, ripped

away in the middle of the year, not even a trickle down to
nothing, something Helene thought a fourteen-year-old could
have borne.

"I can't just stand here," she mumbled, the soft sound
menacing in the country silence. She wished for her mother,
hoping that Queen Ester would come down soon and then
they could pull up kitchen chairs together, knees almost
touching, and Helene would point at childlike handwriting
and say, "Why did you say that?" Queen Ester would smile
and say, "I thought you knew."

The sun rose higher in the sky, lighting what had been in
shadow, and Helene saw a heap of tattered books that had
earlier looked like a pile of colored dresses in the corner. She
moved. Curiosity pulled her toward the old books, where she
crouched, her eyes fixed on pages hanging precariously from
their bindings.

Gowns, less splendid than the one she wore, and half-
packed trunks were scattered about.

It is the Glory of God to conceal things, but the glory
of kings is to search things out.

Her hands riffled through torn pages, and she reached the
bottom of the book pile. In the distorting light she thought
she saw a small boy of eleven or maybe twelve with a bony
chest lying flat on the floor. But then the sun lifted and broke
through the stripes in the curtain, and she saw that there was
no little boy. It was a box, a long red box so dark it could
have been mistaken for a black body. Helene pulled it toward
her, lifted the lid and threw it onto the heap of books at her
side. Letters.

The ones farthest away from her glowed a dim aged yellow; those in the middle of the box were the color of ivory; and the envelopes closest to her gleamed white. Helene reached for those at the back of the box, her hands slightly shaking, and picked up the last one. It had never been sent, had no postmark, but it was stamped and sealed. She held up the letter to see better and read the address:

> Queen Ester Strickland
> P.O. Box 246
> Lafayette County, Arkansas

Helene did not think to herself, This is Mama's and not mine. Desire uncurled inside her, chanting the words: *This is the only way you're going to get what you want. This is the only way to get what you want.* She tore the envelope open as calmly as if her own name and address were printed on the outside. It never occurred to her: don't do this. She heard no chiding voice, only the very satisfying tear of heavy paper.

She pulled, unfolded, and read:

> *Chess done beat Tinnie up under the house. Cause she done told him she pregnant. Her daddy leave her with Chess cause the daddy had to go get back the mama from California. Fore he go, he tell Chess, "Keep Tinnie in the house cause ain't nothing outside but trouble." Then Tinnie run off with some boy, like she don't know what her daddy say to Chess, like she don't know if her daddy beat on her then Chess sho gone hit on her if she step out of line. And Lord, don't nobody move to stop him from beating Tinnie like he did. They hide they nappy heads cause they too scared to go grab the stick he gote. All them children, except Arthur (he the*

one that run and come tell me), looking at Chess go crazy on Tinnie. And ain't a one of them gone go under to save her, cause fore Chess get in there with that stick he look at them all and say, "I kill you too." Mama loves you.

Helene tasted a rushing sugared love as she sat in front of the box; there was bitterness too, just out of her tongue's reach. Queen Ester could have said Chess had killed millions; it wouldn't have made a difference. She just wanted to know where her daddy was from and whether he was surrounded by good people. Helene looked at the letter again. There was no *Dear*, no *Sincerely*, no signature. Mama, what is this? Helene thought. Her mother had set herself down in some chair and written herself a letter, in lovely handwriting as well, and to top it all off, put a stamp on it? Girl, you get your shit and go right now, she thought. Still on her haunches, Helene sat back from the box. "Well?" she questioned herself, sighing at her lack of conviction. She folded the letter and pulled out another.

James done come to see me, and out of nowhere he ask do I remember the first time I ever step out of my house. I look at him like he crazy cause he only seven years old, and what he know about remembering something? Well, I tell him, no I don't remember any such thing, and he tell me he remember the first time he step out of his house. He tell me it was about three years ago and he guess he was about four or five and he say he walk out with his little pants on and his little hat. Then he see some bushes over to the side with some cans under them and he guess that his mama was throwing

cans out of the window when she done with them. Well,
he walked out about fifty or a hundred yards and he
think, Well, looka here, all this been outside all this
time and I just getting to it? There he is standing out-
side, pulling on his hat and all of a sudden, he say,
"Queenie, I see a big old airplane running through the
sky, and I thinks to myself, Lord have mercy."

It was her *f*'s that almost made Helene cry. They bowed
over like old women stirring a pot on the stove. She counted
softly to herself and picked the seventeenth envelope, its color
ivory, and noticed that the letter *M*'s on this page looked like
thrashing waves.

Monroe done kill Wilde, cause Wilde whooped him in
dominoes. Ain't nobody thought about calling the police.
This ain't happened recent—long time ago, in fact—
but I just thought about it now. Monroe looked shame
and paid for the funeral, though. I love you.

Helene read swiftly now, not understanding all the words,
just noting that her mother's *i*'s looked like praying hands.
Putting the letter back into the box, she moved on to the next
envelope and, in her rush, pulled out two letters instead of
one. The first, in her left hand, was clearly addressed to her.

My Girl,
Arthur done burn the house down in the back and Chess
out there tack, tack, tacking all night long. Mama tell
him he can come stay with us, but he tell her she
throwed him out before and plus he trying to be a man
now. Mama say maybe he knocked down for good.

136

Arthur didn't get beat, cause when Chess see his house
and the fire he just start crying. I love you, child.

Your Mama

The second letter was addressed to Queen Ester and, except
for a difference in handwriting, was the same as the first.
That's how they all were, Helene realized: doubled. Mother
and daughter, mother and daughter. Now she knew without
picking up the rest of them that her mother had written in
twos, first to Helene, and then a copy for herself and had
mailed none of them. She did not ask herself why, because
the answer—that Queen Ester was as crazy as a peach-
orchard boar, as Annie b had always said—was not enough.
Being as crazy as a wild pig just didn't cover it.
Even a crazy pig wouldn't set itself down and write a letter
over twice, the handwriting turning lovely the second time
around.

Just thinking on you today. Mama spend all her extra
on Chess. He can't get hungry fore she think to stick a
slice of toast in his mouth. My wanting got to get in
line. First she take care of Chess, then she see to the
folks that come by here for coffee and pie, then she give
a little to Mable, and maybe if I can catch her right
she give some time to me. I done conjured every piece
of nastiness I can and none of it do a bit of good. Last
night, him and her get into a big mess of some sort.
Mama hollering at him and carrying on. Everything
falling over. Crash, crash, crash. Right up till morning.
And you think she'd set him out after that. Cause with
him round here we can't get no peace. But she got a
biscuit in his mouth fore he can say, "Morning." What

she need him for when she got me? I love you. I ain't
a mama just in name.

Helene shivered. Not enough to frighten herself, just
enough so that she wondered whether the door had been left
open. Something light and feathery fluttered in her chest. She
thought of her mother's words and remembered her aunt's
voice, heavy and sour. "Them two women share that man like
a blanket. Nasty the both of them." Smacked with jealousy,
the letter held a sour rivalry and malice. Queen Ester was
ready to do battle. It hurt that her mother's envy didn't reach
to Helene. Maybe her aunt was right and something nasty
had been going on in this house, and what Helene held in her
hands was an invitation to step into the fray, fists raised.

She was on the last pair, the last set of letters. Helene tore
open her mother's copy.

Chess done died. I don't want to, but I dream about
water every night. And I'm watching Mama close. Just
now I'm getting to writing about this, cause every time
I try my hands turn over and look at me like I is crazy.
But I'm glad he's gone. Mama's face all pushed in and
she broke the church up at Chess funeral. I got omens
on Mama. But look like she got omens too.

Queen Ester was coming downstairs. Helene heard the
stairs moan, but she didn't rush to put the lid back on the
box. Her calm hand merely brushed away a layer of dust.
She heard the soft rustle of her mother's housecoat and did
nothing to restore the books' chaotic order. She crouched, listening to the floor heaving in response to the heavy footfall.
Her stomach rolled.

Slowly, Helene turned in Queen Ester's direction. An explanation, Helene thought. Now you have to give me an explanation about Chess and all these people in these letters. But what she said was, "Mama."

The green housedress with blue and orange flowers did not look sleep-wrinkled. Queen Ester shook her head from side to side and said, "Post office damn near thirty miles away, way off in McKamie; what else I gone do? Baby, it was such a trial getting them letters to your place, and Mama look at me funny every time I ask Mable to give me a ride up there. What else I'm gone do? It so hard to get them letters to you, cause every time Annie b get the yard the way she wanted, Ed had y'all up and moved. On the way up to McKamie, Mable telling me the mail ain't no good. Most of the time it get lost or them fellas stick the letters in they pockets cause they just ugly like that. So, what else I gone do? I start writing a letter and pray for the best and then I make a copy for me and I ain't got to pray cause I knowed they in the box."

Helene sighed. "Why did you stop sending the letters to me?"

Queen Ester tugged at the scarf on her head. "Mable done run off to Chicago with her Downtown man. But I keep writing cause I can't break off now. And as soon as I can get me a ride I go and mail what I got. How many you read?"

"Just a few."

"What you reading now?"

"The last one." Queen Ester stooped beside Helene, leaning in close, peering over her daughter's head. "You didn't date any of them," Helene said, wishing her voice could somehow smooth the lines on her mother's neck and calm the trouble she saw in her mother's mouth.

"Couldn't figure out what date I should put down. Ain't

none of it in the right time." Gently, Queen Ester began to rub her daughter's back while Helene sat between her mother's legs. Her mother's hands, old, spotted, danced around Helene's shoulders, while Helene struggled to match her breathing to her mother's and wondered what to do with her hands. Queen Ester continued to press behind her, her legs entrapping Helene, her housedress throwing off a scent of old age, but Helene did not tilt her head back so that her mother could stroke her hair. She curled like a misshapen rock between her mother's knees.

"Your grandmama died seven days after that one." Queen Ester's voice sounded muffled as if she were talking in her sleep. Then she woke up. Looking around, Queen Ester saw her daughter crouching between her legs and the box of letters open in front of them.

"Let's gone back to the kitchen," Queen Ester said, as she straightened up. Her walk back to the kitchen was smooth, mesmerizing, unlike her usual gait, which was a precarious stroll that wobbled as if she didn't know her own feet. Helene followed her, her feet mimicking her mother's, the slide and lift of a funeral procession, with only the chairs, sofa, and cabinet to witness their wake.

Queen Ester found her place against the counter, her eyes set and drowsy and her mouth pulling into a grim and grievous line. "Chess drowned hisself on a Sunday, so I guess Mama thought Sunday was a good day for her to pass too. Didn't hurt her, I think. She got up and cooked breakfast for all us, me and Other and Mable. Lord, Mama scouted around the house and came up with some fresh eggs. How she do that, I don't know, cause none of them chickens worked in the house. She was happy, you hear?" Queen Ester pushed off from the counter and went to the other end of the kitchen. "Your grandmama could walk," she said. "She knew how to take a step in the right way. God-given talent."

She smiled then. Out in the middle of the floor, with her hands above her head, Queen Ester and her half dance, half walk, moved the tile beneath her. Suddenly she twisted toward Helene, her hands still raised above her head.

"See, our preacher was a big-face man—all swollen up. Mama used to say his face like that cause he was heavy-handed with the salt. Well, you ought to a seen Pastor Johnson—or was that Pastor Jackson?—when Mama was making her way to church on Sundays. He see us coming and he say to Mama all uppity like, 'Sister Liberty, I got a mind to see to it you leave first out your house so everybody can follow them tracks of yours.' Well, we just bout in the door and Mama looking over pastor's shoulder—trying to find a seat for all us, I guess—and then she look at him; push a little wind through her teeth and say, 'Morning, Pastor.' Then he step aside and we file in behind Mama."

"I don't know what happened to the pastor, but he see us walking to the church on Sunday and he say, "God don't like righteous women with loose ways, Sister Liberty." Queen Ester threw out her chest, pulling on the lapels of her house-dress as if it were a jacket, to play the Reverend Johnson.

Helene saw her grandmother's stride, steps so small they reminded her of her own. Then she saw Aunt Annie b, her back to Helene's own small eight-year-old face. "I done told you the way," Aunt Annie b said, her hands hasty with the morning's dishes and Helene's lunch sitting on the counter.

Helene saw herself with scuffed shoes and her hair parted and rubber-banded in sections.

"I don't know it no more," Helene had whispered back to her aunt, not wanting Annie b to think she was afraid. Helene waited for her to turn around, pull on one of her braids, and pat her on her bottom, and then together they could stumble out the back door. Instead, Annie b raised her voice to match the hit and clang of the morning dishes. "I done told and showed you the way, now. Helene, I don't need this kind of mess this early in the morning." Hearing her aunt unmoved, Helene did what all eight-year-olds do: she cried.

But Annie b did not turn around, and there was no quiet space between the dishes' crash to tell the child that her aunt heard her fear. Helene stopped crying and grabbed her lunch with sweaty palms.

"You'll get there, all right. Ain't gone be no trouble at all," Aunt Annie b said, a sudsy cup clutched in her hand. She walked Helene to the back door. "You just go on now," she said, and shut it behind her niece. Outside, in the morning's new air, Helene knew that her feet were just not big enough to get her to where she needed to go.

She remembered her little hands full of bologna sandwich and cold baked yam wrapped in tinfoil. She remembered her worry. She worried that the sidewalk with its seams would stretch out forever. She worried that she couldn't hold on to Aunt Annie b saying, Three short blocks down, to the left, and then seven blocks and Helene would see the school; that even if she did get lost, with all the other children coming out of the woodwork looking school-bound she could find her way; that all she'd have to do is watch for the green corduroys hanging in

Mrs. Allecto's backyard, and she couldn't miss those corduroys since rumor had it that they'd been hanging there for almost twelve years on account of a fight between Mrs. Allecto and her husband's laziness.

Helene took a deep breath and walked out to the sidewalk, wishing she could step back inside the blue front door. But instead she counted the concrete stitches in the pavement: one, two, three, four, five, six, seven. Helene hoped the stitches would run out at fifty, because after five and zero she thought of the numbers in the wrong way. She wondered why only clear blue sky and morning silence watched her passing. Why, despite Annie b's promise and the fact that she was on the second block, past Mrs. Henry's house where Helene went on Tuesdays to practice piano, not one school-bound child had even looked outside a door on either side.

Maybe she had left the house too early or too late; maybe all the children had vanished; maybe Aunt Annie b's word had fallen in on itself, so now Helene couldn't even count on the corduroys being there. But she couldn't walk back to the house. She had already taken the left and was on the fourth of the seven blocks. Helene had counted all the way to thirty-seven. Her eyes strained for any sort of green that looked out of place. "Forty-one, forty-two, forty-three," and she still saw no corduroys or Mrs. Allecto, who Aunt Annie b said sometimes stood on her porch and smoked a pipe.

"Forty-four, forty-five," she croaked, and looked around for Mrs. Allecto's husband because she had seen him once before, a fat man with greasy pants whom Uncle Ed called a junkman and Aunt Annie b called a bum. But still there was no one and nothing: no smells of burnt bacon, no sprinkle of chicken feed, no clothes steaming in wash buckets with hot water and soap. She was approaching fifty and nowhere near the school, and after five and zero Helene knew she was lost. So she cried, cried that Aunt Annie b had let her down, cried that Mrs. Allecto wasn't to be found, cried that fifty lay on her tongue but she couldn't say it because she wasn't sure what came next. So she dragged out forty-nine as far as it could go.

Helene's memory fell to the floor in a heap, its place taken by her mother's voice and the hem of her housedress, her wrinkled knees, mimicking the grandmother Helene could only remember as a tall shadow. "So Mama says to Pastor, 'If God sees all, like I think He do, then He seen how I walked out of slavery with this here walk of mine. It done served me then; it gone serve me now.' 'Now, Sister,' Pastor say, 'you ain't old enough to be no slave. You confusing yourself with your mama.' Mama say something back real fast and low, I didn't catch it at all, on account that Duck was blocking all the hearing, but she musta said something like, 'Ain't confusing myself with nobody. If I tells you I was a slave, then that's what I was. Not for long, though. Soon as I found out what I was, I left. This here walk gets me all the way to this church to praise God, and you gone condemn it? It's you who ain't decent, Reverend.' "

Queen Ester brought her empty hands to her face, and pinched her brows together. In the middle of the floor, she stood bereft, grieving. Helene called softly, trying to fool her mother and herself into pretending that nothing had happened, but some suckling memory had come to Queen Ester, who had let it pull at her, thinking it was toothless, some harmless remembered thing with no bite. But it had turned on her. Helene walked over and did what she had wanted to do in the living room. She cupped her mother's elbows, surprised at their softness. "Mama," Helene said, but Queen Ester did not make a sound. "Mama," she said again. Just when Helene thought her mother was dozing, Queen Ester's hands dropped away from her face and revealed that she was seething.

"You don't know how he kill everything. Why? That's what I want to know. Mama had something. When we were down to the quick, Mama had a walk that got us out of anything and everything. And he took that walk. The walk couldn't nobody figure out, he took it. Chess yanked those beautiful legs right out from under.

"He kept bringing his evil self back to our house cause I guess he got tired of being out wherever he was without a roof over his head."

"He had nowhere else to go?"

"Look around, folks round here only take care they own. Chess the only somebody who ain't kin to nobody. So pretty he take every breath away, even Mama's. Didn't have no shame, Helene. Just walked in and tried to steal something that wasn't his. Then we start living like there wasn't never no time when Chess wasn't with us; like the café Mama ran in the living room wasn't Mama's no more, it was Chess's. He was running the house and running the café and all was left for me and Mama to do was cook and sweep everything Chess crashed. You can see that, can't you?"

"Oh, yes, Mama. Yes, yes, I see." Helene felt a hiccup coming. "This man had four legs, not two. Maybe, Mama, maybe he even had two heads." Queen Ester didn't laugh.

"Maybe when he trying to move everything around I should of said no. Like when he come in trying to run something we should of said, "It's ours." But we didn't, and Mama act like she ain't known no man fore Chess. When he should of been outside like the dogs, like anything that's wild and don't know how to mind in a house, Mama tell him, 'Stay on in here with us.'

"Then Mama turned into something I had to take care of and Chess keep coming back and tearing up the house. He pick fights with the men that stop by at the café, look women all in the mouth. When he ain't trying to pick fights or eating us out of house and home, he sleep for days on end and then he go off. After a while everybody asking after him, and I don't know what to say. I can't say a word to nobody without shaming Mama. I ain't gone shame my mama. We give him all we got and when he give it back I can't tell that it's ours no more.

"So then I wait. I thinks maybe Other might say something, maybe Other might stand up and say, 'Wait now. Just wait, this ain't natural.' But everybody go bout they business and Chess mess up our house from floor to rafter.

"Children grow crooked when they live in a house that's unnatural. Chess had this place colder than a motel lobby."

"I'll remember that," Helene said.

"I'm serious. Children can't grow somewhere unnatural."

8

HALLE HAD COME and gone by 1950. After a short decade of birthing children, she grew a tumor into the size of a cantaloupe in her left breast and it killed her. Chess remembered the day well. "I need to lay down," she had told him. "All this running around is getting to be too much." Sure a better life could be found three towns over, for years they had moved from state to state, making babies all along the way. Halle's mother would always arrive and rent a room nearby in time to help deliver her grandchildren. Rose, their eldest daughter, was born in Guymon, Oklahoma; Joseph and Betty in Jefferson City, Missouri; James in Humboldt, Tennessee; John L in Yazoo City, Mississippi; and then Arthur was born as they prepared to leave De Ridder, Louisiana.

Their travels never took them beyond a day's ride from Lafayette County, either by train or car. They needed to be close to Halle's mother's house; when fighting Chess, Halle always managed to maim her husband just shy of needing a doctor and then she headed back home.

Despite her predilection for violence, it hadn't taken long for Chess to decide to marry Halle. That she denied him almost everything made her irresistible. Food, sex, and her kindness were strictly rationed. Waiting in the dark to stab him through the lip, however, didn't keep him faithful. As soon as he married Halle, he met Morning. She had followed Chess whenever she had the money. Aberdeen, Monroe, Idabel: she'd rent a room no more than six blocks away from wherever Chess had decided his family would live until the lack of work moved him to another town. Otherwise, Morning would stay in Lafayette County, knowing that every six months Halle would return to her mother's and, four days after her arrival, Chess would be back in town clutching a wound.

Often Morning wondered how long she'd have to wait until Chess came to his senses and left his knife-wielding wife. The end of every six months held the same promise: "Soon, baby." But when Halle dropped dead at the end of 1949, Chess and his mistress were none the better for it. Without Halle to mete out punishment when Chess came home late or not at all, their affair soured. Over the years, constant adoration lost its power. Morning's homemade pancakes, though eaten, were insulted; her birthdays forgotten. When Chess finally landed in jail for three months, she thought she had had enough. Blue, her neighbor, had tried to court her for two years, bringing her flowers and groceries for no particular reason. She overlooked the neck spasms that caused him to turn his head uncontrollably. Certain afflictions could be forgiven when a man promised the attention Chess had stopped giving. Maybe I've been too good to him, she thought, as she made overcooked meals for his children. With the threat of Blue, perhaps she and Chess could work things out. Get him to keep his promise and marry her.

She was surprised as anyone when, after ninety days of jail, Chess came home and beat her from sundown to sunup. His children stood wide-eyed while the door thumped. True, they had run to tell him all they knew about Morning messing around with Blue, that tall man with the runaway neck. True, with humble hands clenched they had said to themselves that they had to tell on Morning because she'd cheated and had the nerve to bring Blue and pie to their house while Chess was away. And true, with lips biting and runny noses, they heard their dead mother say, "Tell him."

But they didn't think Chess would open Morning's face in the most vicious way. They didn't know Chess could turn the bed the color of roses and smash thunder. And who could have known that the door would thump like that?

"Ain't scared of you!" Morning screamed. Almost contrite, all six of Chess's children prayed that by the time the chickens had to be fed, their father would be tired.

"Don't want you to be scared, want you to mind!" Chess screamed back, just as desperate. His hand rose in the air, landing with a heaviness that brought Morning clattering to the floor. On her back, on her cheeks, on her stomach Chess made rhythm: Blue, Blue, Blue, that no-good nigger Blue.

"Ain't scared of you, Chess," Morning repeated, because everything else that was common sense had been knocked out of her head.

"Don't want you to be scared, want you to mind."

"Ain't scared of you." It took till the sun came up for Morning to realize that, more than obedience, Chess wanted the last word. So she gave it to him. She held her quivering fingers up to her face and thought, If I can stand up after this I'm gone walk, Lord. *Ain't scared of you, Chess*, was suppressed easily. With his fists and feet, Chess made the small house sway.

But who would have known what was happening in Chess's house, except for the children? All the houses in Lafayette County tilted in one direction or another. They held to the Lafayette earth as if they were clinging for dear life, as if the people inside them wished only to shove the houses away because they were tired of living trapped in sagging wood with no windows, doors with no knobs, just holes to stick your fingers through and pull or push. And because of the door situation in Lafayette County, no one was ever able to make a flashy entrance; your fingertips announced your coming. Chess's children knew he was done with Morning when his long fingernails showed through the door.

It was early, and outside the children were murmuring to one another about the quiet in the house while they spread chicken feed. Despite their different ages, they all feared that their prayers the night before had been ineffective. "God gone get us for this," said Arthur.

"But Mama said—" John L tried to defend their actions.

Betty spoke quietly, just loud enough to be heard over the clatter of fodder striking the ground, but they made sure to listen because she might tell them something they did not know. Betty kept secrets under her clothes, and everyone wanted to be there when she decided to lift her dress. "Y'all shut up, we done it already. Might as well just go in and tell her we sorry." Silently, the children opened the front door, wondering whether Morning would roll her eyes. John L risked a look. Her eyes were too swollen to do any such thing.

"What y'all standing here for? This ain't none of your business," Chess said.

Rose spoke. "We know, Daddy, we just wanted to tell you how much we done missed you since you been gone. Me and James and Joe and them got some money together cause we know you ain't got none considering you been in Texarkana." Smoothly, Rose sidestepped the word jail and everyone, including Chess, was thankful. Mind, no one was ashamed that Chess went to jail. Everyone over eighteen had gone, but in Chess's case, something special had landed him in the penitentiary: a leg washed in lye.

The leg went back to 1919, which had been a good year for the Hubbert family. Mr. Hubbert stood only fifty dollars away from repaying his debt to Mr. Sillers, Mrs. Hubbert had been asked to sing at the Seven Mile three times in a row, and late one evening their small Mississippi house couldn't contain the joy. Yelling, laughing, Chess and his parents tumbled around the room. "Come here, little man, come here," his father called to Chess. He dashed under the washing table and Mr. Hubbert's eyes fell on his son's small leg jutting out. He stumbled as he reached out for his son, crashing the table, the water, and lye that was to be soap the next day onto Chess's leg.

That same leg, not quite arrested in growth, dragged behind Chess as constant reminder of his father's wayward happiness. His limp and the possibility of sitting down had landed Chess in jail by tempting him to listen to Five, his friend. Five, who had grinned to the gums and told Chess that moonshining was easy money and no work. The law closed its eyes where illegal liquor was concerned; they could sell it out of Five's shack because no one came down that way; making moonshine was as easy as sleeping, so there was nothing to lose. But the revenuers came. Five ran, losing himself in the trees, leaving Chess in his wake of dust with four bottles of freshly made moonshine, looking at his lame leg in disgust.

Ninety days he spent in the Texarkana prison, jail fat collecting at his waist, staring at the wall in his cell, thinking about Five and watching his nails grow longer than any woman's. For three months, Chess had been imprisoned in the only brick building in Texarkana. Two stories tall, the jail had the deceiving look of a house, complete with wooden shutters and shrubbery on either side of the wooden double doors. Directly inside were wooden floors, and you didn't know where you were until your steps resounded on concrete stairs. Every Thursday, Morning came down with his children. They followed Morning up cement stairs, creaking in their Sunday clothes.

"When you getting out, Daddy?" Arthur said.

"Seventy-six days, boy. Seventy-six days."

"Can't they let you out no sooner?"

"I got ninety days, boy." Chess became angry. "Where Liberty at?"

"Home," Morning said.

"She can't come down and see a body?"

"Chess, she got business to do, and she say that you in jail, not dead."

"Well, ain't that something?"

"She ain't your mama."

"I know that, girl. She send me any money?"

"What you need money for?"

"Cigarettes."

"Chess, you don't need no cigarettes."

"Don't tell me what I need. I need something to help me pass the time."

"Still—"

"Morning, I don't need you to come down here and tell me what I need. If you want to do that, you can stay in Lafayette."

"Daddy, when you gone get out?" Arthur asked.

"Boy, if you ask me that one more time—Morning, why you let these kids come down here?"

"Cause they say they want to see you," said Morning.

"Guess you take them everywhere they want to go."

"Try to."

"Guess you take them to see they dead mama in the grave, huh?"

"See, now, that's uncalled for."

"Do you?" The conversation, before either knew it, became serious and neither knew how to reel it back in.

"Chess, see, I don't want to talk about Halle."

"Answer my question. You take my kids to see my dead wife?"

"Can't say I do." It could have gone on, a conversation about the visitation rights of the dead; Chess was happy to talk about anything, even if it meant a fight; but Morning's mouth had closed with no intention of reopening. They all waited, trying to think of interesting, painless things to say.

All the visits to Chess in prison went something like that,

and by the time the end of the third month rolled around everyone was worn out and someone always walked away looking shamed. Things changed over the three months. Betty moved from the children's room to Chess's room, happy not to have to wait until she heard the sparse breathing of children's sleep to whisper her fury. Rose could wake up in the morning and pretend that she was grown without some adult telling her to stop acting up and be a child.

Their sadness had turned into indifference, and with the arrival of a newly freed Chess they realized they had forgotten to think about him. Their old daddy turned new from three months of separation had bushy brows, big nappy hair, and fingernails that were long enough to remind them of a loose woman. When Rose said, "We done missed you since you been gone," the words came too easily from her mouth, like a sneeze from a tickled nose.

Nevertheless, they gave him money. At thirty cents an hour, three dollars a day, all the children worked the cotton fields for Mr. Carthers. Filled with a sense of duty, each came up with dollars that finally equaled twenty. When they offered almost all the money they had, Chess smiled, not from the gesture but from what lay in their hands.

"You some good kids." Morning spoke out of a broken mouth; her eyes, just slits since her lids were swollen, said different. I gone get y'all for this, she thought.

"Thank you," the children said. Frightened by Morning, they scattered like birds and out the door they sought another place to nest.

"So what you gone do with all that money?" Morning said, testing her swollen mouth with her tongue.

"Spend it," Chess said. He walked to the opened door

the children had just run out of and propped his shoulder against it.

"What? Drinking? Gambling?"

"I think I might go spend it on some women," said Chess, smiling because he knew the words he said lashed. "What? You think I'm gone spend on you?"

"I took care of them children when you was in Texarkana." Why you got to be so dirty? she thought, as she looked down at her hands; they were the only part of her body that still seemed to belong to her.

"And I spose to feel bad about that now? I didn't tell you to take care of them kids. What you think you is, they mama?"

"Chess, I know I ain't they mama. But ain't a one of them full grown. Them boys can't even shave."

"So you want me to pay you back?"

"Naw, I ain't saying that."

"Well, you know what I'm saying, Morning? Bye. Ain't got time to fool with you." And he was out the door, leaving behind not only Morning's broken face but thoughts of her as well. He turned in the direction of Liberty's house. Less than a mile he trudged, through the cotton field that separated their homes. In the middle of the field he looked around in disgust, softly brushing the waist-high cotton that was in bloom.

Don't know why she lets this cotton go bad every year, he thought. He had asked her why she didn't let somebody get out there and pick it—make some easy money. But she had said she didn't need the money. Liberty owned eighty-three acres of land, and not one square inch was dedicated to a sawmill. Such an act was blasphemous. The sawmills covered the land of Lafayette County and black people came to work them, staying in the mill quarters, waking to a constant buzzing. The sound invaded their dreams, rattled their teeth. In church you knew who the mill workers were; they sat in the back and couldn't bring themselves to hum. In the quarters, the women cried for brick, the children prayed for silence, and the men bit their lips because they couldn't stop the ripples in their coffee.

Lafayette County had suspicions about how Liberty had acquired all the land, because not one black man they knew could have laid his hands on so much money at one time. Some rumored she was part Indian and the government must have given it to her people. But how could that be? others asked. Just look at her. Liberty too black to be any part of Indian. The most vicious rumor was one Lafayette men put under their hats because they didn't have enough space for it in their hearts: Liberty had lain down and put those tree-trunk legs in the air to let a white man get in between. Chess didn't care either way. What he knew was, that cotton needed picking. But Liberty kept saying no, so he told her that pretty soon the cotton would kill itself, choke on its own stems.

"Has it?" Liberty had asked, her voice coated with a faraway tone, as if she were concentrating on trying to finish her lemonade and not the conversation.

"Has it what?" Chess said, watching his feet swinging idly on her porch.

"Has it gone and killed itself?" Liberty said, her lips barely moving. She tilted her head back and finished the lemonade and then, like a child still craving the sweet, she stuck out her tongue to lick the rim of the glass.

"No, but—"

"But nothing. That cotton is growing just fine without

me going out and plucking at it. I don't want no bloody hands." She smiled then and pushed the empty glass away from her.

"What you talking bout?" Chess pulled his legs up on the porch floor.

"Come on, Chess. You ever see somebody's hands right after cotton season?" She laughed. Almost yawning, she stood and went inside. Chess followed closely behind, breathing in her scent of dry pine and grass. "What, you ain't picked cotton before?" she said.

"Am I black?"

"I don't know. Is you?"

"Yeah."

"Then you know what it is to pick cotton and I don't want no bloody hands on me. That's it. I don't want to hear about it no more. You hear? Leave that cotton alone." She put steel in her eyes after that, and Chess left, the door banging behind him. That was supposed to be Liberty's last word on the subject, but the conversation was replayed every year when the cotton bloomed. Every season, Chess limped through the sea of white to ask again, until Liberty began to wait on him at the door with a no resting on her tongue.

Well, ain't she gone be surprised when I don't bring it up this time, he thought. Liberty was in the back, hanging the sheets on the line. "No," she whispered, when Chess was less than a foot away.

"See now, I didn't even come to bother you bout that." Chess, too, spoke low. "Ain't seen you in a while." She looked him over, her eyes resting on his shirt, which was covered in cotton. "Ain't you white." Her eyes rose to his hair, coiled and tight, a black rope. "Better go and cut that hair of yours."

"I ain't had the time. Just got out jail, you know." Chess closed his eyes to Liberty's face and to her house, the only one in Lafayette that was painted white and didn't lean.

"Really? I was wondering where you was. What you was down in jail for?" Her eyes danced.

"Moonshine." Chess's voice was curt.

"Moonshine? Didn't know you was into that."

"Well, I got to make money somehow."

"Them kids hungry?" Liberty paused. "Didn't they work for Mr. Carthers when you was in jail?"

"Yeah, I think so. They gave me some money today, but they handed it to me like it was they last."

"Never know, might be. No sense in talking to you about it. Not like you could do much no way." Liberty took the end of a sheet in her hand, stroking the corner. "What you come by for?"

"Just to say hi and ask you why you didn't come to visit when I was in Texarkana." And to tell you, Chess thought, that I missed your wide eyes and the way your feet point out when you stand still.

"You look like you was on vacation. You was in jail getting three square meals a day—more than I eat. Look at you. All them bologna and peas sitting round your stomach. Done gained at least ten pounds from the looks of it." She paused. "You ever figure you too old to get caught up in this kind of mess? Chess, you forty-six years old. Damn near fifty, going on sixteen. What did I need to visit you for? You didn't ask me to come and help you make moonshine, didn't ask for my permission. You grown, came to me grown; I can't hold your hand every time you fall down." She was becoming angry. She knew it and he did too.

"Well, I just came by to say hi, and I'll go now. Next time I fall, I'll make sure to keep it quiet." There was sadness in his face, and she didn't know whether to put it in her heart or beneath her foot. Chess made slow steps toward the cotton field and shook his head.

"Don't go off nowhere," she said, but her eyes roamed the clouds. There was something behind her voice, something that told him to look out. "Watch after yourself. I been worried about you ever since you went off to jail."

"Thought you said I got treated better than you in there."

"Something bad waiting for you in the clouds; when it rains you gone get swept away."

"Liberty, I don't need to hear about no rain. Rain done already come. I got put in jail for moonshining." Chess barely managed a smile. Liberty looking serious didn't help much. She had stopped licking her thumb and put her hands deep in her pocket.

"Mama?" Queen Ester's voice rang out from the side of the house, where she stood.

"Yes, baby," Liberty said, not turning around to face her. Chess kept his eyes on the white cotton.

"I'm gone have lunch. You want me to get you something?" Queen Ester asked.

"Naw, I'm fine for now."

"Mama?" Liberty lifted her head in response. "I was thinking to send out a letter today. You gone check the spelling?"

"A letter, child?" Liberty said.

"To Best, Texas, to Helene." Queen Ester linked her fingers together and waited.

"It ain't her birthday." Now Liberty saw her daughter, her little thing who wasn't little anymore but forty years old, though she still talked like a child, still needed waking up in the morning.

"That I know," Queen Ester said, with a hint of boldness. She unlinked her fingers and slid them into her overall pockets.

"Ain't Christmas."

"That I know."

"Ain't Easter."

"I know," Queen Ester said again. Her words had been defiant, but now her voice wavered.

"Girl, when you gone learn to leave that child alone? She doing just fine down in Best without you bothering her."

"She mine, Mama." Queen Ester's face said, Please, ain't gone beg, but please.

"She know that." Liberty put her hands on her hips. I ain't young enough to put up with this, she thought. "I didn't teach you pen and paper to go off and mess with that little girl."

"I'm a mama now too. I got a baby girl."

"What, you think I don't know that?"

"Like I ain't got no say, like I ain't the mama—" She stopped and swallowed.

"Shut it," Liberty said.

"Ain't no baby no more. Just cause she ain't here don't change that."

"What I say? You want me to come over there and tell you shut it?"

"She mine, Mama." Queen Ester didn't know what else to say. What she knew was that the little girl who had the blue nightgown she had sent to Annie b was hers. She knew the little girl, whose name she didn't know until that child had learned to write and sent Queen Ester a letter signed *Helene*,

was the only thing she had that was right. And she knew her
child was beautiful, although she had only seen Helene once
through a moonlit window, before that bitch Annie b had
sent her away from Pine Bluff with the word decent.

"You don't own nothing. Gone in the house fore I knock
you back in there."

"Yes, ma'am." But a combative stench had risen, and
Queen Ester knew that if she pushed the conversation any
further Liberty would pounce, as good as her word. So she
stopped, not because she was particularly afraid of a fight
with her mother, but because it wouldn't be a fight at all. It
would be a child taking her punishment. Open-handed slaps
that would fall to the middle of Queen Ester's back, then her
mother's fingers would find the soft inside of her thigh, while
her face, absent of anything that looked like rage or jealousy
(never jealousy), spoke the words Queen Ester hated to hear:
this gone hurt me more than it hurt you.

She cocked her head, peering around Liberty's tall frame.
"Oh, that's Chess, ain't it?"

"Yeah, it's me." As Chess spoke he turned to face her, his
eyes staring at the grass around her feet. He smelled the fight
too. "Don't you think you need to go put some shoes on?"

"Naw, I'm fine."

"Thorns out here nasty." Get on out of here, he wanted
to say to Queen Ester, still fixed on her feet.

"I know that, I live here." She moved closer to Liberty
and Chess. Though her mother's eyes told her to watch out,
just turn on back around and do whatever you was doing fore
you got here, Queen Ester stepped closer, until she stood
between them. Her eyes turned bright and accusatory. "Why
you out here with him, Mama? Huh? I can't write a letter to

what's mine, but you let him put candy in her mouth while he say God knows what."

"I ain't said nothing to that girl." And then they were back there, each in his proper place, Chess in the front yard with the child (Doing what? Just what was he doing? God knows), Liberty on the porch with Annie b offering glasses of mint tea and biscuits, and Queen Ester in the house. (No one had told her about Chess and the little girl squatting in the yard together, laughter flowing between them. But still she knew, if not what they said, then at least the form of Chess's back as he spoke to her child.) A four-year-old hurt throbbed new.

"You lying. I don't know what it was, but you said something. And now you out here talking to my ma'am like you ain't got a care in the world. Ain't that right? Well, ain't it?"

"I ain't came out here to argue." He lifted his hands in a gesture of apology.

"Well, here it is, anyhow."

"Ain't gone do this with you, Queenie. Now you gone inside like your mama said for you to do."

"Ain't going nowhere till you tell me what you said to what's mine." The smell of combat was strong now, as if something lay on the ground dying at their feet. Chess walked around Queen Ester and stood next to Liberty, glancing at her for a sign that she would slap Queen Ester back into place. She was curiously blank. All three were thinking of where to go next, how to conjure words that would prick and leave a mark.

Not so in Best, Texas. Man, woman, child gathered at a table some five hundred miles away with turnip greens flavored with smoked ham hock, potato salad with a bit of onion and eggs, and a platter of chicken. After a quick prayer—"God bless this . . ."—adult conversation followed, mundane questions back and forth—"Bill man come by? How your foot getting along?" and so on—until Annie b turned to family gossip. "She done sent another one."

"Who now?"

"You know who." Annie b gave a hard nod over Helene's bowed head. "Don't make no sense."

"Ah, girl, leave that scratch alone. Ain't nobody hurting a thing."

"She got to cut out this meddling. Let it well alone. You say what harm but you know as well as I do, she keep pulling the way she is and ain't nothing gone come of it but hurt. Once in a while is all right by me, but it ain't her birthday all the time. I got a whole satchel worth of them things; she can't read them fast enough. What's so important that she got to get something to her four sometimes five times a week? Lord know what she telling."

Ed slid a piece of chicken onto his plate, looking at his wife. "Them letters ain't what got you going, b."

"Sure it is. That and knowing them two women is nasty as all get-out. I ain't no fool to what's going on down there."

"Up there, you mean."

"All right. All right. Up there. Can't tell me, Ed." Then a nine-year-old voice piped up, curious, hungry.

"What two women, Auntie?"

"I ain't raised you to jump in grown folks' business like that."

"Now, b, let her be. You get to talking like that and anybody gone want to know."

"That ain't the point. Ain't I told you not to listen to grown folks?"

"Yes, ma'am."

"Then what you call yourself doing?"

"I can't help it, Auntie."

"Oh, no, you'll help it all right." The chair Annie b sat in scraped back, and she lifted her hand.

"Stop all that, now," Uncle Ed said. He looked at Helene. "Gone take a plate to your room and finish eating in there." He stared at his wife, her hand still raised. "And put your hand down. Quit on all that. You grown enough to know you can't keep on picking and picking at a thing." He paused to take a bite of chicken. "You don't know what's going on up there any more than I do. Do you?"

"Well, I know—"

Ed cut her off, jabbing his empty fork in her direction. "All you know is that we got they little girl."

Annie b grunted sharply. "I'll keep the peace, but I sho ain't gone turn blind just cause you say so. Nothing stands to reason. If Queenie's the mama, how come she can't stay with them? You tell me that. I got nothing against the girl, but I don't like when folks try to pull one over on me. Something going on *up* there in that house, and it ain't part of God's plan."

True enough, something was going on up there. Mother, daughter, and interloper stood right beside the clothesline, in front of a choked cotton patch, afraid to say a hurtful thing that could knock them all down. Liberty touched Queen Ester's shoulder. She swallowed her stern voice, producing a soft coaxing sound. "I was right there when Chess was sitting with her. He ain't said a thing. Don't you think I would have told you if he did? Don't you?"

"Yes, ma'am."

"Now here you is pulling on some old hurt and Chess just got out. What kind of welcome is that? Gone to the house and I'll see off that letter." Liberty turned to Chess. "Didn't you say you have somewhere to go?" Liberty asked.

Chess lifted his eyes, and relief shone from his face. "Yeah, I did."

After leaving Liberty's, Chess thought he would go to Bo Web's, but Bo's woman worshiped God on Saturdays, so no jook music and no beer. He weighed going to Flip's but it was on the edge of Lafayette, close to Canfield, and he didn't know the people who went there. The places where a man could go and prop himself against a porch were limited. There were no real cafés in Lafayette County, only sagging houses where the owners put in swinging doors to signal that they were open for business. Chess headed back to his house, cursing that he had no car.

"Where you been?" Morning asked, as he stepped inside the door.

"Outside." Chess smiled as he spoke, but Morning had a face that said she did not want to be humored. "Come on, girl, I didn't come home to fight. I need these nails of mine to get clipped." Chess reached out and tugged at her hips, almost dragging her into the bedroom. On the mattress they fell and Chess laughed. "Well, get to cutting."

"Clip your own damn nails."

"Can't you do nothing for a Negro just out of jail?"

"Look at my face, Chess. Who the worse?"

"Ah, Morning, now."

"I can't even feel my face, I can't sit down without hurting somewhere. You done broke me to pieces. Now what? You want me to say thank you? I'm spose to act like nothing wrong, except I done took so much BC powder, I'm sick at the stomach."

"Morning." Chess took a deep breath. "I'm saying please. I can't even hold clippers the way my nails is."

"Ain't got no clippers."

"Gone in the kitchen and get some." As Morning rose, Chess slapped her behind, still smiling, but his grin was fading because she didn't want to play. Liberty's words had gotten under his skin, and in his mind to stop the rain he had to be good to somebody. Morning came back, trying to keep her crushed mouth still so as not to break the scabs. "What you look like that for, girl? Smile, it ain't gone hurt."

"I can't smile, you done broke my face." After Chess had left, Morning had run to the bedroom and snatched her purse from under the chair. Three packets of powder in a glass of water and within an hour Morning glowed. Waiting till she was numb she went to her purse again, grabbing a mirror. What she saw threw her to her knees. A long shaky cut over her right eye, a swollen jaw, her lip slit in three places. "Ain't saying I was right for messing with Blue. But you ain't right for making me look like this. You better hear what I'm saying: I ain't gone look like this no more."

When Morning spoke, Chess's smile drooped to the floor. "Well, you shouldn't have been messing around with Blue. You can't wait for me three months?"

"I'm here, ain't I? I'm here. The next time you get the

notion that you want to beat me and make me mind, I'm gone walk out that door and close it. Ain't coming back."

Morning had said this all before, but it was the burn in her eye that told Chess to say something easy and soothe her. "You want to hear my sorry, well, here it go: sorry. But Morning, ain't gone beg. That ain't my nature."

"Did I ask you to beg?" With a stiff gait, Morning sat on the mattress with a crush and a whoosh, took his hands, and started to clip his fingernails. "Sometime you treat me like sunshine, but then you go off and rain on me. You know what? I'm getting sick. If leaving you gone shake this cold, that's what I'm gone do."

"Well, I see what you saying. You done finish with my nails?"

"Chess!"

"I said I see what you saying. I'm gone try to keep my hands off you as long as you keep your hands off Blue." Chess smiled, pulling Morning into bed with him.

They lay there, the clipped nails on the floor, and Chess asked about the weather and would she like to go fishing with him. "Someone said in Bo Web's that they were in for rain tomorrow," she said.

"What you doing at Bo Web's?"

"Like everybody else, dancing, drinking," Morning replied.

"Why didn't you go to Liberty's?"

Morning thought. Cause I can't stand up to your dead wife, she wanted to say. Because Halle up and died of cancer and got your tears, and I take care of your kids all by myself for three months and get knocked down for it. Because if I lie down in the dirt no one would see me, and Halle passed for white when she felt like it. Because I'm big and Halle was thin as a string. Because every time you had a fight with

Halle she ran down to her mama's and you ran to get her, and when I run off you wait till I come back. Because everyone at Liberty's café knows that.

"Just needed to see some new folks and different food," is what she said.

"Tomorrow's Sunday. We can go to Bo Web's for fish."

"Not the long way."

"Ah, Morning."

"I ain't walking from here clean round the other side of Erling."

"All right. All right. We'll go the short way."

"Cross the footbridge."

"All right, I said."

"Bo Web's wife got pork chops? Fish make me swell up, you know that."

She curled her hand beneath her chin. Feeling drowsy but wanting to talk, she mumbled about her family. Morning was tired and Chess yawned in response. They continued to talk, their voices low and secret, yielding to soft nods and smiles. Sleep came on them without warning, so quick they didn't have time to say good night.

In the middle of the night, Arthur dreamed. He was pulling a small red wagon, and in the back a little girl rode. His legs, fast in his dream, glided across grass as if the girl weighed nothing. The wind pushed on Arthur's hat and played with his jacket, making wings at his sides. Quickly he ran, blurring the sky.

But then the little girl grew heavy, slowing the wagon down. Arthur turned around, asking her to get out and race beside him. The wagon had become too hard to pull. He was shocked by what he saw. The girl's hair turned red, growing longer as he watched. Seeing Arthur's puzzled face, she began to laugh. Open-mouthed, tongue showing, she laughed aloud. Laughter shook her body and threatened to overwhelm her, but she went on, its sound turning dirty, secret. Still her hair grew. Red bounty filled the wagon. The hair grabbed Arthur by the wrist, pulling him down into her red sea, swallowing him in its folds.

Arthur's scream ripped the air.

"What is it? What is it?" Betty said, shaking with fear. All the children woke up, blinking at Arthur.

"What's going on in here?" Morning came in, still in her clothes.

"Something wrong with Arthur," said Rose.

"I don't feel good, I think I hurt myself," Arthur said, lightly touching his swollen wrist.

"Now how you hurt yourself like that in your sleep?" Morning asked.

"Maybe he hit it on the floor," Betty said.

"No, I didn't, it was some hair," said Arthur, looking at Morning.

"Y'all gone to bed. Arthur, can you sleep with your wrist like it is?" Morning asked.

"Yes."

"Well, lie back down. I'll look at it when the light gets here." She returned to Chess's bedroom. "Baby, Arthur all right, hurt his hand on the floor, I think," Morning said. She heard his deep breathing; Chess had not stirred.

On the path to Bo Web's the next day, the sky was free of clouds, and still yesterday's conversation with Liberty scared him. A woman bigger than her front door, she could take down the sun if the notion hit her, but she had looked helpless yesterday.

Had he been looking ahead he would have seen Cookie twisting around the trees. A churchgoer, she was one of Liberty's regulars, a woman with a taste for gossip. Chess didn't notice Cookie in the path and bumped into her.

"Where y'all heading to?" Cookie asked, heaving while she spoke. She bent down to pick up the sack Chess knocked out of her hands.

"Bo Web's," Chess said. "What you doing out in the woods?"

"Figured out a shortcut to Mable's. She said she gone take me to church in Canfield. Got a car her Downtown man let her borrow. So I got to get on the good foot if I'm going. Say, you seen Five since you been back?" Cookie tried to keep her breathing casual. "Folks around saying Five talking about you like you ain't nothing. They say Five was talking about how he should of known better than get involved with you. Talking about how you got caught cause you old and you got that leg. Ain't saying it's true, but that's what I heard."

"That's what he say, huh?"

"Yeah, that's what he say." Cookie turned to leave. "Hi, Morning, didn't see you. I see y'all later." They said good-bye to her back and walked on.

"We ain't at Bo Web's yet? I don't remember it being this far," Morning grumbled.

"We gone be there soon."

"Hand me them house shoes I told you to bring." Morning began to frown. "Don't tell me you didn't bring them." Chess said nothing. "And I guess you didn't bring that newspaper I got from Kansas City either."

"Naw, I didn't bring neither of them."

"See, Chess, you ain't right. I wanted the paper and now I ain't got nothing to do."

"What you read the paper for anyway? I tell you what's going on."

"What you know? You can't even read. You don't even—"

"Morning, I ain't asked you to Bo Web's just for a fight. You that mad about a paper?"

"Yeah, I'm that mad about it."

"Well, gone home. I don't need that kind of mess. Every time I think of something decent for us to do, you go and act a fool. I'm sick of fooling with you. Gone. Gone home, you hear?"

Morning turned on her heel, smacking a couple of trees as she passed them, and wished a couple would fall on Chess and knock him down. She knew come hell or high rain, Chess wouldn't follow her, not even if it meant her life.

Chess watched her leave, shaking his head and wondering whether or not to go after her. If she fool enough to keep on walking, let her walk, he thought. With that, Chess continued falling over hidden stumps, breaking the branches that slapped him in the face, cursing to himself why he was foolish enough to get involved with someone who didn't have enough sense to keep his children at home when he was in prison. "I swear that girl ain't nothing but hassle," he muttered. Now the pinching of his own shoes made him forget about Morning. Those shoes hurt like hell, but they were the most handsome things Chess owned.

He remembered buying them. He felt the pride swelling

as he stepped into Mr. Frank's and pointed at the shining patent-leather wing-tipped Stacey Adamses in the window. Chess just smiled when Mr. Frank said he would have to buy them as is. Chess was figuring that as much as he had been dreaming about them, he would have no problem fitting them. They were two sizes too small.

Half a mile later, Morning realized she had lost her way. Around the trees, pushing back branches, and stepping over fallen logs, Morning thought that if this wasn't the place she had been, it certainly looked like it. Maybe I should turn back and try to find him, she wondered. Maybe I should tell him I don't mind going along, cause it's better than not knowing the way.

Sounds of watery rustling and the crunching of his pretty shoes interrupted Chess's memories. Had Chess looked down, he would have turned back or at least taken off his shoes, which were being scratched by hidden branches that curved up, away from the ground, and tried to trap his feet. But he thought of Liberty and the rain she had spoken of and decided that if he just kept moving forward, the rain would stay where it was supposed to be.

Morning kept walking. She remembered how the children wouldn't eat the food she made after their mother had died. How she tried to wipe their asses and they slapped her hands. If she found Chess, she would tell him that he and them kids don't treat her right and she was tired.

———

There was an urgency racing in Chess's blood, and though he wished to slow down he couldn't. He imagined the laughter that Cookie would share with everyone at church.

Morning was lost and in her confusion she made a semicircle around Chess. Angry steps pushed aside the debris. I been licking my lips thinking about that paper. See, he want me small and in his hands, she thought. Lord, find me.

Chess heard footsteps and tried to replay the sound. Through the forest he was sure he saw someone. The sun glared and Chess was blinded, but he swore he could make out teeth dancing among the leaves. I bet that's Five, he decided as he ran. So he thrashed the trees. What would it be, to leap over the trees.

I'm tired of his hitting me and him thinking everything fine. She went quiet as she heard muffled sounds approaching. If that ain't Chess I don't know who is, she mumbled. But then she ran, with swiftness, her hair blooming behind her into a black flower. When he catch me, we gone tumble. I'll look up at him and laugh and say I ain't got to be Halle and almost white, do I, do I?

That got to be Five, else I'm running like a fool for nothing. I running like one of them children of mine, Chess thought.

As if he had summoned them, his children appeared before him. They laughed, the sort of children's laughter that comes from nowhere. Only children can do that, pull laughter out of the air. But Chess's children swallowed their laughter when he entered the room. One day, he would catch them, empty-handed, with laughter stuffed in their mouths.

Morning shook the bark with the sound of her laughter. And when he catch me, she thought, I'll ask him how he know it was me and he'll say, Cause you my Morning; then I'll tell him that the only reason I was with Blue is that Blue kept after me. Every time I run, Blue run after me; but now you run too, so all that over; see, Chess? All that's gone.

Morning's hands flew behind her and Chess's hands reached forward, so they seemed to be tied together with an invisible string. Leaves whispered in their wake; they rushed by the trees, because nothing could stand in the way of children at serious play. But then, closing in on her, Chess screamed, "Five, I'm gone get you, you dirty son of a bitch!" And if Morning had run before, then she flew. Misnamed and now blinded with tears, she prayed to the woods to lose her again.

He stopped suddenly, trying to give his heart a break, but his heart wasn't listening to his mind at all. Scared, Chess looked around him; it seemed as if he wasn't moving, but his feet flew over the grass. Five was gone. Then he came upon the lake and as soon as his shoe hit the water, he knew Five and his racing heart had both tricked him. By the time his head had caught up with his feet, he was already there, in the water.

He saw a boy flapping and fighting for breath. Small, thin. Chess waded toward him, hot fear coursing down his back as he stepped in the shallow end of Erling Lake. Ain't no pair of lips this time. No flood either. He just a little bit out there; all I got to do is grab him and haul him out. Cold water lapped against the cuffs of Chess's pants, and as he walked deeper, it inched up his calves to the knees. Maybe this the rain Liberty done told me about, Chess thought, and though it was mean, he turned away, about to leave the lake. "Help! Please!" Chess heard the need in the boy's voice; he hadn't heard longing like that since his late wife, the way she had turned the word *please* into sweet beckoning.

He had loved Halle's sound. Not her voice exactly, but the noises that accompanied her movements. The way her zipper hissed going down or the way Halle's breath came out in a whispery rush when she bent over to buckle her shoes. If he kept really quiet, he could hear the sound of her breasts pressing against her knees when she bowed low to roll her stockings over her toes. Chess could even hear Halle's knees object when she finally sat upright, finished with her task. Chess loved the way her legs, entrapped in stockings, swished when they crossed over during church. At home he would hit her so he could hear the thud of her falling to the floor. She never fell alone; Chess would follow her to the ground, pressing his ear close to her mouth, listening to hoarse breathing, smiling, loving the sound of it.

Chess returned to the boy, jumping into the water fully.

He hadn't expected the rush of cold water, and for a moment he was stunned. The lake closed over his head while he grabbed the boy's foot, then tried to climb on top of him to reach the sweetest air in Lafayette County, the kind that lay right on top of the water.

His legs sawed back and forth, trying to lift him above the lake, but their movements had the reverse effect. The more they sawed, the more they pulled him under, entangling him in the long grass that grew on the bottom. Almost out, he thought; he could feel it, the sun bright and hot above him.

Chess took a deep breath, thinking he had reached the surface, praying he was on top of the water instead of under it, because he just couldn't hold out any longer. He didn't feel the water enter his lungs, disguised as air. His body was twitching uncontrollably but his mind was calm. The last thing he saw before his eyes closed was his dead wife looking just as good as she did ten years ago. Just wait till I tell Liberty I kissed Halle good-bye.

The dishes were almost done when Liberty's knees buckled. She fell down quick, a tight yank to the floor. Her flower-print dress hitched up to her thighs and her legs jerked as if they were trying to walk on air. Struggling for breath, she gasped her daughter's name.

Queen Ester came running. "What is it, Mama, what's wrong?"

Liberty growled softly, her mouth opened and closed, trying to breathe.

"Mama, I can't understand you, what's wrong?" Queen

Ester yelled in her ear. Liberty stopped moving, and Queen Ester lifted her hand, about to strike her mother back to life.

"Run to Erling Lake." Liberty's voice was clear and tranquil.

"What you talking bout?"

"Chess done drown hisself and something innocent too."

9

IN A THATCHED-BOTTOM chair, her legs crossed at the ankles, Helene watched Queen Ester resume a story that would not cease until she did. "You know Chess was with us off and on for twenty years? When I think on it, don't look like it could be that long, but it was. Twenty-two years. Not straight through—sometimes he take off. Be gone for a week or a year, sometimes three years at a spell. Wouldn't tell nobody where he run off to. Never even pack a bag. Sometimes it take a couple–three days to find out he left. After a while Mama don't even look for him. She could just tell by the way the sheet crumpled in the bed that he gone. Twenty-some years, baby. That's almost as old as you." She paused, tucking her head down and blowing air into her housedress.

Helene wasn't quite prepared to hear that Chess had been

in her mother's house almost a lifetime. She'd thought he'd flickered in and out quickly, maybe two years at the most. No one needed that much time to stir the sort of devilment that her mother claimed Chess had.

"Mama, I'm hungry." As she spoke her stomach rumbled.

"Sound like it. Well, if we gone have dinner, we got to get those dishes done."

Helene stood up, her feet tingling from the movement, and walked around the wooden table to the sink, where the floor had been worn to a shallow depression from the sturdy feet that stood there. It was a double sink, both tubs large enough to wash a child, the white porcelain worn thin, black steel peeking through at places.

"What you got a mind to eat?"

"Oh, anything you have, Mama," Helene said, taking the dishes out of the sink to make room for clean soapy water.

"Well, we got eggs and bacon and bread."

Helene looked at her watch. "Mama, it's six o'clock." All this time has passed, Helene thought. We've spent almost the entire day saying what could have been said in two hours. Maybe if I'd asked Mama for breakfast at the beginning, we would already be at Uncle Ed's house, Mama soaking her feet in warm water and Epsom salt, complaining about the air-conditioning in my car and saying she had brought the wrong pair of shoes.

"Well, Cookie brought by pork chops and greens, couple days back. Them pork chops in the freezer, but I'm guessing it wouldn't take too long to thaw them out." Her voice was echoed by the opening of blue-painted cabinet drawers. "I haven't had someone over to eat in so long, I'm surprised these pans haven't rusted away."

"Mama, don't worry, I can't tell you the last time I used

a pot." Queen Ester placed two saucepans, a glass dish, a plate, cups, knives, spoons, and forks to her left. Helene turned on the faucet, filling the sink with hot water and liquid soap.

"Ain't you got no man?"

Helene thought she had not heard her mother right, over the haste and hurry of the water from the faucet. She sucked some air between her teeth and held it before she answered— not because she was embarrassed that she didn't have a husband or someone to call to, when she was home alone, but because Queen Ester sounded like a mother. "No, Mama, I don't."

"Why not?" Queen Ester looked surprised. "You a pretty lady."

"It's hard for me to find a man I like. All the men I meet aren't that great, or they're fat or too skinny, or they have three children."

"Don't you like children?"

"Mama—" Her mother pulled her head out of the cabinet and Helene saw that Queen Ester was trying her best not to choke on laughter. "I don't like children that much, Mama."

Queen Ester responded so swiftly that Helene barely realized how easily she had turned the conversation away from what could have been dangerous to them both. "Well, Annie b always did care for pork chops."

This is what hope is, Helene thought, a flash of fire that slips through the flesh and settles in the stomach so quick it burns. She and her mother played with it, speaking around hope as if they'd always had it.

"Cookie still around?"

"Lord, yes. I don't think she ever thought to go farther than Canfield, where the church is. I suppose the way she see it, if you can find God in Canfield, why would a body want

to go anywhere else?" Queen Ester smiled before her face
vanished into the freezer. Puffs of cold air escaped out the
open freezer door as she continued to speak. "Still gossiping;
ain't changed, but I suppose she ain't got that much to talk
about now—everybody leaving and all. I told you Mable left
to Chicago, and Chess's children, they was gone almost right
after Chess get dead. I think Morning the only one that come
by the house and say good-bye." Her hands pulled out the
pork chops and set them on the counter.

"Mourning?"

"Morning and Chess was together. From the way I see it,
Chess might as well of had two wives, cause he go with
Morning about a year after he marry Halle, and even when
Halle die he don't get rid of Morning out of shame. Morning
stay with him till he died." She joined Helene at the sink
and dipped her hands in the soapy water. "I wash if you
rinse. Anyway, Morning told me at the door that she had to
see Mama, and she looked mad. Mama ask where she off to,
and Morning say she was thinking Kansas City or maybe
Texas somewhere. She got a girlfriend down in Texas. Then
Morning take Mama by the shoulders and look at her like
she gone shake her, but she let go, like whatever living thing
made her put her hands on Mama like she was drunk or a
man just up and died.

"She left and I look out the window and she ain't got no
car waiting on her or nothing, she just keep going straight
out into them woods, not even walking on the path Mama
had beat out. Mama says maybe Morning feel like she need
to walk a spell, and that's the last time I seen her, walking
into them woods like there was a road laid through it. Last
I heard of her. Course, Cookie tells me she went to Texas and

fell out with the folks she was staying with and then she and that girlfriend went up north to New York."

"Really?"

"That's what Cookie say. But I say, poor Morning."

"Mama, how did she get a name like Mourning? Was that her real name?"

"As far as I know, it was. I think Morning's a right pretty name."

"I guess." Helene looked at her mother again, and Queen Ester shrugged her shoulders.

"You like gravy?"

"Oh, yes."

"I make a good gravy to put on pork chops."

This calm, this is hope, Helene thought. Standing together, her hips lightly brushing against her mother's, the commonplace talk drowning in the dishwater. This is what it's like, unneeded laughter, talk without meaning. "Mama, are you really not going to come?" Before she knew it Helene had turned serious. "You should get out of the house, Mama."

"Well, it's too late for all that." Queen Ester whispered her answer.

Helene didn't grasp her mother's quiet, her reserve, besides the gurgle of the soapy water.

"Oh, you don't know the trouble with greetings," Queen Ester went on. "It's always the women that's trouble. Try to be polite. 'Hello, Mrs. So-and-so,' and then look out. 'Oh,' she say, 'Mr. So-and-so been out and about without me, and so on.' And then I look at the mess I done got myself into by just saying hello. You don't want me to get in that sort of mess, do you, baby?"

"No, Mama, but you have to come to the funeral. I need you there. I'll tell you about the women and who's married and who isn't and why; I'll tell you all that while we're in the car, Mama, I promise." What to do about Annie b's funeral was something they could turn over in their hands along with the dishes. Helene felt their hands touching through dirty plates and cups, around and over through the soap. "Mama, you need to get outside." Not just around back to hang clothes on the line, not just in front to push leaves out of the yard, but somewhere that required her to put on a coat, fix her hair, and pay attention that her stockings didn't roll down below her knees. "Come on, let's go to the grocery store."

"We got everything we need for dinner here." Queen Ester took her hands out of the water, letting them dangle on the edge of the sink. "Everything we need is right here."

"Mama, when was the last time you went somewhere— anywhere?"

"What, you race and go all the time?"

"No, but—"

"You think I don't know what's going on outside? I been outside. Everything I want, I can get right here in this house. You sound like Mama—"

Queen Ester did not finish, because Helene snatched her mother's hand and plunged it back in the dishwater. "We'll never get dinner if we don't finish."

Queen Ester took up the fork and the sponge and began to scrub. If I can forgive the number of years you sent me away, you can look past my wanting you to step out of this house, Helene thought. Shoulder to shoulder, their arms rose and dipped, the pads of their fingers touching when Queen Ester passed her a soaped-clean plate or cup.

"Done," Queen Ester said, stepping away from the sink. She leaned against the table, wiping her wet hands on her housedress. "Now for the collards."

"Where are they?"

"In the fridge. We looking at a big mess." Helene walked to the refrigerator, which growled with age. It stood in the corner, large and rounded at the top; the cursive silver letters *Frigidaire* sat on top of an arrow shaped like an old Cadillac. When the door opened, the fridge moaned in response. "Pull up the whole door and it won't act like that." Peering in, Helene saw a bottle of ketchup and mustard, two blocks of butter, a carton of milk, tomatoes still on the vine, a brown hair comb, and three tubes of lipstick. Don't even ask, she told herself and pulled out the collards that poked from a big brown bag.

"I don't let Cookie clean them for me, cause that's just a waste of water."

Laughing, Helene said, "Lazy?"

"Naw, talk too much." Queen Ester raised an eyebrow. "You know how to clean collards?"

"Aunt Annie b made me clean them every Sunday in the bathtub."

"In the tub?"

"Yeah. I couldn't reach the sink until I was twelve."

"Why not outside or on the porch?"

"Aunt Annie was funny about me being outside alone." Helene felt her face settle into a pleasant smile. Their conversation dropped, then languished.

"Let's go on the porch and see to the collards," Queen Ester said, after a silence, taking the bag out of Helene's arms. The porch was enclosed with three large window frames that held no glass, just screens to keep the flies out so sunlight came in from both sides. A slim door was in the back, as if placed there as a last and fleeting thought. The wall was covered with maps: Texas, Arkansas, Oklahoma, and Mississippi held up with yellow and green thumbtacks, smaller maps of Washington, D.C., and Chicago fastened with gray masking tape, and a framed map of the New York subway. On the floor close to the wall were more maps scattered: New Mexico; Kansas; Louisiana; Atlanta, Georgia; Seattle; and California. An old washer and dryer sat in the corner, and in the middle of the porch was a large copper bucket. Green crawled and circled around the bottom of the bucket as if it had stood in water for a long time. The wooden floor buckled in places. A thatched-bottom seat like the ones in the kitchen and a wooden rocking chair painted pink perched in another corner.

"Pull out the chairs," Queen Ester said, and Helene picked up the rocking chair and placed it next to her mother. "You take the rocking chair, I ain't that old." A vacant smile tugged at Queen Ester's mouth. She dumped the collard greens on the floor. "Look between the washer and the dryer, and you'll see the water hose." Helene pulled out the hose. Standing up, she turned the knob for the water. The hose slithered alive, rising from the floor from the sudden pressure, splashing and spraying water all over the porch, all over Queen Ester.

"Turn it down! Turn it down!" Queen Ester yelled. "Ain't nobody trying to take a bath." She was soaked through.

"Mama, I'm sorry. You should go and change." Helene tried not to, but she couldn't help laughing.

"It's all right." Queen Ester laughed too. "Lord know, I ain't gone melt cause no water."

"I didn't know I had turned it that hard."

"Suppose be washing the collards, not me." Her mother

picked the hose up from the floor, handing it to Helene. "Fill the bucket so we can get started." The tub filled quickly, and they put the collards in. Helene watched Queen Ester take a large leaf in her hands, wringing the two sides together as if it were cloth. The dirt collected in the middle of the leaf, and Queen Ester dipped the collard in the water again. Taking hold of the stem, she pulled it away from the leaf, folded what was left, and rolled it up to cut later on. No sound was heard except the whispered tear of leaf from stem and the lapping of the water in the tub.

"Why are all those maps there?" Helene asked, pointing a wet finger at the wall.

"I put them up."

"How come?"

"Folks always moving, and I never knew where to. Every time somebody go, I got a map of where they done gone to. That way, if I ever get to one of these places, I know where I'm at. Mable got most of them for me. I got the Chicago map on my own, though, cause Mable and her man was the ones that went to Chicago."

"Are you ever going to go?"

"Where?"

"To any of those places?"

"Ain't ever had no reason to. Ain't nobody ever wrote or called for me to come. I can't go all that way to see folks who don't know I'm coming."

"But Mama—"

"Don't start, Helene. You know what I'm gone say, so don't start." They were halfway done with the washing. So close to being finished, when memory saw the blank and leapt in. Helene heard the collards in her mother's hands try to hush her memory: *shah, shah, shah*. But she still saw in her mind a wooden fence with shrubbery all around, three paths decorated with broken glass and colored brick that converged into one. Helene watched herself, eighteen and agile, jump on a wooden crate. The timing off, she had lurched when she shouldn't have, banging her leg viciously on the fence. If I jump just so, *just so*, I'll land to the left, which is good, *good*; and if I run quick enough the crunching of dead leaves will not wake a soul; then the kitchen, the bathroom, the hallway to my room—that's all. Helene opened the door without a sound and, untroubled, she walked through, past the kitchen and bathroom (so close, so close), but Annie b had been waiting for her, sitting in a kitchen chair pulled into the hallway for that purpose only, placed in the sharp turn, and without seeing the white of her eye or her teeth Helene bumped into her aunt.

"Where you been?" Annie b said, still in the chair, not bothering to stand up, growing with that unstoppable rage that only adults can have, the sort that jump-starts itself from past incidents that do not always have anything to do with the person being addressed. In Annie b's mind, her niece had broken the sanctity of her home, had been in a place she shouldn't have been, at a time when she shouldn't have been there, and her aunt's anger sprang not only from Helene having been out, and drinking, but also because at one o'clock in the morning her niece was in the hallway and should have been in her bedroom.

"Aunt Annie b, I just been out, that's all. With some friends."

"Out where?" She stood up. Helene noticed Annie b wasn't in her bed clothes but was dressed in jeans and a T-shirt.

"Aunt b, just out. I mean, at my girlfriend Kiesha's house."

"She got a mama?"

"Yeah."

"So you gone stand here and lie to my face and tell me Kiesha mama let you stay up in they house till one o'clock in the morning?"

"Aunt b—"

"Don't lie to me, girl. You think I don't smell that shit on your breath?" Annie b stood erect with rage in her pocket, but Helene's anger was there as well, the nameless and thus helpless fury of an eighteen-year-old who had been kept in the house for so long she knew of no real trouble to get into.

"Just a couple of beers, Aunt b."

"And now I suppose to believe Kiesha mama let you have some beers too."

"Aunt b—" Annie b's open hand came out of nowhere. Helene felt the fast whirl of air before she saw her aunt's fingers curl in the air and land on her collarbone, but that was the last clear hit Annie b would have. Helene ducked and came up with a fist of her own—two of Helene's thumps landed on Annie b's hip and chest—and her aunt came back with two blows to Helene's ear, making her niece stagger. Between the slaps, slivers of their argument bellowed in the hallway: *You turning into nothing but a slut*—three blows lashed out, making Helene fall back a few feet from her aunt; *That's what you want me to be, but I ain't*—Helene's foot came off the floor and she kneed Annie b in her crotch; *Get pregnant and work for nothing but a dollar and change somewhere*—her aunt's hand caught Helene's hair in a fist and she jerked her face close to her own.

"You can't pull this kind of shit in my house, you hear me? I ain't raised you so you can be nothing." Her hands tightened in Helene's hair, her forearms locking Helene's face inches from hers. Even at eighteen, Helene was dwarfed by Annie b, so that only one foot touched the floor.

"B, what you doing to that girl?" Ed came out of the bedroom in his underwear, struggling into a shirt.

"You gone back to bed, Ed. I got this."

"Ah, b, let the girl alone."

"Uncle Ed, tell her to let me go."

"Let her go, now." Helene heard him breathe behind Annie b, before he stepped forward. "I say, let her go, b." Ed was right beside them now, although Helene could only see his right shoulder. They were no longer yelling; Ed was concentrating on prying Annie b's forearms from Helene's face, and b's breath came in staggered gusts. Then she let go and Uncle Ed fell back.

"I ain't the one, b. You let the girl git to sleep."

"You say she right coming in my house at this hour?"

"Naw, but you ain't got to beat on her. She grown now. Eighteen years old."

"She grown when she move out my house. She want to drink and lay up with some man that ain't gone do nothing but use her and get her pregnant, she know where the door is." She turned to Helene, her lips already swollen from the fight. "Front or back door, make no difference to me."

"Just come on to bed and let things alone."

"You want to jump in now? You ain't got no right when you never here. I'm the one that take care of her. You got no right!" She was screaming, but Uncle Ed wasn't looking at her; he had turned to Helene, his mouth open and moving, except Helene didn't hear him at all....

The porch reappeared plank by plank, left to right, with

the slide and pull of a curtain being drawn. "Helene?" Queen Ester said. "Helene, baby? Change the water, so we can finish."

The soundless words of Uncle Ed still ringing in her ear, Helene hauled the bucket to the back door. It swung open. With no fence, the backyard seemed to stretch on and on. Grass and trees leapt toward the house like a jungle. Weeds that had forgotten their place ripened into half-grown trees, dandelions and wild bush reached up and beyond the knees, and fifty yards out, decaying rampant cotton mingled with wild Kentucky bluegrass and white three birds and Solomon's seal fairies that waved their bright blue petals. A person with shears wouldn't know where to begin, where to stoop and make the first trim. Helene walked down the steps and turned back to her mother. "Where do you want me to dump it?"

"Right on the end of the steps." Helene splashed the water where the grass didn't grow. It made a low arc, leaking over her feet.

Walking off the steps, Helene could see the back of the barn, with its wide doors hanging off their hinges. In a small space where feet had stomped the grass to dirt a sundress hung on a clothesline, red in the folds lifting and falling with the wind, the straps shiny like ribbons. The dress seemed too small for Queen Ester. Beyond the cotton field was a shotgun house with its door flung open; squinting, Helene saw through the house to another yard beyond. She returned to the porch and, reaching again for the hose, began to fill the bucket.

"Whose house is that?"

"What you say now?"

"That house. Behind the cotton field."

"Ours." Queen Ester pressed her lips together and began

to hum as she pulled a collard's thick stem away from its leaf.

"You shouldn't let it go like that." Helene took the leaf from her mother.

"I'm too old to get way out there and take care of it."

"You could rent it." Helene watched her mother's nimble hands tear another stem.

"Still mean I got to go out there and get the rent."

"You could make the tenant come to you and give you the rent."

Queen Ester snorted. "You know somebody that just come and give money without somebody pushing on them for it?" She picked up a fresh collard. "You gone close the door?"

"Can I keep it open?"

"You want to go outside?"

"No, but I thought we could have a breeze."

Queen Ester looked guarded. "Ain't nothing gone come through that door cept flies."

"I guess that means I should close the door."

"Guess you right. Plus the porch ain't nothing but open windows, what more you want?"

They said nothing for a while. Maybe after dinner we'll get into my car, Helene thought, and with the windows rolled down I can ask Mama to put all her words in the right places. But then Queen Ester picked up the story again as if it were a folded dress that needed to be shook out.

"Fore Mama died, I thought all dying did was take your breath away. Like all the dying folk just lay up in bed looking sick and sad, and when they almost ready they say, 'Well, bye, now.' But that ain't how it is." Queen Ester paused. "It ain't like I ain't never seen no dying fore Chess come, maybe

I did, but I don't remember now. I just remember his and hers; everybody else just fell away." She looked at Helene. "Turn the hose back on and hold it over my hands, so we can get finished."

"You want me to empty out the tub again?"

"That's all right, let the water spill on the floor." Helene held the hose, the water spilling over Queen Ester's hands and the clean collards. "If he would of let her die natural, I think by now I would of forgot who Chess was. But he couldn't let her be, even gone." Helene's hand slightly trembled, and the water waved from the hose.

"You know what Mama's last words were to me? Not Bye, baby, I'll see you on the other side. Don't nobody think that maybe I needed Mama to say, 'Baby, I sho don't want to go'?

"But I don't get nothing. On the last breath she conjure she tell me to get out. My own mama tell me to get out: get up and get out."

Helene took the last leaf and wrung it clean, then turned the empty collards bag upside down and shook it. Gathering the washed collards back in the bag, they both stood. "Maybe she didn't mean it." Helene saw the words crawl out of her mouth like puffs of smoke that curled and sat in front of them, full of nothing.

They passed through the porch door (it did not shut behind them) and went back into the kitchen, the story dropping again for the moment, unheeded. "Go to the pantry and get onion and potatoes and cut them up." Queen Ester looked at Helene, waiting, as if her daughter would know where to find the vegetables, as if upon stepping into the house Helene knew enough not to bump into a stick of furniture. "Right there, behind the curtain."

The curtain, a sheet, hung next to the refrigerator. Lifting it, Helene walked inside and the sheet fell behind her. A smell, cool and woody, surrounded her; the top two shelves were lined with canned fruits and vegetables—peaches, strawberries, cucumbers, peppers—pickled eggs, and pigs' feet.

"Hurry, now. The potatoes and onions are on the bottom shelf in the back." Helene heard her mother's voice again, along with the sound of water filling a pot and the whisper of a striking match. Stooping, she smelled the dirt from the potatoes and melting butter from the stove. And then, with potatoes and onions clutched in one hand, she lifted the curtain and saw a knife and a newspaper laid out for her at the table.

"Sure nough, Chess die on a Sunday." There was just the almost soundless scrape of knife against potatoes. "Ain't no passing like the kind that got to be taken care of midweek. And it was hot. Maybe that's how things got turned around. Cause like it or not, you can't wear all them heavy dark clothes in the summer. Folks not dressed for a funeral, so they stop acting like they was at one. Mama tried to hold it all together, put on the only dress she owned, so folks should of known better. But Mama's dress was red, with two ribbons on the side to hold it up, so I guess it looked like she was at a party. But that was the only dress she owned, so what was we gone do?"

"Is that the dress outside?"

"That's the dress. Mama wore the dress that Wednesday and washed it the same day. She start dying fore she got to take it off the line." Queen Ester took the onions from the table, the knife in her hand gleaming. With one hand she pushed the onion out of its dried skin, like a tongue thrust out of a mouth. She doesn't cry when she cuts onions, Helene thought, just like me. Setting the onions aside on the counter, her mother scooped up the potatoes, browning on the table, and dunked them in the boiling water.

"Porch put on a record, somebody slid back a rug, pushed the couch into the corner, and fore I could blink we had some kind of party. Folks decided a funeral was as good a place as any to cut up a dance floor. Mama had a stack of records but not that many, and didn't nobody want to hear the same song twice. So we went to the house in the back where Chess lived, crashed through all the cotton, made a path where there wan't none."

Queen Ester turned to look at Helene, her palms and elbows lifting in bewilderment.

"Helene, he didn't even have no real furniture. All them children and he didn't have a bed frame. But he had music. Had records stuffed everywhere. And we found them all. Under the mattress, behind the loose walls, under the sink. I don't know what possessed Mama to search all them places. It took till six o'clock to finish all Chess's music. And it started to look like folks had done worn themselves out—like they was gone go home. But then Mable said she had a couple of records her Downtown man had bought her as a present, and as soon as she said it folks were pushing her out the door and yelling for her to hurry it up.

"Maybe folks didn't know what to do with all that quiet, and was too stubborn to put the same songs on again. I don't know what it was. They start talking. Nothing serious at first. Just about how well the funeral was done and how the new reverend really outdid hisself on the eulogy. Then I think it was Banky who said it sure was a pretty day, too bad it had to be messed up by going to a funeral. And then out of nowhere, somebody asked, 'Member how Chess loved blue skies?'

"And even then there was a space of quiet where folks could have sat down and behaved themselves. But not us. All of a sudden we was up, one pair of feet back through the patch of cotton, not taking the way we had made before. It was like we was lost all over again, and for no good reason, cause by now there was a path already laid down in the cotton field. I don't know who was at the front of the line; all I know is that I was in front of Carol Lee, and she screaming, 'Where the hell are we?' Nobody wanted to get left behind, so instead of stopping and picking the burrs out of our clothes we just keep on. All that white cotton and thorns and no way out, just moving in circles."

Queen Ester shook her head, but Helene only saw her two hands flashing as if they were four—light, quick, taking down the jar of bacon grease and splashing some in the pan now that the pork chops were done, then reaching over to a large clay jar, pulling out pinches of flour, shaking in salt and pepper and something else from a bottle that was not labeled.

"When we finally got out of the patch, everybody was white and cut up. But none of us minded a bit. We went through the back porch, and all us went into the living room that was still the café. Even then, Helene, we just could of shook off and said to us selves, 'Well, look here,' then held our heads down in shame, and still God would have thought it was sadness.

"But they just wouldn't let things be. They went on and started talking about Halle, the yella gal didn't not a one of them know. Porch and Buttermilk got to talking about the wedding party Mama threw for Chess, and Halle's white dress with the slit up the side, and how Chess was singing in her ear like a piano. But nobody say how Halle had that dress with no drawers on."

Queen Ester carried the boiling pot of potatoes to the sink, where the colander was waiting. Hot steam licked at her hands and elbows. Helene watched her mother's profile, cheeks drawn, mouth puckered, while she blew to keep the steam away.

"No brassiere on neither, but who was I to say, cause she was dead by then, and I can't talk bad about a dead woman." Opening the drawer by the sink, Queen Ester pulled out a spatula and a large fork. From the refrigerator she took out a carton of cream.

"And we just kept on, do you hear? The music was gone now and they just words, sounding like pages out of the Bible. The blue sky opened and shined down on Him, and He was Glory—He was the Miracle—there was no living and dead. There was only Him, Chess, living and dead, on the water and under the water. That's what we sounded like." Helene saw her mother pouring cream and butter over the potatoes and wasn't surprised when Queen Ester turned to her, holding the fork like a knife.

10

BY 1959, LAFAYETTE had gone through two churches
and six pastors. It wasn't the town's resistance to religion that
kept the pulpit bereft of sermons. They prayed like any loose
body of people for cash crops to come to fruition and for state
taxes not to find them (which was in fact a wrong-headed
prayer, since state taxes would have brought them paved
streets), but the churches never captured generations or even
an entire family. First a Lutheran church appeared, built by
Germans who came through the county in the late 1800s in
covered wagons—a century late, but filled with wanderlust
and headed for Texas freedom. The congregation they left
fell apart before it ever came together. Then the Baptists took
over, trying to assemble as many mothers as possible, but to

no avail. Yes, the mothers came with young children and the old arrived with a visiting nephew, but a complete family never. Those who fled the town, carrying everything under a black arm or tucked in a kitchen apron, took with them a rumor of Lafayette's sacrilege: idols lay hidden under beds, conjuring was done without the help of God. Untrue. The people of Lafayette just didn't have a full understanding of a church's potential. They grumbled when they tithed (which afflicted them again, the first three pastors filling their own pockets and the fourth drinking it all away). They couldn't see that Sunday's collection could have been used for new pews and doorknobs.

Still pastoral trust, never questioned, flowed implicit, and even after the fourth one, Reverend Johnson, stumbled out of town drunk while boarding the train, that trust never diminished. The fifth and sixth pastors saw the dust on the pews and hymnals and turned around and left. With Little Rock so far away, the town reverted to some primal understanding of God or gods, depending on your neighbor and religion. It took the time of a child's yawn for Lafayette people to read the yearly almanac as a second set of scriptures, and they never went to bed without sweeping the dirt out the door. Superstition came on the heels of desperation. Everyone chewed baked chicken on the right side of the mouth, and each and every foot in the car lifted when crossing railroad tracks.

The Reverend Doctor Robert Claire Mackervay stepped into this state of affairs; while walking to the church, the railway conductor spat over his shoulder because he and Mackervay split a pole. Unlike the six pastors before him, however, the Reverend Mackervay carried ambition with his scriptures. Young, heavy-lipped, he sought to galvanize the entire county. Though the pastor's first sermon would be a funeral eulogy, which should have damned him immediately, he filled himself with hope because he wouldn't have to search around Lafayette looking for congregants. They would come to him, mourning and humbled, seeking solace at his pulpit. Amid the swooping crackle of tissue-thin parchment, balm for grief would be found. The sheer possibilities of what could be done with all the newly assembled—rapture bound, ready to be consoled, on the brink of baptisms—made him shiver. Reverend Mackervay knew he would not have so many people united again unless somebody else died soon, and from what he saw they seemed like a resilient bunch.

The sermon had to hold out redemption and hope, stroke the living, and respect the departed. But before Reverend Mackervay could deliver his sermon, he had to convince Liberty to embalm the dead. An open or closed casket shouldn't have been his concern, but a closed coffin meant a missed opportunity to console the grieving. Reverend Mackervay had plans on how to use a viewing to draw in the congregation. A solemn greeting and a good-bye at the door wouldn't be enough. He needed to stand next to the stricken family gleaning precious information while visitors filed past the coffin offering the bereaved condolences. "I know you was gone come by and help plug my roof, but ain't no need for that right now" or "I know you like rhubarb pie just like my Uncle Willie" were the sort of insights Reverend Mackervay hoped would slip out of their mouths. Who wouldn't come back to a church where the pastor not only offered redemption but was willing to help fix a leaking roof?

Three times in two days he went out to Liberty's house, trying to coax her into letting the undertakers prepare the body. By the time Chester Hubbert died, coffin making had been given its own special room in the furniture store, and the staff showed respect by a change of aprons. Where formerly the dead had been prepared on their own sheets, now this was the province of practical hands. But Liberty wouldn't let them take Chess out of her house. She had heard stories, she told the reverend: how they cut the dead under their arms and turn them upside down, treating the dead like a hen during slaughter. "We do it the old ways in this house," she said. "Death doesn't need something extra." People in town had lied to her about having mothers and uncles prepared. Liberty fought Reverend Mackervay with a calm stare that fixed him to the door while she bit her nails in his presence. She fought him not just for her own sake but for the entire county. So when the reverend said that Mrs. Cecil had been embalmed—hadn't she liked the way the woman looked?—Liberty replied, "That ain't so, at least the family's saying different." The reverend tried wheedling and then admonishing, but nothing got him or the undertakers past the living room. The argument kept Chess above ground—bloated from lake water, teeth stained with blood, shit and water oozing out of his asshole—until the smell of dank rotting flesh forced Liberty to let the funeral men move the body from the house.

She stood in the doorway while they lifted his body into the back of a truck, frowning, smiling, embarrassed, while Reverend Mackervay stood beside her, fidgeting with his hat. "How bout tomorrow?"

"What about tomorrow?" he said.

"You got him now. Ain't no sense in wasting time."

"Now, I don't know about that, Sister Liberty. The men they got stuff to do and—well, I ain't had time to prepare something appropriate." He turned the rim of his hat between his thumb and forefinger. Six feet two inches, Reverend Mackervay stood as high as Liberty's chin, her height casting a dark shadow over him.

"You got the rest of the day and all the night, don't you?"

"You right about that. Sure enough, you right about that. Still, I think tomorrow is too soon. Ain't told a soul the funeral gone be tomorrow."

"We got Mable; I tell her. But you don't sound like you can deliver." Violence shimmered beneath her words, even though she looked tired. "You can't deliver, I take him back."

"No, now. I can deliver."

"One o'clock, Reverend." He looked at her blank face and saw the rim of her nose flare. "None later." She stepped back in the house and shut the door before Reverend Mackervay could say yes.

Once inside, Liberty slumped against the door. Suddenly, she bent in two and coughed, harsh and dangerous; a spew spread wide and clacked like death in her chest. Thick veins appeared on her neck, and her eyes watered. The sound floated upstairs. Queen Ester could smell Liberty's fear all the way in the back room.

"Mama, that you?" Queen Ester called down, camphor oil in hand.

"You know it is."

"We got to do something bout you. Call the doctor. Something."

"Doctor way off in McKamie," Liberty said, with tight laughter. Queen Ester came downstairs and took Liberty by the arm, leading her into the café, which had begun turning slowly back into a living room as Liberty grew sicker and steady customers fell off one by one. By the end of the week there wouldn't be a single person to slide pie to.

"You sit down, Mama."

"You gone go for me or ain't you?" Liberty's voice trembled.

"Might, if you ask right."

"I'm your mama."

"I'm a ma'am too, remember?"

"You holding on too tight," Liberty said, trying to shake her daughter off.

"You hear me? I'm a ma'am too," Queen Ester said, still clutching her mother's upper arm.

"You don't let nobody in this house forget, Queenie."

"Who in this house cept you and me, now? Ain't nobody can stop us, if we got a mind to do it. You let her come back, and I'll go get that doctor right now."

"Right now?" Liberty pulled away from her daughter's hand and searched her face.

"Won't even put my coat on fore I walk out the door."

"Too hot for a coat anyway."

"You know what I'm saying."

"Yeah, I guess I know." Liberty let silence crawl between them.

"Well?"

Liberty began slowly. "I been a good ma'am to you. Can't a soul fault me. You ain't never gone hungry and ain't never want for a thing." She stopped and coughed harshly into her hands. "And now you sitting here trying to be mama over me; want me to trade something you ain't got no say over. I shouldn't have to ask you to gone and get me a doctor; you should know to go and get one. And—"

Queen Ester cut her off. "That don't mean you can't ask right."

"What I'm saying?" Her voice desperate and wavering. "You ain't gone nowhere. Ain't been nowhere in five years and then some."

"Well, maybe I'll be somewhere tomorrow." Queen Ester smiled.

"Stupid bitch." They rushed apart, and Queen Ester left, walking back upstairs to her room, leaving the camphor oil on the table. Liberty picked up the bottle and lifted the cap. Beyond the slight stench of camphor she smelled mostly vegetable oil and water. "Ain't gone yet," she yelled, and slumped against the couch, looking through the window outside where the reverend and his men had left so quickly the dust hadn't even time to rise in the wake of spinning tires.

"Crazy, ain't she?" said one of the men in the cab of the truck, as they drove back to the furniture shop.

"Grief-stricken," Reverend Mackervay said to him, and sighed. "Just grief. We'll take care of that tomorrow." The truck rolled on until a mile from the furniture store and the reverend asked to get out. "I'll walk the rest. See you tomorrow at the church at one o'clock. Even if it means a closed casket." Once out of the truck, the reverend thought about the sermon. First Corinthians came to mind; the bitter wrath of God's words through Paul the Apostle loomed over him on the street and carried him to his office.

Charity suffers long, and is kind. Charity envies not, is not puffed up, does not behave itself unseemly, seeks not her own, is not easily provoked, thinks no evil, . . . bears all things, believes all things, hopes all things, endures all things.

He loved Paul, his guidance, his steadfast words to a lost and tortured congregation. Sitting with pen in hand, Reverend Mackervay wove into his sermon consoling words to the poor and imagined the hardworking and sick falling to their knees, weeping. He smiled, his heavy lips curling above buckteeth at the thought. Only he had the grace to feed them God's words.

"You coming or what, girl?" Liberty called up. Though tired, she made dinner, not trusting her daughter. Reverend Mackervay with his men had worn her out, Chess's death sickened her heart, and her first love was trying her best to kill her mother through careful neglect. The camphor oil bottle full of water was just the latest thing Queen Ester had done. No pillow in the middle of the night or kitchen knife missing, just Queenie doing everything within her power to make her mother change her mind. Liberty sliced that thought before she was carried away by it. Queen Ester wanted the child to come back, as if nine years could be turned into just a minute. Didn't the girl already have a home, people to care for her like her own kin? And now (although it was not now, it was always, but Liberty wouldn't admit that to herself), Queen Ester wanted to haul Helene back into their lives because she said she had a right to. No, sir, Liberty thought, let my first love do what she will. Knowing Liberty needed chamomile, Queen Ester gave her Lipton tea instead and laughed. It felt like malice, glittering, harsh, but it was also a misplaced thought, assuming that sickness ignored will be forgotten and that, with no one to mind, illness goes away.

Liberty had neither the strength nor the inclination to confront Queen Ester. She simply stooped when the ill will came too near. A child's mind and a woman's pair of legs. Together, they would kill Liberty by the end of the week. Queen Ester's child desire had gone awry, become strong enough to choke the life out of her. At the foot of the stairs, Liberty called out again. "You hear me?"

"Yeah."

"Well, come on."

"Mama, I am."

Liberty lingered at the bottom of the stairs. Then she called out what Queen Ester was waiting to hear. "Down to eat, child."

Queen Ester appeared at the foot of the stairs, apparition-like, smiling, laughing. "Mama, you know magic words."

"Just come on."

"I'm here."

"I see." Together they went into the kitchen. Cold tuna salad and fresh apples waited for them at the table, and each woman perched on her chair, her mind whirling.

"Heard the funeral at one o'clock."

"You was way upstairs."

"Ain't deaf, though."

Liberty said nothing more until they finished the salad and started on the apples. "So, you going?" Liberty asked, suddenly resentful that her daughter wanted to share in what she thought to be her own private mourning.

Queen Ester picked up her apple, red and gleaming. As she bit into it, its juice ran down her chin unchecked. She smiled, her mouth full of crushed pulp, the red skin of apple poking out between her teeth.

"Oh, yeah," she said.

Liberty reached over the table and slapped her face, and Queen Ester took the blow without flinching. It took more out of Liberty than Queen Ester, who tipped her chair and let herself fall, still chewing the rest of the apple. She lay on the floor, her feet and arms outstretched, enjoying the cool tile beneath her and sucking her teeth clean.

"Get up, get up, get up," Liberty whispered, her lips chapped and split, arms stretched wide, pulling Queen Ester off the floor.

The same question and answer ("So, you going?"; "Oh, yeah," but without the grief and violence) echoed throughout Lafayette County. Exchanged by Poo-Poo and Banky while sipping beer, out from the grin of Carol Lee as she rolled her hair, through the pursed lips of Pat while she cooked up a batch of collard greens. By the time Mable walked through Liberty's front door, everybody in Lafayette County was accounted for; they just needed to know the exact time. Mable came and went, staying long enough to learn when the service would happen and squeezing Liberty on the shoulder for comfort. She was shaken by Queen Ester's smiling—the grin uncalled for and sassy, with a touch of glee. Grief showed itself in different ways, she thought. Only God can know anguish.

The Reverend Doctor Robert Claire Mackervay thought the same thing at three o'clock in the morning. Braced awake with black coffee, he sat in front of his notes and his Bible. Don't start with grief, he thought, as he had been taught in seminary. It scares the congregation, a mother might break, and then the sermon is lost, the seminary pastors always said. Start them off small, lead them to grief, and pray the men stay at home. A woman's grief is common, the scream of a dress ripping, the weeping, and whatnot; religion knows what to do with it. A man's grief liable to topple the coffin; then what you gone do? What indeed? Reverend Mackervay yawned in spite of the coffee and wrote a phrase in his notes: *Still water and holy Jesus.*

On the other side of town, Liberty's face was etched with torture, till finally she struck a fist out of the open window. Every night for the past month, a slow pain began in her stomach and moved upward, catlike, grabbing at her breasts, until it squatted on her face, clenching its thighs. Her only solace was the window; it allowed her to cough and not be heard. She had seen people die the way she was dying— constantly tired, their weight a sin, coughing until bright blood appeared.

She slid her hand out farther, till her elbow rested on the sill. The wind kicked up, promising and soft. "Didn't I have enough love for all, Jesus? And now my first love won't leave to save—" but then she felt a shattering knock, cold and persistent, starting in her chest.

Frightened, she leaned until she hung halfway out of the window, head down. Liberty coughed, unceasing; bright green phlegm streamed from her mouth, hanging straight and stretching a foot away but still attached to her bottom lip. The seizing in her chest passed. "I done too much for you to ask. You know that. And now you trying to make love look like sin. Are you there?"

Her head still down, she closed her eyes. "Don't ask tonight, all right, now? What I done ain't a sin; God know it ain't." She rested her chin on the windowsill. "Her blood is mine, his too, even though he ain't kin. I gots to take care of everything under my arm, ain't that the way? Theys all fit. It ain't my fault I'm bigger than the rest."

Who cooks for you? She heard a voice, the question damning. *Who cooks for you all?* She knew what lay outside the window. It would look like a small monkish man with black eyes, a barred owl screeching from a perch beyond the cotton field with a songbird in its claw. *Who cooks for you, who cooks for you all?* The owl shrieked again, the question booming across the unpicked cotton field, knowing the answer Liberty would give, a smirk in the question. Her face a fatigued gray, Liberty propped her arms on the windowsill and saw the bird rise into the air, its wings two commas, still crying, *Who cooks for you?* The inflection of the question turned with every stroke of its wings: Who *cooks for you all? Who cooks for* you?"—the songbird, still clasped in its claw, living and singing a persistent rapid chatter.

Liberty's breathing became tattered as the end drew near. Too tired to leave the window, she let her muscles relax, hoping the dead weight would pull her back into the house. She answered the owl, half flailing over the ledge. "I did. Maybe that's the problem—" breaking in the middle of her answer, not quite crying, the lungs sucking deep and wretched. She wondered how Queen Ester could sleep while she suffered; how her daughter could lie in bed, hrrring with her mouth open, deep in a child's dream full of bliss. Liberty finally fell asleep close to dawn, still hanging out of the window, the owl gone.

The rush of it all began the trouble. Sleep pushed aside, the women of Lafayette County spent all night cooking potato salad, shit-on-the-shingle smothered with beef gravy, oxtail and onions. No one had time for chicken gumbo. Amid the hurry and with so little time, small things went awry. Who had the time to add bell pepper to the black-eyed-pea salad? Women wore stockings with runs from the ankle to the thigh: the good dress, dark and below the knees, couldn't be properly cleaned; ties forgotten, suit jackets with Thanksgiving stains, babies with uncombed, ribbonless hair. An entire congregation was tattered, brooding, and angry without knowing it, sensing the missing formality. At noon a small crowd gathered by the church steps with lukewarm food on plates covered with aluminum foil, talking among themselves. Women in torn black-veiled hats and Easter bonnets bobbed their heads, jostling children and Bibles in their arms. The sun directly overhead, dresses dampened, hat brims wilted, but no one went inside. Without being told, they waited for the truly grieved to lead the procession, to set the tone. Liberty, Queen Ester. The women who would walk into the church with proper hats and shoes, duly teary.

And then there was Morning, the mistress who really should have been called the unmarried wife, who cooked and cleaned but didn't have the children to show for it. Who knew whether Morning would arrive? No one had seen her since the drowning. Mable had checked her house twice but, finding it empty, went to the mother's in Canfield, only to come across an old woman who wouldn't let her past the front door. In Morning's absence, the rumors swirled. She had taken to stalking the woods, crouching behind bushes, pissing with her panties pulled up, shoving fistfuls of paper into her mouth: true grief—the sort that howled in meter, rent clothes, and tore hair from the scalp in a fit of loss. Minutes passed, and then at 12:32 a fight broke out. Afterward many said it started because of the town itself, the way buildings and land came together, and with all the grief involved it couldn't be avoided.

Lafayette County was a labyrinth straddling a sloping hill and surrounded by water. With nothing but wayward footpaths to keep the trees apart, they crowded every structure except the sawmill. So Lafayette County people were forever destined to step out of shadows, spring out of bushes. Every action took on the taste of fear. Thus no one was prepared for the appearance of Liberty and Queen Ester. They just emerged, Queen Ester's hand supporting Liberty by the elbow and both of them sullen. Queen Ester looked like the poor cousin in khakis and a too-tight shirt with the first three buttons open. But it was the red dress that shook them. Or, rather, the dress and Liberty in it. "Couldn't she do no better?" the crowd whispered. Harlots, both of them. High-heeled shoes and painted faces, but the crowd saw the dress before they saw anything else, cinched at the waist with a matching belt: nipples pressing like pebbles against the thin cotton, Liberty looked like a whore. The humble congregation seethed that anyone would come to a funeral dressed that way. Never mind that the church's flock were frayed at the elbows, patches rubbed thin—at least they tried.

"What you-all waiting on?" Liberty asked.

"You, girl," said Mable, stepping out of the crowd. "Just you."

"And me too," Queen Ester said. The crowd swallowed them, surrounding both women.

"You too," said Mable. Queen Ester and Liberty stood just an arm's length away from the church doors. Coolness and the casket, along with the Reverend Mackervay, waited for them.

"Well, now. We all here." Liberty took a deep breath. "Let's go."

Sly and quick, Queen Ester let go of Liberty, her face pushed out and stern, and with the sudden withdrawal of support, Liberty staggered. A free hand followed by a worn white cuff emerged from the press of people, but it wasn't fast enough to catch her and Liberty fell to her knees, scraping her palms in the fall. A bowl dropped to the ground and cold gravy spilled into the dirt. The whole crowd heaved to come in closer, to see the look on Liberty's face; Bibles slipped, tossed out of sweaty hands, feet were stepped on. Soft shoving rocked the congregation.

"Good Lord, girl. Look what you done to your mama."

"Ain't done nothing," Queen Ester said, wishing she could button up her shirt.

"Ain't that the truth." They all turned to her, leaving Liberty folded on the ground.

"Somebody need to slap that face."

"Knock you over the way you done your mama."

"I got a hand for it," said the blue dress with black pumps and gloves but no stockings. Morning. The crowd sighed, because at least she looked the way the grieving should. Wearing a hat pulled down over her left eye, Morning said to Queen Ester, "You want to knock somebody else down?"

No one was quite sure who landed the first punch. What

was certain was that Queen Ester took a step toward Morning and that's how the fight began. They circled each other like men, no nails or spitting. Elbows tucked in close to the ribs, forearms locked, knees bent, fists raised to the middle of the chest, Morning and Queen Ester exchanged sharp blows. Queenie got in the most punches because she had dressed in pants. Not a word from the crowd either, no catcalls or rooting, just hands on their hips and a fast sidestep when the two moved too close. For safety's sake, mothers moved their children to the grass beyond the semicircle of people. In the end, Queen Ester lost. The quick movement of a shoulder jostled a breast free, and in the moment she took to look down and arrange herself, Morning brought up a fist that tapped Queen Ester's left temple, lifting her off her feet. Queen Ester lay sprawled against the church doors, legs wide, the heel of her shoe broken off. Both women took in gulps of air, heaving, their precious clothes torn. Three men stepped away from the crowd, hands dangling at their sides, waiting. Then Morning got a second wind; she stepped forward, pulling off her gloves. But the men who stood beside her knew her thoughts—Crack open the skull, I want to see the bloom of blood—before Morning could throw a final punch. Two of them grabbed her elbows, while the third wound his arms around Queen Ester's waist and yanked her to her feet.

"You done now?" Mable said to Queen Ester, and then she remembered Liberty, still crumpled like cloth on the ground, her face turned away from the fight and the church. "Somebody get Liberty," she called out, not trusting herself to kneel and hold her broken friend in her arms without weeping.

"Got her." Buttermilk and Carol Lee pulled Liberty to her knees. They gasped. Prepared for a face torn by tears, grief, and anger, they found nothing of the kind. Instead, the woman whose red dress had slipped up to her underwear wore the glow of a child in deep sleep. Disgusted, the women unhooked their hands and let her fall back to the ground. She came to then, pushing herself up on her elbows.

"What?" said Liberty. "What happened?" From the church steps came Queen Ester's rich deep laughter. Hands on hips, head thrown back. A couple of people spat in the dirt and waited for her to finish. But the laughter went on, resounding against the wood of the church. Liberty picked herself off the ground, shouting, "That's enough, now!" But Queen Ester ignored her mother. Reverend Mackervay heard her from inside the church. The sound pulled him down the aisle. He opened the door and the laughter stopped.

"What's all this?" he said, looking at Queen Ester, her eyes still merry though her mouth was closed. Mable stood at the bottom of the stairs and behind her two women hovered a little way from Liberty; he noticed the dress immediately, one strap slipped down over her shoulder, stray grass and dirt clinging to the cloth, her face starved and confused. Finally, his eyes came to rest on his congregation. Arms were folded, every face was clouded, and except for Morning, who strained against the two men holding her by the arms, no one looked particularly grief-stricken. "What's all this?" he asked again.

Queenie smiled and said, "A funeral."

"That's right," he said, looking past her to Mable for help.

"Well, now. We better get on with it," Mable said, and reached up and took the reverend by the hand. "Everybody, come on."

Reverend Mackervay pulled open both doors, and he and Mable walked in first.

"Six children got left behind cause you know the wife got

dead," she said in a low voice, her feet shuffling on the carpeted aisle, the entire congregation following behind.

"Don't say it." Mackervay lifted his brows in surprise. The new information disturbed him. Ten minutes of his sermon, written solely with the pained widow in mind, were now lost.

"I'm saying it. Wife name Halle."

"Ain't heard nigh word."

"I know you ain't."

"But I thought the wife was . . ." He hoped Mable would finish his thought.

"Seem like it. But she ain't."

"What of? The wife, I mean." They now stood at the pulpit together. Behind them the pews groaned with the weight of the assembly. Queen Ester crept farther and farther along the aisle, elbowing parishioners out of her way. Mable grabbed Mackervay by the shoulder and pulled his face close to her mouth.

"Broken heart," she said, her voice serious. "And another something you ought to know—"

But then Queen Ester caught Mable by the hand, jerking it from Reverend Mackervay's shoulder. "Come sit by me, fore all the sitting gone."

Mable turned, looking helpless and scared, and sat down on the pew in front. The reverend walked around the pulpit to face his congregation. He coughed loudly, and began.

"Dearly beloved, we are gathered here today to give witness to Chester Hubbert, father and beloved. Yes, Lord, I want to talk today about a passing. A good man. But fore that, Jesus, fore that, my brothers and sisters, let me tell you what I heard today." He stopped and waited for the shifting in the pews to cease, wondering, What word, Lord, what word? He thought of the word *laughing*, its sin uncertain, but then he settled on *grumble*. Common and mean, the word gave him room to bend inside of it.

"I heard grumbling outside the Lord's house today." He looked down, expecting to see guilt creep into their faces. Nothing happened. More than a dozen people were bent over with sleep. "Yes, beloved, I heard grumbling outside the Lord's house, and it knocked me down. You see, not today. Not when we laying down our own. Evil done saw that grief is on all sides and slide up in our fold fore we know it. On the very day we lay down a father to somebody, a brother, a husband." He concentrated on the very old, knowing that if he could get an *amen* it would come from them. "Should of known. Look in them pages. Stories of evil following grief everywhere. Lord didn't say it was gone be easy. Raising six children, and a wife that fell down fore he did. Chess knew it wasn't gone be easy. Halle knew, fore she passed away, that it wasn't gone be easy. Don't bring grumbling inside the Lord's house. Don't take it in your houses. Cause therein lies evil. Somebody say Sweet Jesus." Grief poked through his sermon, the advice the seminary taught him fell in on itself.

"We all are here today to mourn the loss of a friend, of a friend who loved us all. Nobody can say that Chess Hubbert didn't love." A row of women's lips spread wide. "Can you say Hallelujah? Praise the Lord. Somebody give the Lord his glory!"

Weak and scattered confirmation sounded in the hall. Frightened, the reverend watched his congregants restlessly fold their hands in their laps. The smiling women closed their mouths and fixed their hats; men stole glances at their watches.

"Chess looking down from the gates of Heaven and he saying to me right now, 'Take care of these children that I done left behind.' We are forsaken and not forsaken. But we got to look for the path, beloved. Just cause the Lord is with us don't mean He gone hold a hand. Take the grumbling out your lives and find a way, beloved. You better hear this." He paused, sweat dampening his collar. His temples glistened, the white handkerchief inside of his jacket pocket waiting to be pulled out, so he tried again, his voice licking at the crescendo to come. "You better hear this, beloved. Glory is the place you make. It is a dwelling spot made with your own hands, and there the Lord is." What had happened outside? he wondered. By now they should have been swaying. He wanted to reach in his pocket for his handkerchief; the sweat was now standing on his brow and he couldn't wipe it away. His next words, unprepared on the tongue, held his wrath.

"Vanity of vanities, said the Preacher, vanity of vanities." Midday and summer, the church burned in the heat. Reverend Mackervay coughed. "Right outside the Lord's door—vanity. I'm telling you, brothers, and bow your heads underneath the Lord's power, one generation pass away and another generation come—but the earth abide forever. And still you grumble outside the Lord's door. All the rivers run into the sea, yet the sea is not full. The eye is not satisfied with seeing; nor the ear filled with hearing.

"And the Lord as my witness, I stepped out here, one foot out the train, Jesus, and lo, I heard what you-all done done to this man and his water. And I said in mine heart, God shall judge the righteous and the wicked; for there is a time for every purpose and for every work. You done found evil in God's work. Don't you know, beloved? There is a river, and God is in her, and she will not be moved. And that there is where Chess went for refuge. Beloved, hear me! All!—" his hand lifted from the pulpit, the palm upturned—"all are from the dust, and all turn to dust again. We are troubled on every side, yet not distressed; we are confused, but not in despair; persecuted, but not forsaken; cast down, but not destroyed."

A man, sixth pew back, sat open-mouthed, his eyes rolling up white as laundry. There was not a word from anyone, no hum raised to the sky, but the reverend knew he had them. His stomach cramped in excitement, his words, the sermon, rolled out of his mouth. "Jesus, Jesus, bless it now, not tomorrow but now."

Contagious, the spirit caught a woman two pews down; she yanked a songbook from her purse and fanned herself, her light dress lifting and falling in response. The spirit jumped up three rows, where a lady in a green skirt shot her hand in the air, the action repeating, flaring up all over the church. Psalms flew out of the reverend's mouth. "It is not the place for man to know the works of God. Beloved, hear me. For our light affliction, which is for but a moment, work for us a far more exceeding and eternal weight of glory. We look not at the things which are seen, but at the things which are not seen; for the things which are seen are in time; but the things which are not seen are forever. That's right, beloved. Forever." Three entire pews—hum, haw, hum—full of tight anguish; Mackervay sank his sermon into their chorus, not even coherent now. A harsh sigh taking up most of his voice, Mackervay stretched out the word *forever*, a dangerous term among Negroes, and mistook their grief for affirmation.

Mable and Morning fixed their eyes on the reverend, the handkerchief out of his jacket pocket now flailing at his face like a washcloth, dabbing here and there, while Queen Ester swayed back and forth in her pew.

"Chess is up in the sky, looking at us all and saying, 'This is forever.' Still water and holy Jesus. Always and forever, amen, Jesus. The blessing of Jesus, now and forever. One word—" but the Reverend Robert Mackervay didn't finish, Queen Ester shot up before his sentence was through, the sermon tangled on his tongue coming to a close, while Queen Ester felt a primal naked fear build in her chest. *Forever* and *now*—their meaning was clear to her: to be doomed to wait with the dead in a church that smelled of a tomb, and the blessing of the Lord was cast aside.

Liberty watched her daughter. Not now with my leg half asleep, she thought, too tired to get up and stop her. Queen Ester raced down the aisle, stopping halfway. "I knew him!" she shouted. "Me! Me!" It took a moment for the congregation to find their outrage. "I knew him!" Queenie's loud voice mingled with their own. Most thought she couldn't take the mixture of heat and grief anymore and was heading outside for fresh air.

When she turned back toward the pulpit, as if preparing to topple the coffin, women began screaming. Frightened, their children took refuge under the knees of daddies and pews to escape the sudden roar. Still Queen Ester kept shouting, "I knew him!" and her voice soared above the congregation. Mackervay slumped over the pulpit, his congregation lost. Mable did not return his gaze but merely kept her head down, her arms hooked around the shoulders of two of Chess's children. The preacher was at a loss for what to do.

But then Liberty's foot woke up. A tingling shot up her leg to the knee. Sick as she was, rage became a cure. She grabbed Queen Ester by the neck, lifting her clean off her feet. "You want to act out? You want to act out now?" Liberty hissed in Queen Ester's ear. She pushed her daughter toward the door, and the congregation began to follow them back to the house—a parade of sorts.

Alone, Reverend Mackervay chanted the final words to the dead: "The Lord bless thee and keep thee. Surely goodness and mercy shall follow me all the days of my life, and I will dwell in the house of the Lord forever." Mackervay looked over his shoulder; and seeing no one, he resumed. "The Lord make His face to shine upon thee and be gracious unto thee. The Lord lift up His countenance upon thee and give thee peace. And they shall put His name upon the children and He will bless them." And then the Reverend Robert Claire Mackervay wept as a stricken mother would.

But who heard the howling of an ambitious preacher when the people of Lafayette had run out on him to follow Liberty, the truly stricken mother? Her strange sleep in front of the chapel was seen as theatrics, something done to wrench attention away from Morning, who had the love but not the children. Hadn't the town tumbled into her house and she outdanced them all? The rumor that she was sick, even that Liberty had shat blood, seemed farfetched, a myth told merely to show that even Liberty could fall on hard times. Now her fellow mourners left her house, while she stood in the door, waving good-bye, and told them not to come back anytime soon because she had to clean up the mess they made. She was about to step inside the house again and let out the long breath she had been holding when Morning stepped out of the wilderness, still wearing her torn blue dress.

"I want to talk to you," Morning said.

"What about?"

"Goddamned fornicator—"

"Where you get that at?" Liberty laughed softly.

"The goddamned Bible." Morning moved closer to Liberty.

"Stop all that goddamned," Liberty barked.

Morning was chastened, as well as a bit frightened. "Well . . . fornicator."

"You wasn't his wife neither. Mind that." Both fell quiet. "You want a lemonade or something?"

"I didn't come out here for that."

"Well, at least take a seat on the porch. I been standing all day." Liberty took Morning's hand and led her to the edge of the porch, where they both sat down, letting their legs dangle. "What you come out here for?"

"Why was you sleeping?" The question blurted out unexpectedly. Liberty raised an eyebrow. Didn't Morning want to ask Liberty something altogether different? Morning couldn't remember what she had meant to say, and now a question pregnant with potential shame sat still between the two women.

"You come way out here to ask me that?"

"No, but since I'm here, gone and tell it."

"What I got to be awake about?"

Morning gripped the edge of the porch with both hands. "You could of stopped her. She made fools out of everybody there."

"Of you too?"

"No, you did that on your own." Morning sucked in a deep breath. "He love me."

"Gone and tell yourself that."

"I'm telling you, ain't I? He love me." A frantic defiance lit her eyes.

"He ain't loving neither one of us now."

"Don't go skipping off. I'm telling you: he love me."

"He took you cause I wouldn't let him have me or my baby girl." Liberty pulled her knees up, about to rise, confident that she had claimed the last word.

"Ya'll share drawers, too?"

"Wouldn't you like a whiff. You gave him everything, and ain't got a child nowhere. Or maybe Chess didn't want no dark-as-night children on him and did something to his self fore he lay down with you." Liberty smiled, knowing she had won, since Morning pulled back from her, looking struck. She trudged out of Liberty's yard dazed.

But Liberty walked back into her house feeling broken and petty. Perhaps she should have let Morning have Chess's love. It shamed Liberty to think she could be so small over a dead man. The strength that had carried her through the funeral, the party, and then the cat fight with Morning vanished. Now she could barely hold her head up. Gripping the banister for support, she crawled upstairs and fell asleep, fully dressed on the bed. The next morning, with the last bit of ugliness she'd dealt to Morning still in her mouth, she almost welcomed the delirium that swirled around her. She stuck to her bed, the sheets soaked with sweat and drops of blood because Liberty refused to be bothered with that owl right outside her window. Who cook for you? I do, goddamn it.

It took three hours for Liberty to get dressed and make breakfast. The morning toast tasted like blood and so did the coffee. What had she told Mable yesterday when she asked if she was okay? "Girl, I'm fine. Just a little tired. Maybe sick at the heart, but that ain't never killed nobody." She saw the worry scrawled over her friend's mouth and hoped she didn't look as bad as Mable's face said she did. Dozing while slowly eating her breakfast, she woke with a start and found that two of her fingers had slipped into her warm coffee and she had pissed on the floor. Self-pity flooded her, because she knew she didn't have the energy to wipe away the smell of her own urine. Lord, I don't want to leave like this—wearing clothes I done messed in and smelling my blood on everything. Where was her daughter when she needed her? Queen Ester had disappeared after the funeral. I'm just too old and Queenie can't care for herself, cause I wouldn't let her for so long, and now what? she thought. I still got to cook for them all, never mind that damn bird. Except Liberty didn't believe her own convictions; the worry and grief had worn her out, and now this sickness seemed poised to knock her down.

For two days she slept whenever and wherever she stopped moving. In the middle of drinking tea she would wake up and find the cup grown cold; on the way up the stairs she would wake and notice her back had grown stiff. By Sunday morning she knew she wouldn't be able to get out of bed, even if the house were burning to the ground. A sour scent floated up her nose and Liberty woke, slightly gagging, watching her daughter's mouth move.

"You hear me, death ain't nothing. Ma'am, you hear?" Queen Ester shook Liberty hard on the shoulder.

"You gone to bring her back to this house? That what you telling me?"

Queen Ester watched her mother's eyes cloud over. "I ain't done nothing yet." She shook Liberty, who seemed to be fighting sleep. "You hear me? I ain't brought her here."

"I ain't said you did. I said are you gone to bring her

here?" Liberty panted and tried to push her daughter away. "Sit me up." Queen Ester hooked her arms underneath her mother's and hauled her up roughly, patting the pillows around her so she wouldn't sink back down the bed. "You need to brush your teeth. Your breath stink."

"Sorry." Queen Ester covered her mouth with her hands.

"You hear me? I said, you want to bring her here?" Liberty repeated.

"She mine. She yours too. Don't that count for nothing?"

"Go get me some water."

"No. I gone get you nothing till you tell me Helene can move back."

"That girl ain't gone get nothing in this house but heartbreak."

"Chess gone; now you on your way out. Who I'm suppose to be with? Who gone be here to mind me?"

"You got to mind yourself."

"You leaving to spite me."

Liberty looked at her daughter and Mable's advice returned to her, that pretty soon Queen Ester would turn foolish and she would rue the years that she tried to keep her child in a cradle. Now a brick of regret crashed onto her chest. She had just wanted her small enough to carry, small enough so no hurt could prick. Look what happen, Liberty thought. She can't wipe her own ass and don't even know she trying to kill me. "You got to learn to wipe your own ass, baby."

"Ma'am? What you say?"

"I said, you got to learn to wipe your own ass." Liberty saw the confusion on her daughter's face and almost cried. "I need to get away from you. You done let your own ma'am die."

"That ain't so. All I ask is for you to let me get my baby girl. You tell me I can, and I go to the doctor right now."

"Too late for the doctor."

"No, it ain't. I go get him right now, you tell me I can go get my baby."

"I can't tell you nothing. You can't see that? I been trying to tell you to go get somebody to help me, and you ain't moved cept to crash the church."

"I ain't mean to."

"You need to get out of this house. Move on away from here and be on your own. Maybe you can take that job Mable was telling me about. Move me up on the pillow, baby." Queen Ester reached over again and pulled Liberty higher on the bed, readjusting the pillows.

"What job?"

"Mable was telling me about some work at the beauty shop."

"When she tell you about it?"

"Oh, that night we went and got Chess that first time. Member that?"

"That time we went to Bo Web's?"

"Yeah."

"Mama, that was twenty more years ago." Queen Ester's eyes grew wide at her mother's mistake.

Liberty crinkled her forehead. Time had folded upon her like a sheet and she hadn't noticed it. "Shut your mouth."

"It's the truth."

"Lord Jesus have mercy on my soul."

"And that beauty shop done closed down, anyway."

"All right."

"I think that lady who ran it went off to Kansas City."

"I said all right, Queenie."

"Well, I just thought—"

"Lord as my witness, you just gone talk right up till I drop dead, ain't you? Shhh. . . . Somebody on the stairs. You hear that? Gone and see and come back." She watched Queen Ester walk out of the door. At least I can have peace while she gone, Liberty thought.

"Who that?" Queen Ester called down the hall.

"Yeah?" Other's deep voice carried itself up the rest of the stairs.

"Other, that you?"

"Yeah?"

"What you doing here?" Other walked down the hall toward Queen Ester. "You checking on Mama?"

"Yeah."

"She all right. Gone die, though. I can tell it." Queen Ester watched Other quicken his step and blocked his path. "Don't go and bother her. Ain't nothing nobody can do. She told me she ready to go and she don't want nobody messing with her till she gone."

"Yeah?"

"Yeah, she did." Queen Ester licked her lips. "Now you get on downstairs." But Other stayed standing in front of her. "You hear me? Get on out of here. You think I can't take care of my own mama?" Other opened his mouth, but Queen Ester didn't let him get out his customary phrase. "You think I let my mama stay and get sick? You think cause you see everything, you know everything? I know my mama, and I ain't gone stand here and let you tell me I'm a lie. You hear that? I know you get what I'm saying. I see you walking around here like you don't know how to put two words together. That's just something you pull to get over on folks. I see through you." Her voice climbed higher, trying to wipe away Other's look of concern.

Liberty had sunk again farther down on the bed, pillows

toppled over her, she struggled against drowning in her sheets. Panic lifted her voice. "Queen Ester, gone and get the doctor. Helene can come back if she want to. Queenie?" The brick of regret seemed heavier; she felt a tight crush on her chest. "I was the one said ain't nothing gone get left by me. I was the one who said that very thing. But she ain't mine, is she? That little girl ain't a part of the three: Queenie and Chess and me." But her voice sounded unconvincing, even to her own ears, a flat and begging noise. "I ain't begging nobody for nothing. Last time I begged for something was Georgia— no, on the rails, when I was begging Sweets to get off. But that don't count none cause wasn't no need for it nohow. He wanted to get off the rails just as bad." She paused, taking her last ragged breath, unable to finish her thought, that the Negro lived a life of three and that her three was done.

11

WHILE THEY MADE dinner in the kitchen, Helene wondered about her mother's biblical tone. He was the Miracle? He was Glory? Chess? Nobody spoke like that, she thought, watching Queen Ester pick up a fork as if it were a knife ready to be plunged. "Only so long a body can hate, and sometimes mine too tired to keep up with somebody that's dead." She slid the fork onto the table and turned back to the stove to fiddle with the heat. One hand stirred, and her head dipped down to the skillet to smell the pork chops.

"Sometimes I forget," she started up again. "You stay in one place in this house for too long and you forget. I forget why I got this knock-down hate for Chess. It's like all the memory I got goes away and what I got is right now, and that ain't enough cause I'm alone. But you know how I remember?"

"No. How do you remember?"

"I just look around this house. I look around and I see him everywhere. My life, my whole life."

"Mama, what are you talking about?" Helene asked, suddenly worried that she wouldn't get to eat the dinner her mother promised. I won't even get to see how she arranges food on a plate.

"I can't start from scratch cause it's my whole life."

"Mama, nobody's asking you to start over."

"Ain't you? You the one that wants me to run off to Stamps."

"Mama, I just want you to get in my car. You don't have to go the funeral, you could stay at Uncle Ed's house and wait for us all to get back. I just want you to get in my car," Helene said, her tone now begging.

"Are you trying to get me out of my own house? This house is me. How could you tell me to get out of my own house?" Taking a step away from the stove, Queen Ester pushed her finger in her daughter's face. Helene knew her mother couldn't see her. She was either Chess, leaning back in a kitchen chair with broken shoes and an open shirt, or she was Liberty, wearing a red-ribboned dress that couldn't hold all that spilled out of it.

"Wait a minute, Mama, I know this is your house. We could just take a walk or a drive or something, that's all. That's all."

Queen Ester didn't look at Helene; instead, she pointed at the wall as if it were not a papered surface with blue and yellow flowers.

"Mama, what are you looking at? Mama?"

Queen Ester turned her head away from the wall and looked beyond her daughter. Helene thought, This isn't real, she's not even moving; it's like she's trapped in a painting, with the stove, the sink, and blue chipped cabinets as the frame. I'm dreaming because she's standing in front of me, mid-stride, with her arm pointing in my direction.

"This wall, that wall right over there, that's my life. All these walls, they my life. You don't understand that. You acting like you do, but you don't." The words—*this wall, that wall, you do, you don't*—seemed to come not from her mouth but from around her, from under her housedress, from the sink, the stove. She did not drop her finger as Helene had hoped—yes, the daughter still hoped—instead, her four other fingers uncurled, so now she held out a full hand in accusation. Then, running, Queen Ester dashed over to the wall, touching it, and Helene swore (and ten years later she would swear again, looking into her husband's unbelieving face while they lay together in bed) she saw the wall touch her mother back. Like a handshake (and later she would use those very words), just like a handshake. How do you do? the wall said. And her mother replied, as cordial as she would reply to the mailman, "Oh, just fine, and you?" Just like that, as if her mother and the house were old friends who'd run into each other at the grocery store. But she did see it, just as she saw it now: the house with a mind of its own held her mother's hand fiercely, and her mother held it back. Then quickly, so quickly Helene did not quite see the movement, her mother began walking back and forth from one wall to another, driving herself mad.

Helene was frightened, frightened of this house that could grab hold of what it wanted and frightened of this woman. A wild thing had thrown its mad self inside her mother, so maybe what she felt before wasn't hope at all but fear, waiting, finding its place between the makings of dinner. Old legs with mad blood ran back and forth from wall to wall. Queen Ester's mouth moved all the while, but the only words Helene could hear were *my, my, my*, and in helpless return her heart beat *me, me, me*.

Up and out of the chair before Queen Ester finished a turn, Helene took off down the short hall that led to the door and the stairs. She stood in the hall, choosing between now and memory, the door or the stairs. Helene took the stairs; at the top, knowledge waited for her to embrace it. "One, two, three, four," she murmured, feeling as if she had done this before, except now she knew exactly where she was going. Queen Ester stood at the bottom of the stairs and called her name, but Helene didn't turn around; she would not stop. Running up the stairs, she wondered what had gotten her there. Maybe I'm not here; maybe I'm standing on the porch waving goodbye; maybe I'm driving my car back to Stamps and just remembering what I wanted to do.

There wasn't a sound behind her, not the swish of a dress or the thump of Queen Ester's feet: nothing. Then her mother spoke, in a voice light and fragile, out of place, as different as a change of coats. "Down to eat, child."

Helene was tempted to turn around and scream *What?* Queen Ester called her name again. "Helene. Baby girl." She thought she must be imagining this, since there was nothing on the stairs except her and the call of her name and a phrase that seemed plucked out of a book. But Helene wouldn't look back because she'd have to see her mother's face and know that Queen Ester wasn't her mother at all but some woman with splayed hands and a mouthful of wild teeth.

Queen Ester spoke again, this time almost in Helene's ear.

"Helene, where are you going?" She stood only a couple of steps away, her arm wrapped around the banister as if to hold her steady, her upturned face not full of rage as Helene thought—hoped? feared? The two things were the same if you squinted your eyes.

"Where do you think I'm going, Mama?" she yelled.

"I don't know, girl." I don't know either, Helene thought, not a clue. Why upstairs? Why not the living room? Where am I going? Don't play dumb; you know where you want to go: his room. Just to see if there's an impression left of him in the bed or a scent in one of his shirts.

"What's in Chess's room, Mama?"

Her mother's face shifted from an expression of questioning to determination. "I'm asking you now, Helene, don't go to that room."

"Why not? What's in there?"

Her mother's arm grabbed at the back of Helene's dress, pulling her down. "That ain't none of your business, Helene. You come down from here."

"What's in the room, Mama?" Helene tried to twist out of her mother's grasp.

"Why, Helene? Dinner downstairs." Helene's dress still in her hands, Queen Ester yanked it downward, as if she wanted Helene to sit. "Don't make me ask you twice, girl."

"Dinner's done, Mama."

Helene didn't push her, she just turned all the way around, the dress tightening, so it felt as if she had it on backwards. "Let go, Mama," she said, placing her hands on Queen Ester's shoulders. And Queen Ester did. The grip on her dress unfastened and Helene tottered back a few steps. Her mother smiled, not a full smile but a closed-lipped grin that rose higher on the left side of her face.

"All right, all right. Gone on, then." Her hands went up as if she had surrendered or wanted Helene to see her palms. She wore a resolute face, the sort of face you have when you need to wring a cloth or pluck the meat from a chicken neck. "You want to go, so gone on."

"I am, Mama." Helene reached the doorknob, gleaming with sweat from previous hands or furniture polish. She twisted it and heard the soft click; in the hush of the hallway, Queen Ester heard it too. The door opened with a cry, as the refrigerator had downstairs. Expecting a dark sour must, Helene held her breath, but there was no need to, for despite its disarray the room smelled of dry clean wood and soap. Small tables were overturned in corners; a bar counter ran the length of half the wall, and on top were fourteen blue-colored glasses filled with liquid. Four pairs of brown khaki pants were draped over empty chairs, along with two white shirts and a blue bottle-necked dress. A small stove sat on the floor. With the curtains pulled back, the room was flooded with light. Through the three large west-facing windows, the falling sun cloaked everything in orange and purple. Helene took it all in, this room that looked and smelled as if it waited for an ice cream social.

Why the chase up the stairs? To have a peek at a room Queen Ester wouldn't let her see—and why, because of the mess it contained? There was no bed where Helene could find the faint outline of Chess, no dresser where she could touch a comb or mirror. It's just a storage room, just a stupid storage room. She fought back the rising disappointment. The room wasn't messy at all, as she had first thought, but had a disturbing order all its own: the furniture seemed overturned with care; the four pairs of pants lapped over each other, shirts and dress, were cleaned and ironed; the liquid (gin?

tea?) in the glasses was measured. Helene turned around, an apology ready on her lips.

Queen Ester was waging battle over whether to explain the room's centerpiece. "Listen, you..." She let the words linger, wracked with indecision. Should she say what had come to mind? Mama let him suckle her like a calf on her teat. Stepped tween you and me even when it meant killing her own self. And him. Chess had his fingers in my mouth searching for shame. It ain't right that I got to be the only one to bear witness. Ma'am and Chess, they got to stay above ground and be witness right along with me.

"Mama laid up in that bed and died all day long, Helene, and Mable and Other was there, trying to get me to do a funeral real quick, like the quicker I get her in the ground, the quicker I forget about her, my own mama, the woman who spilt me out in the river. Did you know that? I was born in a river. Mama told me that, and I forgot clean about it till both of us was standing here. But I told Mable, didn't I just get over burying the dead. Can't Mama stay in her own bed for a while, fore we scoop her in the dirt? And Mable say, 'Ester, it gone get to stinking soon.' I told her, standing right there over my dead mama, 'What "it," Mable? What "it" you talking about? Cause I know you ain't talking about Mama like she a old chair we's got to throw out.' And Mable looked real shame then, cause she was thinking on throwing out her best friend like she was trash. So she say, 'It just ain't right to let a dead woman lay in the bed she done died in; it ain't religious.' 'You think I don't know that?' I told her. 'She ain't gone lay in this bed forever; I just needs to rest. I don't want the kind of funeral we gives Chess. That what's ain't religious.' Then she say, 'You ain't said that at first, Ester. The way you was talking before, I thought—' but I cut her off fore she got to say what she was thinking, and I say to her, 'Girl, what you thinking? You crazy? You think I let my dead mama lay up in the bed she died in forever? I ain't crazy!' So then Mable start crying, and Other, he don't say nothing; his eyes just roll up in the back of his head. I walked them both to the door, and fore I even got the door closed good, I just start laughing, cause Mable thought I was gone let Mama lay up dead in that bed forever."

"What year was that, Mama?" Helene asked, suspicious of the soliloquy. Queen Ester's account of her mother's death had moved beyond harmless telling, the repeating of stories that gave Helene time to find memories to match them. She wanted to know the date, if for nothing else than to figure out how old she was the moment her grandmother died.

Queen Ester didn't answer her question. Instead, she walked over to a long high table, yanking it until the edge touched her chest. "Come over here."

Helene crept close and peered over her mother's shoulder.

"See?" Queen Ester pointed to a sturdy-looking wish-boned stick sitting on a dust-covered stool. On the floor, covered in an elaborate cobweb, were a pair of brogans.

"What?" Helene asked.

Queen Ester turned to her daughter, noticing Helene's look, calm but confused. "The flesh that works the hardest is the last to go—the skin on the knees and elbows, the thick white part on the back of the heel—sometime theys don't go at all, and the skin turn to jerky on the bone. Mama died on me, and by the time I seen Mable and them out and got back upstairs, Mama done got cold and hard. Rigor mortis, that's what the doctors call it, set up in Mama face first, then spread down to the chest like a summer cold. I was scared then, cause how I'm gone get Mama where she need to go when she a piece of wood? But I wait it out, and by the time I see her in the morning, she folded right up in my hands. Chess, he stayed in the water for a day and a half, so he was kind of puffed up when we fished him out. That why he ain't got no skin left; ain't no fault of mine.

"I got a truck from Banky and took Chess right out the ground. I was strong then. He was heavy and soft in my arms like dirt. He might have been a little thing, but he had some weight on him, let me tell you. Took me all day and half a night to get him just in the house. Carrying both them was like holding a baby. Like you. When you was little, and I had you for them first couple of days, I held on to you all the time and you'd get heavy on me, like a watermelon growing a pound a minute, then I had to put you down.

"Lord know I sure didn't want to. You never cried when you was in my hands. You cried something fierce when Mama had you, but when you was with me you was like a baby.

"Chess was hard, cause I had to get him up those stairs. I dragged him the first half of the way, and in the end I dragged him the rest of the way, but I sure tried a lot of different things in the middle. I take a rest; when I can't do no more, I put two buckets full of rocks up by him, so he stay still while I go get some tea or lay down on the couch.

"You gotta see I couldn't just up and have Mama and Chess under the ground with a cross on top of them. I know for sure that Mama wouldn't stand for that stuff. That's what I didn't bother telling Mable and Other. They don't know Mama. One time Mama got mad at me cause I threw a sheet on top of her for play. How you think she be if she got six feet of dirt on top of her? And far as Chess go, Mama didn't never let him leave, she keep him in the house, cause she know that the only way he gone learn something. He need somebody over him, telling him what to do. Why he get to leave the house just cause he dead? What being dead got to do with anything?"

Helene had staggered away in horror during her mother's rambling account, it coming clear to her, slowly, that where she saw a stick, brogans, and flapping khakis, her mother saw bodies: Liberty and Chess, not in the ground, not buried but right here.

"Mama, Jesus. Mama!" Helene's voice rose, taut and shrill. "There's nothing there, you know that, don't you? Just so fucked up, Mama. Just fucked!"

Queen Ester's face closed like window shutters. Helene saw her mother not next to her but through eight-year-old eyes, standing on a porch with her hair wild. She spoke through a child's voice, trying to say the only thing she knew for certain would bring Queen Ester back to the room. "Mama, Mama, be—"

Queen Ester pulled the word from Helene's mouth before it was said. "Decent. Decent?" The memory of Aunt Annie b, her hair shorn and manly, stood between them. Queen Ester opened her lips wide enough that Helene could see the three decaying teeth in the back of her mother's mouth, but she didn't make a sound. They were almost out of the room when Helene tried to take the word back and make it unheard, knowing even then that she couldn't.

"No, Mama, no." Her mother's arm rose above her head. The sleeve of the housedress slid back to reveal an elbow no darker than the rest of her arm, elbow and forearm all of a piece—straight, unbearable.

Helene wanted to stop her there and say, Look at us, our stale arms open and empty. I bet her arm's like that from years and years of reading Sears catalogs, Helene thought, looking at dresses she can't afford while resting her elbows in halved lemons. She wasn't prepared for Queen Ester's arm to fall on her like a crowbar thrown out of a window.

Helene ducked.

Like stairs anywhere, it did not take nearly as long to run down them as it did to run up. Queen Ester ran too. Helene heard her mother's feet right behind her and imagined her arm raised again sharply, housedress lifting and falling. Queen Ester called out, but the words—"Wait, wait"— sounded strangled.

The front door did not slip out of Helene's hands when she twisted and pulled; though large, it swung open easily. Out the door, off the porch, in the swept yard, Helene turned back to look at the house. Still the same, squatting on the land like a grounded bird. Queen Ester appeared in the doorway.

"Mama, I'm leaving," Helene said, her hands clenched at her stomach as she moved backward toward the car. At the edge of the yard she began to cry and then to hiccup uncontrollably, her feet full of thorns. Fumbling in her purse for her keys, she said, "You hear me? I'm leaving." Helene felt for the door handle and yanked it open, climbed inside. The car roared to life.

"Good," Queen Ester said softly, as she tiptoed closer to the edge of the porch. "Good," she said again, clearer this time. "Good, good."

12

SHE CRAVED SHOES most of all. On her knees, with her ass high in the air, she had chewed six pairs of shoes into unrecognizable lumps—all on the sly, of course. The leather soles of brogans, with just a trace of dust, she loved best, but they were hard to find. Sunday shoes and bedroom slippers were reduced to piles of leather scraps. She sucked at the tips of shoes like sucking out the marrow from a chicken bone. Dutifully, Liberty would leave her daughter ketchup in a bowl and pickled eggs swimming in red dye, open boxes of Argo cornstarch, and Queen Ester, trying to please, would dip a finger into the bowl and lick it clean. But what she really wanted were shoes—perhaps with the heels worn away and shards of grass tucked into the groove between the sole and leather—or even a work boot, though the rubber aggravated her gums, if anyone were to ask. The first three months she gnawed away at a pair of bedroom slippers and her single pair of loafers; but after the fourth month of pregnancy her house shoes lay at the foot of her bed, unidentifiable. Queen Ester grew swollen and picky, every undone and gone-to-sour thing Liberty could think to give her daughter remained untouched, until finally Liberty handed over an old pair of garden shoes.

Nobody spoke about him.

Not quite gone, Chess and his almost-absence had seeped into both women's dreams. Queen Ester's belly, of course, didn't help matters. First stranger, then son (her baby boy, all her own), then—before Halle's death—finally lover had leapt from the mother's arms to the daughter's and, not satisfied with that sin, had topped himself and made a baby. At least that was what Liberty told herself. Maybe not leapt, she thought, but stumbled. But when? Almost nine months ago, unable to put him completely out of mind, Liberty put him out of reach. Beyond her hands but not beyond her sight. Like Chess's stumble (hmm, yes, she liked that word) into Queen Ester, Liberty too had blundered into Chess. Watching her daughter's swollen stomach, she didn't like to recall how eagerly she had shared him, just barely, with his wife Halle and his black night mistress.

She wondered how he had managed all of them. Wasn't Halle demanding (especially at the end, when she couldn't help but be), Morning sullen, and Liberty greedy? She had felt satisfaction that he loved her best. He had said Halle was a sore he couldn't help picking, and Morning—Morning just kept in his path all the time. And herself? "Oh, I love you, baby. As soon as—" Liberty had put her hand over his mouth then, not allowing him to finish, knowing he wouldn't be able to stand up to his words later on. But now?

Now nobody spoke about him.

For years he had flickered in and out of their lives, him and that wife of his, Liberty thought. Though Halle had stayed just long enough to have six babies. Then she dropped dead, some said from heartache. Hah! She could dish it out better than anybody. Halle fought dirty and more often than not won, leaving Chess to pant in a corner somewhere, licking at a cut she had just inflicted. Heartache? She was the wife and the bitch and that was all. Yes, Liberty knew Chess felt Halle was a sore he couldn't help but tear at (wasn't he the same for her?), but Halle, at least in Liberty's mind, had possessed a streak of meanness that could turn clever and hurt in unexpected places. Though Liberty (and Morning) hated to admit it, Halle proved to have a stronger hold dead than she had ever had while living. Her ghost (prettier and sweeter) slept between the sheets of both of Chess's women and smiled when they and Chess argued. She wasn't that nice when alive, but her ghost was a saint. Don't believe it? Just ask Chess. Liberty did constant battle with a dead wife's memory.

Now, though, nobody spoke his name and Halle wasn't even a thought.

Nine months had galloped past them all with only Queen Ester's swelling stomach ticking off the time. When her water broke, a clear mucus running down her legs, Liberty's first impulse was not to catch her daughter, slumped over the table, but to race out the door through the cotton field and snatch up Chess. "She ready now and I want you to see," she said, as they stumbled back through the stretch of land that separated their homes. His feet fumbled as she dragged him along.

"All right, all right, I ain't fighting you, is I?" Chess gasped, afraid to say another word because this was the first time Liberty had spoken to him since she had opened his face with her hands and then put him out of touch. Queen Ester in labor—this was to be his punishment for impregnating her child, she said. As far as Chess was concerned it wasn't that much of a punishment; hadn't he seen his own wife (God bless her) grow with child six times? Granted, he had never been in the room with Halle when she had given birth; she always went away to her mother's house and would come back to Chess a week or so later with something swaddled in her arms. But he didn't think Liberty would really put him in the room with Queen Ester. No, he thought, as he watched Liberty's long legs saw back and forth through the tall grass, his punishment was the absence of Liberty; he missed the way she untucked her laughter. Morning had become complacent these past few months without the threat of Liberty stepping through the door to pluck away "her man." She had become lazy in bed, telling him no when she felt tired, something she never would have done if she thought Liberty lurked around the corner. "Say, slow down," Chess said, as he stumbled for the second time.

Liberty broke the bolt she'd begun at Chess's house. "Better?" she asked.

"Yeah." Chess panted. "I done missed you," he blurted. Both he and Liberty were surprised by how quickly she turned with her hand raised ready to strike.

"What you say?"

"Nothing. I ain't say nothing." He took a small hop back

from her. Liberty turned away, almost running toward the house.

Queen Ester had crawled into her bed by the time Chess and Liberty entered the house. They took the stairs three at a time, and both lover and beloved paused when they heard Queen Ester's heavy moan behind the closed bedroom door. "You stay on here, I got it." Liberty let go of Chess's hand. "No, maybe we should—" She stopped. "No. I got it. No. Wait. Go get Other and tell him—"

"Where he at?" Chess interrupted.

"Well, shit, I don't know. He can't be far." She licked the inside of her thumb.

"Sure he could."

Both heard Queen Ester's mewing again. "Just shut it, Chess." Liberty scowled.

"Well, goddamn, baby," Chess said. "You need to hurry up on whatever you gone do."

Her nervousness created a wall between them, and Chess hadn't the faintest idea how to climb over it. Instead, he watched, fascinated, as Liberty paced up and down the hall, her thumb inside her mouth, saying the one thing she knew to calm herself, "All right. All right, all right." Finally she stopped in front of the door. "I done this before."

"When?"

"Okay, maybe I haven't, but gone and get me some hot water and some rags from the kitchen. Gone, now." She walked into the bedroom and closed the door behind her. For the next three hours, Chess stayed alone in the hallway without a chair to sit in.

"She done yet?"

Liberty didn't bother to stand up and walk to the door, she

merely yelled out, "You get some respect, Chess. And no, she ain't done."

Chess smiled lightly at what he thought was Liberty's conversational tone. "You know, Halle would go to her mama, stay a week and come back with a baby. Just one, two, three."

Liberty stepped out and slapped Chess lightly, and he saw something playful and joyous in her face. "She at her mama's. That's me."

Then they were four, an awkward number easily broken. And only Queen Ester could stand it. They kept the baby for just seven days. Seven solid days of Queen Ester's heavy cooing and oh my's that even she, full of new-mother bliss, knew wouldn't last. Mama planning, she thought, and I ain't got the know-how to stand up to her like I should. She was right. Liberty spent those seven days thinking there were some things a body couldn't bear and, Lord be a witness, shouldn't have to bear, such as your lover making a baby with your daughter, and then to have that baby plus lover plus daughter all under the same roof. No, she thought hotly, nobody should be called upon to bear that. Big as she was, Liberty wasn't big enough for that sort of nonsense, and she knew someone would have to go.

Those seven days, when Queen Ester was wrapped in a thin cocoon of rapture, Liberty thought of the man she was going to pass off as the father, husband to Queen Ester except that he died too soon. Duck didn't have the decency to stay alive for eight months. Nevertheless, she prepared for Annie b and Ed, two people she had laid eyes on only once in her life, with a faith that in spite of everything things would work out. A letter full of looping handwriting had been sent out to Duck's kin and they were coming, on their way to see what Duck left behind, and thank you for sending the body so promptly. Liberty planned for their arrival, stalking her house, making everyone bend to her will. They were three and baby be damned. On the seventh day, early in the morning, she sent Chess to fetch Mable and Other. Liberty stepped into the bedroom, already mid-speech even though she hadn't said a word, Queen Ester couldn't pretend surprise. "It ain't even got a daddy," Liberty told her daughter.

"Yes, it do."

"Duck dead, baby."

"I ain't talking about him."

"Well, that daddy already got too many babies of his own. And I'm too old to be taking care of no brand-new children."

"I ain't ask you to mind after what's mine."

"I ain't said you did."

"Well?"

"Well, you telling me that you can mind after what's yours, but who mind after you?" Liberty walked further inside the room. "That's right, I do. And you ain't even got a job."

"I can gone and get one."

"Then who gone take care your baby while you working?"

"Mama."

"Duck people's coming down here today. I want you to stay on up here."

"Ain't." Defiance laced her voice.

Liberty moved, striding across the small room. She crouched over the bed where Queen Ester lay and yanked her daughter's shoulder, shaking her furiously. "You hear me? I said don't you come down when they get here." She pulled back and raised her other hand. Her palm and fingers waved in the air, poised to strike. Knowing she was beat, Queen Ester laid the baby, too small to be named, in her mother's arms, sighing gently as Liberty closed the door behind her.

She walked downstairs, baby in her hands. Mable waited for her friend in the café. "Chess come and got me. Other outside on the porch." Mable saw the baby tucked in the crook of Liberty's elbow. "What's going on?"

"I need you to do something for me." Liberty's voice came out, flat and mean.

"What, Liberty?"

"Some of Duck's people gone come by and pick up the baby, and I want you to give it to them."

"What?"

"You heard."

"Liberty, what's going on?" Mable's concern sat naked on her face, but then both women heard a cranky rumbling enter the yard. Together they stepped to the window. "Who that?"

"I told you, Duck's kin coming."

"To take the baby?"

Liberty held the sleeping child out.

"Do they even know Duck dead?" Mable's question hung between the two women. Mable already knew that if Duck was the daddy she was Chinese. Nothing escaped her notice.

"Course they do."

"Why don't you—" But Liberty cut her off.

"I can't. Chess can't gone out there. Look at her." They peered through the window at the car and saw a man and woman get out. "She ain't no fool. One look at him and she'll know."

Now it was Mable's turn to feel nervous. Panic caught at

her throat and shook her hard. "I don't know about this, Liberty. You think these folks outside just gone take a baby when the mama above ground?"

"Just listen. You tell her Queen Ester ain't right. And when she say, What you mean? you just nod your head, real slow. You hear me?"

"Liberty."

"When she ask after me, tell her I'm too old to take care of no child, plus—and Mable, say it just like this—I didn't want to say, but Duck and Liberty never did get along. I don't know how he would feel . . . then trail right on off." Liberty shifted the baby in her arms. "Now take this baby and get out there."

"Liberty, I don't know."

Liberty played her last card. "Since I done known you, I ain't never asked you for a thing. I'm asking you gone and do this one thing for me. How many times you done told me yourself that I need to look out for Queenie fore she turn foolish on me?"

"All right, all right." Liberty passed Mable the child and opened the door for her. Other waited on the porch and Mable spoke to him while walking down the stairs. "Come on, Other, I just need you to stand by me."

And, well, Liberty was right. Annie b. Taylor was nobody's fool. She took one look at Mable and Other and knew something was awry. Where's the mama? she thought, watching the two come closer. Here we are, getting a welcome from some lady who I know for a fact ain't kin and a nigger big as a bull. Liberty could of come out. Who ever heard of meeting family in the middle of the yard? No one asked them how their trip went or invited them to come on and sit in the cool for a spell. "Something smelling sour," Annie b whispered to her husband.

"Hey there," Mable said, smiling as she approached.

"Hey yourself."

"I'm Mable and this here is Other. And"—Mable moved the child higher in her arms so Annie b and her husband, Ed, could see—"this is your little niece. Can you say howdy to your auntie?" Mable cooed.

Annie b didn't look at the child. "Where Queen Ester at?"

"She laid up right now, sleeping, I think."

"I bet." Annie b snorted and spat carefully behind her feet. "And where Liberty?"

"Well, somebody got to see after the brand-new mama." A wobbly smile pulled at Mable's face.

Annie b turned to Other. "What? You can't say nothing?"

"Other ain't much for talking. He just came out with me cause I asked him to. You ain't even take a good look at the baby. That's what you came way out here for, right?" Annie scared her, and Mable couldn't put aside the creeping fear. It's the hair, Mable thought, looking at Annie's shorn head.

"You got this dumb nigger with you, like I don't know no better from a turd. Humph!"

"Miss b, you know what they say."

"What's that?"

"Don't run off and kill the messenger." Mable coughed a faint laugh and shifted the baby from one arm to the other.

"Yeah, well, you know what else they say? Mama's baby, Daddy's maybe."

Ed brought his hands out of his pockets and moved closer to the child, peering into the bundle Mable carried. "I think that's a right fine-looking baby, b."

"I bet you do."

"Sure do seem to sleep a lot."

"They do when they this little. She ain't no trouble at all

and that's a fact. Just sleep and eat. Ain't never seen a better baby. Lord as my witness, I think she look just like you and Duck, Miss Annie," Mable said, as she put the child in Ed's arms.

"My eye she do." But they took the child anyway, Annie b's suspicions be damned. She could see Ed had fallen in love with the child in his arms, and she felt it wasn't her right to deny him what she herself couldn't give. Together, the new uncle and aunt drove away with the baby.

Thus began years of corrections: I ain't your mama, I'm your auntie, answered with a shy *Yes, ma'am.* They took the child. For Helene, only the letters offered solace. At six she would peek inside the Christmas cards scrawled with, *I love you. I love you.* Helene's desire to see her mama wouldn't quit, despite Annie b's shooing and hush-all-that. "She ain't here and she ain't coming" was a common refrain. At least Queen Ester had had seven days of bliss. The letters, instead of soothing Helene's want, jump-started her desire, and Annie b, gruff and almost mean, didn't know what to do with a child that small and needy.

Who knew what would have happened to the child had she stayed in that house? With both the mama and the granny set against her, the child might not have survived. Annie b knew what was going on, never mind that she hadn't put a foot inside the door. She knew. She smelled it as soon as she stepped out of the car—soured jealousy and craziness cooking on a stove. Can't tell me, she had mumbled on the way back home. If Duck was the daddy, I'm a monkey.

13

HELENE WOULD HAVE sat there listening forever—
wept in all the right places, held her mother's hand when
she looked shaken, gulped it up like a good girl. She had seen
enough movies to know when to raise an eyebrow, quiver a
chin. She didn't have to show me that room, Helene thought.
But she didn't; I went up there on my own, ran up the stairs,
and kept looking when I should've stayed in the kitchen and
clipped Mama at the knees, tackled her until she calmed
down. Helene stopped, slowing the car down, because she
could hear herself talk like a Southerner, her voice rounding
out each word as if she were choking on it; she sounded like
her mother. "Good goddamn," she whispered. "I don't. I can't
sound like her in just one day. I'm wrong and I'm scared. But

I'll take care of it when I get home. Maybe I'll move to New York after the funeral and get rid of all this forever." She took me up there, Helene reasoned, just as if she had led me by the hand. She wouldn't show it to me in the first place, which set my curiosity going, and like a child I bit into the first thing I couldn't have and ran to the room Mama didn't have the decency to lock.

Helene now had what she wanted: knowing, not yet complete but she couldn't imagine a time of not knowing. She rolled down the car window, rested an elbow on the ledge, and remembered Aunt Annie b saying gleefully, "Your mama done turned like milk set out." Queen Ester's face suddenly struck her as if it were rotting fruit, gagged her so that she heaved and thrust her head out the window. Not until she crossed over a footbridge did the clacking of tires on old wood jolt her out of her reverie. The road before her was deepest black, night wrapped around the landscape like a wool blanket, and she realized she had lost her way.

She had paid no attention to the numbered farm market roads. Helene had seen Queen Ester vanish in her rearview mirror but still she hoped, never mind her mother's craziness or the dead she imagined living in her house. Perhaps Queen Ester had secretly left the porch without Helene noticing and was trotting behind the car, saying, "You didn't hear what you heard, and even if you did I'm sorry about it." But the gravel from the road sprayed out beneath her wheels, tearing down all imaginings, including her phantom mother. Roads turned into circles that led Helene nowhere. The farm road signs stood in corners, their wisdom shrouded by bug-clogged streetlights. Now, unlike the morning ride, Helene saw not a single house.

When she spotted an old man, the only person she had

seen since she left Queen Ester's house, Helene slowed down. She thought of Uncle Ed, alone in Stamps without her or Aunt Annie b. The old man sat in the dark with his pants rolled up; his shoes, tied together at the laces, were slung over his shoulder. When Helene's headlights flashed on him, he got to his feet as if he had been waiting for her, thick strong fingers resting on his knees, a full plastic bag at his side. Girl, what are you doing? she thought, stopping to look at him. She got out of the car, thinking maybe he could point the way through the trees and get her back to Stamps.

"Hello there," she said.

"Yeah."

"Are you lost?"

"Sho nough." He smiled, his words flickered with laughter.

"Okay." She smiled back at him. "I'm trying to find my way to Stamps."

"Sho nough."

"Yes, well, could you help?"

"Yeah." She waited for him to give her directions.

"I was visiting my mother," Helene volunteered, surprised she said the word *mother* so easily. "I just took my eyes off the road for a second." She paused for him to speak. "And there you have it."

"Sho nough?"

"Yes. Queen Ester Strickland. Do you know her?"

"Yeah."

"Yes, well, my aunt just recently passed and—well, I came out here to let her know."

"Yeah."

"So I did—let her know. And somehow I thought she would come back up to Stamps with me. Maybe if she had I wouldn't be lost right now." Helene rattled on, knowing that if she could step outside herself and look at the two of them standing in the road, she would hear herself, not letting him get a word in. For the life of me I can't stop, Helene thought. It wasn't just because she'd found some old man sitting at the side of the road as if he were lingering there just for her sake. His manner, his yeahs and sho noughs, coaxed her on. Soft and melodious, their sound dipped and rose, questioned and answered, prodding her until Helene stuttered to a close. "So I left the house. I couldn't stay, could I?" They had stepped away from the lights of her car, or rather he had moved and Helene had followed, still talking, her voice full of anguish.

"Yeah," he said, beckoning to her, pointing toward the darkness of the woods. She gripped his forearm, noting that the skin felt loose and thin while the muscle underneath was taut. She spoke in a softly persistent chatter, churning the question over and over. "I mean, I couldn't just stay there and pretend with her, could I?"

"Sho nough." But his eyes said different, and Helene felt shamed that she had left her mother alone in the house.

"Where are you pointing?" she asked, when he pulled at her as if they should both plunge into the woods. "That's the way back to Mama's."

"Yeah." She could have shaken him off, pushed at the arm that moved like paper across a clear desk, but she didn't.

"Isn't Stamps the other way? That's the wrong way, isn't it?" Again he said nothing, and Helene only heard the crunching leaves beneath their feet and a wrinkling of the plastic bag he clutched at his side. "What's your name? Do you hear me? Tell me your name."

"Other." Helene heard him breathing. "Other."

Queen Ester watched Helene leave as she had always left, flying from the house with the quickness of a getaway. She didn't wait for Helene's car to round out of her sight before she walked back into the house, still singing the word *good* in measured tones while she closed the door.

She was amazed Helene had stayed as long as she had. The daughter had come, twenty-six years grown, with her hair parted down the middle and feathered at the sides in soft curls; yes, the daughter had come at last, her forehead high and round, the color of pecans, eyebrows plucked, wearing the sort of dress Queen Ester thought she would wear— dark green and cinched at the waist, the length licking the calves—her daughter who had sat down with her and listened.

"Just a little bit more and I would have got what I wanted," Queen Ester said aloud. They had been so close to having dinner and then Helene had turned on her, just like Liberty. "You would of loved my gravy." Sorrow kicked in as Queen Ester thought about the fat separating and rising to the top as the gravy grew cold, and she began to cry, ravenous tears welling in her eyes and streaking down her cheeks.

She lifted her hand and smeared the back of it across her face. "She don't see," she said, her head tilted, hearing the sound of Helene's feet on the stairs; not the thud of a woman bent on opening a door Queen Ester had never closed in the first place but the soft patter of a child, complete with pigtails and something messy in her hand, a malleable child with "Yes, Mama" on her tongue. She loved that daughter, a fiction of a child, not the pecan-coated thing who had tried to strike at her with the word decent. "As if I ain't," Queen Ester said.

Still standing in the hallway, she thought again about dinner and decided she would go hungry tonight, not wanting to eat alone what she had made for two. "But y'all still here, ain't you?" Queen Ester called upstairs, then touched the wall smiling, her imagination as strong as the surface she leaned against. All the way upstairs, she saw a dead hand, in repose, lift and wave back to her. She took to the stairs, humming softly. "I know she look like me, but she ain't just mine, Lord, she ain't all mine." Tightly holding the banister, she swung one heavy foot in front of the other until she reached the top of the stairs. Without meaning to she softy mumbled a dead man's name: "Duck."

Her mumbling grew as she willed the madness (which wasn't madness at all but a cultivated, flexible memory that allowed Queen Ester to take out and replace the events that displeased her, so already while moving up the stairs she wiped clean the image of Helene inside the room, scrolling back her daughter's visit, erasing the ugly words and replacing them with *I love you*). Queen Ester wished the madness that fell warm as a cloak would hold her even tighter. "Duck," she said. "My husband."

Sterile, with nothing but a pair of worn pants where his sex should be, he never consummated their marriage. Instead, he took the train to Little Rock and courted prostitutes for weekends that climbed into Tuesdays every month. She never asked outright, but she knew what he did: playing house, she heard some people call it, paying some woman three dollars a day, a field hand's wage, to cook and rub his head while calling him baby or honey. From what Mable told her he saw one woman—Bell, that's what she was called, now, ain't it?—so often she and Duck learned each other's last names. Liberty provided Duck's money for the prostitutes, knowing that her daughter still slept in the single bed next to her own room while Duck slept across the hall.

Worn dollars passed from hand to hand. Queen Ester would give him the money that she got from Liberty. No words were ever exchanged, just bills piled neatly atop each other left on the dresser. Duck got to keep the money he made at the sawmill for other things, groceries that refused to grow in the garden. According to the logic of the house, he shouldn't have to pay for his women, since Queen Ester had decided she wouldn't be touched and neither she nor Duck had really wanted to get married in the first place.

Liberty had conjured up the idea. Queen Ester was pregnant and so should be married, the order of these two things being irrelevant. And since Duck was always prowling around (Liberty found him in her barn twice), she figured marriage was as good a way as any for him to earn his keep, and he had been after Queen Ester anyway, as far as Liberty could tell. Didn't Duck toy with dreams that he would one day own the house and land? He couldn't get them without wedding someone, Liberty reasoned. Maybe marriage would keep Queen Ester occupied with something other than keeping Liberty under constant watch.

Duck had always been around (after Liberty had run him off from the barn, he'd taken to the cotton field, and she'd let him stay there), the thief who stole their broom to sweep their porch, the poor mouth whose thievery meant his victims had to feed him. Queen Ester didn't often remember him as her husband—the marriage had been too short, too sterile;

Duck the husband was truly a brother but not even graced with friendship, since to be friends they would have had to know each other better.

"What you say now?" was his version of hello, as if the person he greeted had just said something that Duck had failed to catch, so the beginning of a conversation with him always felt like the middle. He was the only man who thought to call her girl, the only one who refused to be scared off by her mother. She would give him a bite of her lunch. "Them sweet fingers of yours make it taste so good, girl," he would say, ready with the inelegant persuasion of a lover. Every compliment was fumbled, but Queen Ester didn't notice, because Liberty had done such a thorough job of keeping away every man save the few who came to the café, and even then she ordered Queen Ester to stay in the kitchen. He became her husband, even though she had already thrown away what she called her "nothing." Duck just smiled and said he didn't need it.

They had the discussion one Wednesday. (Why always a Wednesday, a would-be church day had any of them been churchgoers?) Liberty picked the day and the dress. "Well, you done done it now," she said, "so you got to go and get a daddy." She instructed Queen Ester calmly, holding the dress on a hanger.

"It already got a daddy," Queen Ester said, with complete naïveté. She sounded amazed, or maybe it was just anger with nothing to cling on to.

"Well, that daddy already got a wife." Liberty handed Queen Ester the dress. With utter control, Liberty thought swiftly of all the places Duck might possibly be at that time of day. She rehearsed what she would say to get him to wait on her porch, weighing her words and their lilt, and decided she would offer him lemonade. Touching the doorknob, Liberty called back over her shoulder, "Iron that collar and be down on the porch quick," and opened and shut the door before Queen Ester could say another word.

Liberty found Duck sitting in the corner of her cotton patch where she thought he would be. "You gone to the porch, I got lemonade in the kitchen," she said. Duck looked up, trying to understand the meaning behind her words, not trusting the lazy sound of her voice, since she had in fact almost pounced on him.

"All right, then," he said, but Liberty didn't hear him as she spun around to trot to the kitchen, where a pitcher waited for her sweating hands. She stood in front of the counter, her eyes searching the ceiling, squinting to see Queen Ester dressing above her, willing the prayer, "Get up and gone to the porch and be still, boy," over and over. Liberty directed imaginary hands to push Duck to the front porch and stay put, not wander off to the barn for a nap or to look for a beer that she didn't have. Hearing Queen Ester's steps, she poured two tall glasses full of lemonade, and met her daughter at the foot of the stairs.

"Took you long enough," Liberty said, pushing the lemonade into Queen Ester's hands.

Queen Ester leaned close to her mother, clutching the frosty glasses. "And what if he say no? What then?"

For the first time since Liberty had thought of marrying Duck and Queen Ester, she looked uncertain. Then her doubt fell away and she said, "He won't."

Duck sat and waited on the porch, surprised to see Queen Ester in a dress with a collar and lemonade in her hands.

"I got it now," he said, taking a glass from her. Queen Ester looked at him and smiled, saying nothing, since Liberty had forgotten to give her the words to convince him without shaming herself. She didn't know how to use flirtation to win him over, undo the important buttons, slide the cloth down her shoulder, blink slowly to make her lashes catch and pull apart. Instead, she thought, If I was in a car with the hood up, Duck would come running cause men like to fix what's broke.

She sat down on the porch, knowing that Liberty stood just inside the house, listening through a door over an inch thick. Unable to hear a thing, Liberty pressed her forehead against the wood, trying to feel the vibrations on the porch to know where Queen Ester and Duck were sitting or standing. Queen Ester wished Liberty had followed her outside, because without her mother's guidance, she thought the only way to trap Duck into marriage was to present him with a broken chair. She decided on the truth, the only thing she knew. "It's gone."

"What?" Duck asked, wiping the condensation from the glass onto his pants.

"My nothing, it's gone."

"Girl, what you talking about?"

Queen Ester's face burned. She slumped a bit, put the glass down next to her, and pressed her hands to the middle of her dress. As she looked at Duck, he smiled, his dimples appearing, and Queen Ester felt a searing start at her chest. His coaxing felt like scorn to her. He too put his glass down and muttered, putting his hand on top of her own, "You women the devil's confusion," a soft chuckle escaping from his mouth.

With hopelessness overwhelming her, she looked up, letting the sun burn the back of her eyes. "Duck, I'm trying to tell you. My nothing—it's gone."

"Just what that mean?"

Her dry tongue licked cracked lips. "I'm having a baby."

Now he smirked openly, it was the look she had braced herself against before she'd stepped out the house. They sat quietly, silently asking and answering each other's questions: So you need me now? You know I do; need you bad. And your mama, for all she is, had to stoop low and catch me. Yeah, she done stooped low and got you. No more cotton field for me? No, you right, no more field sleeping for you. I knew it, I knew it.

"Ain't too partial to bloody sheets no way, girl," he said. Queen Ester gasped. Well, I asked; I can't do nothing now, she thought. Though she was prepared for the smirk, the comment knocked her back. Even Queen Ester, whose mother's control had rubbed her down to a dull glow, had pride. And Duck's words had pricked it. She wanted him to drop to his knees and beg, even though she didn't love him. Still, as childish as she was, she had enough sense to know the begging wasn't coming. She would have to settle for Duck patting her hand and calling her *girl* two times in a row. "Me neither," she said softly, struggling to grin.

Liberty rushed through the door, stood before them, and stared directly at Duck, taking Queen Ester's expression for granted. Why waste time looking in the mirror? she thought. Although absent, she had taken her part in the exchange and, not wanting to see her own regret in Queen Ester's face, spoke only to Duck. "We got to make a date. I gone get the license, ain't no need to send away for it. Maybe we can get Mable to take us on down to Texarkana. Let's start off early on a weekday, maybe Thursday or some such. They got that court-house right off the highway, and if we hurry we can make it back here fore supper." Duck, thinking he would one day be the man of the house, lifted his glass and said nothing. He swallowed half the lemonade, clinking the ice against his teeth, and looked at Liberty over the rim.

"You free then, Duck?" Queen Ester asked.

"Yeah," he said, not taking the glass from his mouth. Liberty saw his scorn, knowing that if he could reach over far enough he would put his thumb on her neck, but she smiled; Duck would find out right after he moved into the house that he'd taken charge of nothing. Her daughter wouldn't even take his last name. So now they were three, even four if you counted the unborn child. Liberty made the arrangements, except there was no excitement or joy in her voice, just determination that Duck mistook for desperation.

Queen Ester, shamed again, didn't know who to be angrier with: Duck, who didn't have the decency to hide his ambition to rule their eighty-three acres, or her mother, cold and dauntless. Where was Queen Ester's fury when she needed it? Maybe I spent it on Other, she thought.

Other had been watching Queen Ester (while she swept the yard, picked tomatoes, threw sheets over the clothesline to air) and she him (over the length of a table, while running errands at the two general stores). For days she would turn quickly and catch him looking at her with blank or apologetic eyes. All that week he would capture her gaze, then drop his eyes to her shoes and fumble with the lint in his pocket. His yeahs and sho noughs had become full of import. Finally, she cornered him in one of those dark spaces where she stood keeping an eye on Liberty, luring him there on a false errand. "You gone and get some shoestring for me, Other," she said, already knowing his answer. She tugged at his collar as she whispered, "What?"

"Yeah?" Other said, crouching to accommodate the pull.

"What?" she said again, twisting harder. He looked away, placing his hand on the wall to steady himself.

"Sho nough," Other said, waiting for Queen Ester to state her need, tuck coins or a list into his fist, and let him go, but she said nothing. He resorted to his second response, since "Sho nough" only made Queen Ester's hand tighten. They stood for a while, Queen Ester with a bruised look in her eye and Other trying to pass as deaf and dumb, unable to bring himself to face her.

"I know you know, I know you saw it, so won't you just gone and say it?" Queen Ester lashed out, clutching Other by the shoulder. "Somebody broke my door that night." If I could swallow him whole, I'd do it, she thought.

He had never seen her in the dark before and, frightened, he shouted shrilly, "Yeah, yeah!" Unprepared for Other's voice to rise above a murmur, Queen Ester let go of him, but he remained crouched.

They both knew that Liberty stood somewhere in the house, so she cupped her hand around Other's ear, speaking in a low conversational tone. "Other, you know. You know. You ain't dumb. You think I don't know you can speak? You say it. Tell me you the one that crack my door in two." Angry, Queen Ester shook in her dress, her mouth resting near his cheek and ear so that they appeared to be lovers trapped and grunting. "You, goddamn it," she said.

As if he had been sleeping, letting Queen Ester have her way with him, Other suddenly woke up and struggled under her grasp. He tried to tear his shoulder from her hand, but she held on all the tighter, whispering all the while, "You say it, you.

"Cause if you did see, then you just as much to blame," she went on. "You the one that come out of closets and whatnot with your yeahs and sho noughs. Can't beat you at trying to fetch what folks want, but you didn't do nothing for me. You is bigger than he is and could of stopped it."

Queen Ester heard an unfamiliar sound start at the back of his throat, and she realized she didn't want him to say what he had seen: the pushing up of her flimsy nightgown, the taking of her nothing before she had time to withhold it. Other opened his mouth, but she quickly placed her hand over it and smothered the words. "No, boy, you forget that, cause I'm gone to."

The day after, Queen Ester and Liberty walked with their heads bowed, their brows dark and serious as if they were speaking about a bank robbery or a murder.

"You is a liar, girl," Liberty said. She might as well have said, Take that, for the harshness in her voice, as if she meant to slap her daughter. Queen Ester didn't bother to say, No I'm not, since she didn't lie and her mother knew she didn't. Liberty's accusation was merely a formality, a space, an opportunity for Queen Ester to clap her on the back and say, Yeah, I am.

"Now what you gone do?" Queen Ester asked, rubbing her hands together as if she stood out in the open snow, cupping one hand in the other and blowing into them.

"I don't know yet," Liberty said. Queen Ester took a step back, unprepared for the remark, wanting instead for Liberty to yell, I'm gone kill him, kill him dead! or some such declaration from a Western: Wait till sundown; When the clock strikes twelve.

"What you mean, you don't know?" Queen Ester said, and Liberty's eyebrows rose with surprise, as if her daughter had just tossed her a gold ring. "I just told you what I told you, your only baby girl, and you tell me you don't know? That's all?"

"What else you want me to say? You grown now. I can't stomp down every fuss you get into."

"I didn't get into nothing. And I ain't asked you to go off and slap some schoolboy that I done got in some tussle with. Is I now, is I?" Queen Ester grabbed Liberty's hand, squeezing it. "Is I now?"

"No, this ain't no schoolboy mess," Liberty said, softly trying to pull her hand away from Queen Ester, but her daughter held her fast, both of their hands growing sticky. Liberty couldn't decide which was worse, the sound of Queen Ester or her touch, since the sound alone—a harsh anguished whisper— allowed her to believe their conversation was simply a dream. No, Liberty thought, it's her touch that's the worst of it.

"I know it ain't. So what you gone do about it?" They stopped again. Queen Ester brought Liberty's hand to her lips, and her mother almost cringed at the gesture.

Liberty looked at her daughter, her eyebrows still raised as if they had been taped to the middle of her forehead. For one brief moment, she almost said, You should be glad you gone have a baby, if that what come of this. Why you care how you got that way? Finally, tugging her hand away from Queen Ester and wiping it on her pants, Liberty said, "Where he at now? You know that much?"

"He in the barn, I think; at least that's where he was fore

I start talking to you." Queen Ester's voice was reproachful, accusing Liberty of not behaving as a mother should, for not responding with heaving anger that would break dishes and chairs while covering the guilty with blood. Liberty turned away from her.

"Where you going to, now, Mama?"

"Where you think?" Racing down the stairs, Liberty almost tumbled on a bucket that sat at the bottom. "I'm gone move that bucket, soon as I take care of . . ." Her voice dwindled as she snatched the door open.

Liberty ran through the swept yard and into the barn, yelling his name all the while. "You, Chess! You here? You, Chess!"

Pitching hay, he spun around at the call of his name and tossed aside his pitchfork, smiling as he walked toward her. "Girl, here I am." A pail sat in the middle of the barn, full of cold water and bottled beer. "Guess what? I got to talking with Bo Web and told him I'd cut his hair for six months for a bucketful of beer. And he went on and gave it to me. Sho did. Gave it to me straight out. You should of seen his woman. Hot, I tell you." He let out a slow easy laugh. But then he looked up at her. "What is it now, girl?"

He ain't acting like he done what she said he done, Liberty thought, but my baby girl ain't gone lie to me. He asked the question again, except now she didn't hear him (or if she did, she heard his voice the way a person hears crickets sawing in the night, faint and constant). She saw his hand resting at the small of his back, his smile faltering but still in place, his eyes shifting back and forth between her face and the pail full of cooled beer. She spoke finally. "What you done done?"

He laughed again. "Girl, you mad that I went to Bo Web's for the beer?" As Chess spoke he moved toward her, swinging low and grabbing two beers in his fist. "It ain't my fault you ain't got beer here. Plus, I got it for us two. I can't drink no bucketful of beer by myself." He moved with a graceless shuffle full of bravado, the bottles thudding softly against his thigh, still smiling though he smelled her fury.

"You hear me? What you done done?" Liberty said again, quieter this time, stepping away from the door and into the barn.

"Damn, girl, what you mean? I'm out here moving hay for you, not me; got us some beers for when I'm through; and all you can ask me is what I done. I done a lot. What you done done?"

"Don't you, Chess. You hear me?" Liberty closed the distance between them.

"If you ain't got a mind for beer, you don't—"

She cut him off. Lifting a hand, her palm curling inward to make a half fist, she signaled him to silence. "You think I came in here for some beer?"

Chess looked not at her face but at the hand that was raised. "We can share it with Queenie if you got a mind—" He didn't get to finish, because Liberty knocked the beer from his hand.

"There's your beer." The two bottles fell and rolled to the ground. "Let's talk about what you share with Queen Ester."

"What you talking bout?"

"She came to me and told me what you done. So, what? We all share with my little girl?" She pushed him, and he fell to the ground.

"You believe her?" he asked, sprawled in the dirt. He's not denying it; he ain't said not me, she thought.

"You get on up."

"Ain't." Chess started to pant even though she had only pushed him.

"You get on up, I said." Liberty put her hand on her hips. "Get on up from there."

"You the one that got me down here," Chess said, and Liberty smiled, bending toward him with her hand extended.

"I got you," she said softly and he took her hand. Chess tried to laugh again, but Liberty smiled and said, "I'm gone beat you to hell."

He shook and licked his lips. "I'll leave. Go right now."

"No. You gone stay. Let's see what you done in nine months to my little girl."

He knew what Queen Ester had told Liberty, but still he went along. "What she done told you?"

"You done pushed yourself on my girl."

"Ain't done no such a thing. She tell you that? She a bold-face lie."

Liberty spoke on as if she hadn't heard him. "On my little girl."

"How can I go and push myself on her when she grown like she is? She ain't little no more, Liberty. She grown." He was whispering now in a soft beseeching voice, his body limp and doll-like against hers.

"That don't matter, she mine." Her voice trembled. "You got Halle, you got Morning." She paused. "You got me now. You was spose to be mine. I took you in and gave you me, cause you told me the wife ain't enough, and Morning ain't enough either. So I gave you me and now you lay down with my child, and I might as well say my tree, my table." Liberty barked out the words. "I know it. If the table would of said you did what you did, I still be out here in this here barn. Cause I ain't enough, and why ain't I?" She wound an arm around his waist, and they stood for a moment gasping together like dogs. "I ain't enough?" She lifted her fist high and brought it down, smashing his mouth. Chess fell to the ground, pulling his knees up, but Liberty bent over him, sawing her fists back and forth across his face, relishing the spread of blood on her hands.

14

BOTH ME AND Mama had our hands on Chess. Mama had him the longest, but I got him once and that was all it took to get me a little girl and for Mama and me to fall apart. Seem like she can't treat me right less Chess there, stirring shit and smiling at the same time. I told her she got to quit on that, trying to be with me and Chess too, but she told me she can't give Chess up. The only time she pay me any mind is when Chess around, so I guess I don't want her to. Whenever he run off, Mama tear up everything in reach. And I can't make her stop. For myself, I just wanted a piece, a small slice of Chess to chew on. I can't remember when it start, but I done look up and all I can settle my mind on was Chess and how he look in them pants. He got Morning and Halle (for nine years) and Mama too. Lord knows who else he with.

I figure a man who can handle that many at once can't mind one more. I want Chess more than I done ever want another thing. He come in from where he was and, well . . . well, I can't look nowhere else. I been trying my best to do different, but if Mama come in right after him, something rise up in me that I can't push down. I want to knock her out, put her under my foot. Maybe even make her call me ma'am. Lord as my witness, I can't help myself.

Mama fix a meal and I watch over her, make sure she do it just right, you know. Little sprinkle of salt in this or that. Collards can't be cooked for too long. She ain't said nothing, but I think she know. She know I been pulling after Chess. Maybe soon he gone pull after me, cause he a man and can't go contrary to his nature. In the end, though, maybe Mama the one that get to bend over laughing. Cause I didn't really know what I was hankering after and she did. He come to me one night and just lay right on top of me. Don't say a word, just pull on up the covers and slid in. My heart gets to going quick—bang, bang, bang! All I can think is I want what ain't mine to have. But then I smell him. He sweating and I breathe it in. Something sour on his mouth and I feel like I'm gone get sick to the stomach right then and there, and I don't want his laughing mouth all over me. I push on him, but he don't get off. He bite me on my shoulder, humping tween my legs. Like that ain't enough, he pull his head back, open his mouth, and bite on me again like I'm a dog. I open my mouth too, screaming; not a word in my mouth, just a sound.

Chess act like he ain't heard a thing. He rub two fingers over my lips, not like he trying to shush me, though. They just ride my lips back and forth. He go still after a while and slide from the bed. Not get up, you know, pull back the cover and walk away, but slide down to the foot of the bed, like a rug that need to find the floor again. With my gown all pulled up and my legs thither and yon, I ask him right there, "What was that? What was it?" He don't even look back at me. He say, "It was nothing."

15

FIRST OF ALL, both of them got they hands on me. I can't get no peace with nobody. All of them fools. Cept my wife, God bless her. Even she was sometimes . . . Well, I ain't gone talk bad about the dead. Morning done gone crazy, watching me all the time. Liberty wants to fuck me one minute and then be my ma'am the next. And Queenie—I don't know bout Queenie. All that kid shit, sometimes I think that just show. Liberty love her better when she think Queenie can't wipe her own ass. Other times, I think she love her the way she is—a grown-ass woman who been six years old for twenty-five years. That first time we meet she was staring at me like she knew what I ain't told a soul—my daddy's thumb and the mouth it rubbed cross. I ain't never told Liberty, and I tell her damn near everything.

Some days, I don't get a taste for it, you know, a batch of love and hate cooked up all together; then other days I can't think of nothing else. That's why I let Queenie get to me the way she did. She kept after me like she didn't know what to do with herself. I wasn't gone pay her no attention, but then we was sitting in the kitchen together, not saying nothing, and I notice her mouth. Looked real good. You know how you can look at a thing, years and years' worth of looking, and then one day you catch a peek out the side of your eye and it turn brand new? That's what I saw, hurt and happy laying quiet on her mouth all at the same time. She just need somebody to push on it.

I reckon I couldn't help myself. Came to her in the middle of the night, and she was waiting on me. Bedclothes pulled down, legs open. It's dark and I can't see a thing, but her breathing showed me the way. Not a peep out of her, do you hear me? Cept for the shape of her mouth I could have been fucking the dead.

Anyway, maybe she flipped me all of a sudden and I fell out of bed. Knock the wind clean out of me. I almost laughed, curled there on the floor, pants round my ankles. But I don't say nothing. Struggle over to the door, and then she call out to me from the bed, "What was that? What was it?" What's a nigger spose to say? That's me trying to touch what my daddy did all them years ago? And I didn't know I could get it from you till I looked at your mouth? I wasn't gone tell her that's you and me passing over your mama, that's you and me shaming Morning and my dead wife. I knew even fore I was through that I ain't gone let Liberty and Morning go. I figure maybe I done her a favor, give her what her mama been trying to keep her from. But I don't know who broke her door like that. It wasn't fucking me.

16

SHO NOUGH, I broke Queenie's door. Broke it clean in two cause it let something pass that it shouldn't of. Liberty spend three nights helping Mable pack up and move to Chicago and she leave me in charge and look what happen. Chess walked out the bedroom and Queenie's in the room crying. Look after Queen Ester, she say. Stare at me real hard and put her hand on my cheek. If that ain't saying to watch out for Queenie, I don't know what is.

I owe Liberty, cause she help me out when I come to Lafayette and she ain't asked for a thank-you. I had this run-in with two white men when I was at this place, the Inn in Knoxville, Tennessee, picking up trash. One named Cowlie and the other one name I never did hear. They was talking about something like who's smarter than who. One of them

turned to me and said, "Well?" I was minding my own business; can't catch me staring in some white man's mouth.
"Excuse me?" Just like that. But him and his friend said,
"Well?" Now I can tell both of them mad cause they had to
repeat theyselves. "I ain't heard the question. What's the
question you done asked me?" I guess they must of thought
they heard sass, cause they hauled me outside and the one I
never caught the name of pulled a book out of his jacket the
size of the Bible and feed it to me, binding too.

I took fever after that, sick all the time. Peeing ink. Wasn't
no good for nobody for a while. But Liberty take me in and
get me well, though sometimes I think the curing was worse
than being sick. Mulberry leaves, sugar, turpentine, and hot
water. Like to kill me, but I swallowed it down. Liberty got
this way, make you liable to do just about anything to keep
her from being mad. Queenie can get that way too.

While I was mending I got to thinking. What in the world
them two men could of asked me? Whatever it was, I didn't
have no words for it. I figure can't no fight be had from just
yeah and sho nough. I laid in that bed getting well and figured them the last two words in the world that got trouble
streaked tween them.

Sho nough, I was right. That ain't to say folks can't come
up with some foolishness. Got me running here and there
with they wants. "Other, you come help me with these bags;
Other, gone go run this down to the boss man." But I say
this: I ain't never got into no trouble behind yeah and sho
nough. Cept till now. I was only gone for a second. Queenie
think I saw it all, but God as a witness that ain't true. Banky
ask me to go and pick up his baby girl and take her over to
her mama's, and by the time I get back, all I see is Chess
closing the door behind him. I should of saw Chess coming,

that way he always looking at a nigger when he think ain't nobody watching is some queer mess. And I swear Queenie been looking at him like she can't look nowhere else. Cut her eyes at Liberty every chance she get. So, yeah, I broke the door down.

17

SHE WALKED STIFFLY, passing her own boarded-up bedroom door, haphazard wooden shingles fastened to its frame, the nails protruding and bent. The door had let her down once but never again. It had been built up better, stronger, hers. Light-headed, she crept down the hall until she reached Chess's room, its door still ajar the way Helene had left it. Only inside those four walls could she feel safe. This place was a creation all her own, every object in it nowhere else but where she wanted it to be: the sewing machine in the corner, the rug rolled up next to the long counter table, a portable coffeepot turned on its head, the toaster and iron in the closet.

The only time Queen Ester had thought to fix the disarray was when she remembered Liberty's sickness and the filth that had taken hold in every room as Liberty had grown weaker. She always believed that illness hadn't taken her mother. Liberty had the power to say things and make them come into existence, the way God said Let there be Light and it was so; Liberty had decided to get sick, said "Let Me take Ill," laid down in her bed, and died.

Queen Ester dipped her fingers into the glasses filled with honey-sweetened water, adjusted the chairs and tables. Stooping, she grabbed the leg of the sewing machine and lifted it, finding the carpet underneath bright and shiny, unworn from exposure. She loved that spot, the place where time had no meaning. Reverently, she fingered the carpet.

Staggering to her feet, she approached the countertop, her hands outstretched as if even now she held the wood between her fingers and thumb. "Hello?" she said, nervous because she couldn't smell the softly sweet odor she was sure had been there, with the dead bodies. "Helene done shook something loose, and now here I am stuck with it all, too old to make room," Queen Ester said. She hadn't scared Helene senseless, she thought; in her own way had urged Helene to stay the way you force a mule to plow a straight line with a heavy hand, since if you make the mistake of being nice, stroking its hind end, cooing in its ear, the mule will eventually kick you in the chest.

She looked closely at the bottom edge of the counter, and where there should have been a leg there was nothing. Her eyes slammed against the blank wall behind the bar. Don't fret, Queen Ester told herself. I pulled the bar just so, I think. No, that's right. So maybe they is still behind there and I just don't see. But even if I pulled it—and I ain't saying I'm wrong—I should see them from right where I'm standing. Even from here I should be able to see something. Sweat spread across Queen Ester's chest, washing over her sunken breasts and dampening her housecoat.

"If they ain't here, where is they? Helene ain't carried nothing out with her." She held on to the counter. "Well, move in close so you can see if they is where you left them at." At last, she leaned her head over its edge to see the other side. They were gone. Even the depression where they had sat had vanished. Queen Ester shuddered. She believed what she had told Helene—"What being dead got to do with anything?"—but she knew they could not have gone anywhere without her.

Turning quickly, she fell, scraping her legs. On her hands and knees, Queen Ester tried to close her jaw, but the muscle beneath her chin was slack. Gripping the side of the bar, she pulled herself to her feet, her thoughts still clear, methodical. "Well, just where could they be at? Mama's room? Mine? Kitchen? Living room? What's that sliding? You hear that?"

She saw her left foot was limp and twisted as she dragged it toward the door. "That me?" She locked the door behind her. "All this time, I ain't never done up Chess's door. Well, ain't I a day late and a dollar short? Where to first, upstairs or down?" At the head of the stairs, she felt a draft, soft and insistent. "If that ain't wind, I ain't me," Queen Ester said, towing her foot behind her. "Here I am looking a mess with the front door wide open."

She took a first step, tripping again, and reached for the hallway carpet to steady herself. From where she leaned, she saw the walls curve and then Liberty's door curl itself into a bow before her eyes. The bow looped itself into hands, feet, legs, black men, some of whom were equipped with unflagging strength and could triumph over rivers and railroads. A woman paced back and forth on a dirt-packed floor, clutching at a handbag crammed with camisoles and undershirts, desperation and desire. Shaking hands wrapped themselves around a Colt revolver and blew a hole in a chest, big enough for a fist to fit through. The draft blew harder and the door creaked. "Sweet Jesus," Queen Ester gasped, stretching with both hands to touch the wooden doorframe, wheezing. "Sweet Jesus."

18

THEY CRASHED TOGETHER in the dark toward
Queen Ester's house. Her hand inside the crook of his arm,
Helene squinted to see Other push back an overgrown branch
as if he were pulling out a chair for her. All the while she
kept up a chant of words. "At first, I didn't know why I came.
I mean I knew I wanted Mama, just to look at her and not
be pulled away by someone. But it wasn't just that. I could
have driven down here and sat inside my car and stared at
Mama to my heart's content. But I wanted to know what was
going on down here, why everyone seemed to stand in our
way." She panted while they tramped on. "You know, when
I saw Mama today she seemed happy to see me? She said
hello as if she meant it and then we sat down and I didn't
have to tug at her for a thing. She just spilled out her life,

although she lied about my daddy. Whoever he is, he's dead. That's what I want to tell her now. Whoever he is, Duck or Chess, he's dead. Aunt Annie b's dead and Grandma too. Everybody's dying on me and I can't do a thing about it."

She stopped. "You hear that? I did it again. I sound like Mama. I sound southern," Helene said. They were running now, stepping lightly over underbrush and around branches that stuck out from trees like tables. "This morning——" She stopped again, amazed that it was only this morning when she had woken up with the scowl of sleep and the only weight she had carried was her curiosity. "This morning——" She tried to remember. Am I old or tired or crazy? she thought. Maybe all three, and that's why I'm out here running in this country darkness to who knows where. "Other? Other, you still here?"

"Yeah."

"Don't," she said, anger in her voice. They ran side by side, clutching on to each other. "Don't do that. Say something else, okay?"

"Sho nough." Helene pulled hard at his shirt, dragging her feet till they stopped.

"Don't, Other. I need you to talk to me. You have to say no sometimes. I think sometimes people don't know what they are until they say no to something or break something over their knee."

Because they were in the dark, Helene didn't see Other's face crack and fill with words, as it had when her mother barked at him—"You say it, you say it, you"—in the upstairs hallway. Helene didn't know what she was asking for; her words were just there to chase away the loneliness of her voice out in the wilderness. Maybe, had Helene seen the rage that her mother had seen, maybe she too would have said, "No, boy, you forget that, cause I'm gone to."

"That's what you plan on doing?" Other spoke suddenly. "Breaking your mama over your knee? Because you can, you the only one left that can do it. Break her right in half if you have a mind to." His words, brimming with disapproval, split the night. "I know you. I was there in the yard with Chess, with that piece of candy hanging out of your mouth. I was there when Mable handed you over to Annie b. You want to come in your mama's house and make her lay down. Shame on you, girl. She's so weak she can't hurt a soul even if she wanted to, and you want her to stir up an old ache, just so you can see for yourself. And why? Because you're the daughter? You think you got a right to know? Queenie ain't the only fool in your family. You a fool too. Fool to come down here and try to make your mama mind. Who are you to make an old woman lick at a hurt she's been trying to forget some twenty-odd years? Who are you, Helene?"

"Hello? Hello?" Queen Ester said, tugging her limp leg behind her like luggage. Where had they gone? Well, they sho ain't downstairs taking tea and laughing over biscuits, she thought. Two bodies couldn't get very far without someone to help them along. Maybe Helene come back and I ain't seen her.

"Helene?" She turned, straining to hear any small scrap of sound. "Helene?" she called out again. A light thump echoed in the corner, the same dark nook where she had shaken Other, daring him to say what he had seen. "Helene? That you, girl?" She heard the sound a second time. "Helene, that's you, ain't it? You can't be coming in here, messing with my house. What you do with them two? You hear me? Lord Jesus, you gave me a fright. Come on out of that corner." Something thumped again. "All right, you get on out of there. Making all that racket."

Helene stepped out of the bend in the hallway, arms outstretched, accusatory, the way she had been when she ran up to the one room Queen Ester had not let her see.

"What's in the room, Mama?" Her daughter's voice shook the house. Queen Ester trembled. "You know what's in the room. You done saw it yourself."

"What's in the room, Mama?" Helene said again, and this time she moved. She stood inches away from Queen Ester, her manner wild, frenzied. "What's in the room?"

Queen Ester shouted, afraid of her daughter, who seemed poised to strike. Queen Ester clapped her hands over her ears, now yearning for quiet, and Helene vanished.

"Well, I'll be. She wan't never here, that's why her hair looked so nice," Queenie mumbled, not frightened by Helene's ghost but, rather, happy that her daughter's shadow was able to step out of dark corners or maybe even closets. Without an ounce of pushing on Queen Ester's part, Helene had moved into her mother's house. All things considered, she thought, that ain't so bad. Ain't got to press on her to stay, cause she already here.

Queen Ester advanced, a slow shuffle, listening for something that might be two bodies walking in an old house. "Where is they? Chess and Mama both having crackers and sardines somewhere." I done made a good-looking girl, she thought, the hair parted just so and curled up at the end. Not a ribbon in sight but good-looking just the same. My baby sho looked good coming out of the dark like that. Queen Ester threw open the door to her own room and it was as if the three of them, Liberty, Chess, and Helene, were waiting for her quietly, not the ghost of her child but the loveliness of Helene's hair; not the shot but the thumb; not the leaving but the door flung ajar; not the violation but the words said directly thereafter; not the father but the Mary Jane dripping from a child's mouth.

The wild grass stood almost thigh-high. Only the sharp report of branches snapping in two broke the quiet. Helene played back Other's words, this time slowly shifting through, because something he said tasted bitter. I didn't ask Mama to lick at an old hurt, did I? Mama never said, Don't ask because it may knock me down. I never pulled on her, never. I don't care what he says. Maybe I wanted to, but wanting and doing sit on opposite sides of the road. I didn't shake her, make her lick an old hurt. She was talking before I stepped on the porch, and that's the heaven's truth. But that doesn't account for the bad taste on my tongue.

They ducked together under a branch Other could not move and, untucking her head, Helene remembered what he had said—I was there when Mable handed you over to Annie b—which opened a bottomless dive of questions: Who gave me to whom? Where was Mama when I was handed over? Was my daddy already dead, and if he (if Duck was my daddy) had already passed, why did Aunt Annie b and Uncle Ed come out here only when I was born?

No longer chest-to-chest with Chess (her father, hers, hers) in the middle of the yard, a five-year-old Helene stood next to Liberty, not tall enough to reach her grandmother's knee.

They were on the porch and the deep rolling voice she had always thought was Uncle Ed's came out of her grandmother, washing over her.

"Yeah, this your house, baby girl, more yours than anybody, cause here, right inside the door, right upstairs, you was born." Liberty's hand slid from Helene's head to her chin. "Your ma'am push something fierce to get you out. She sure did, and when she got to hollering she scared me bad. Didn't know what to do; and if you know your granny, which you don't cause you too young, you know that Granny always know what to do. I walked up and down the hallway, without a clear thought in my head. And that ain't never happened to me. At least not since I been grown." Liberty laughed, and the five-year-old Helene lapped up the sound. "You the only one born in this house. Now what about that? Ain't that something?"

Liberty suddenly crouched, scooping the child up in her arms. "I told myself I wasn't never gone kiss some little thing under the neck, but here I go. You want some sugar from your granny?" Helene, frightened because she felt she was on the verge of being devoured, nodded dumbly. Liberty felt Helene stiffen in her hands and turned mean. "When somebody ask you something, you say yes, ma'am or no, ma'am, not shake your head like you some dummy. B been keeping you in a barn?"

"No, ma'am."

"Now, you want some sugar from your granny or don't you?"

"Yes, ma'am."

"All right, then. Raise your head up." Liberty slowly touched her lips to Helene's exposed neck and the child, feeling her grandmother's wide mouth and the tiniest bit of her tongue, erupted in laughter. With the laugh, Helene tickled Liberty's nose, so she shook along with the child.

"My, my, my," she said, when she had caught her breath. She lifted Helene high in her arms. "You is a pretty one, that a fact. Sure is. You want to come live with me?" Helene, still laughing, didn't hear the question, so Liberty repeated it. "Say, baby. I asked you if you want to come live with your granny."

There was no pause. The child's voice turned breathless. "Yes, ma'am. Yes, yes!"

Liberty heard the desire, and she put Helene down. "What you say?"

Helene, still panting from the laughter and her grandmother's tongue on her neck, spoke louder this time. "Yes, Granny. I mean, yes, ma'am."

Liberty stepped back, wrinkling her nose as if a bad smell rose from the child. Her voice swelled rapidly to a crescendo of anger. "Somebody come get this baby girl. Ya'll need to go home. Now." She fled inside the house, closing the door behind her. Helene heard a battle of hushed voices.

"I know a lot, you think I'm a fool. Lord know what you two carrying on down here," Annie b hissed.

"All right, b, enough of all that," Ed said.

"I think you better watch for your mouth when you in somebody's house."

"You think cause you bigger than me, I'm gone run off scared?"

"I don't want you to be scared, Miss b."

"You and your girl up to something."

"B, now——"

"Shut up, Ed. You got Queenie upstairs, but I been up there to see, and even with the sheets covering her she look strong as a ox."

"I done already told you she take sick from time to time."

"My eye."

"Your brother told me he want his little girl to be with you-all."

"Who say, you?"

"You calling me a lie?" Their voices grew louder.

"All right, the both of you," Ed broke in. "She ain't deaf. She right outside the door."

"I know it, I left her there." Liberty's words strained against decorum.

"I'm telling you, Ed, that girl healthy as a horse. They live in this big old house without a care in the world. So why come we the ones taking care of that little girl, just tell me that?" Had they known that the same little girl had stopped trying to sort through the adult argument and turned her attention to meddling with the hem of her dress, her small fingernails tugging at brown thread, perhaps they would have raised their fists along with their voices.

So I knew the story all along, Helene thought. I'm too late to change a thing. Why did I come in the first place? What I thought I wanted I already had. If that doesn't beat all. So why am I here? Because I wanted to make Mama laugh and feel blessed to have a daughter like me. Because I wanted Mama to lick at a hurt she's been trying to forget for some twenty-odd years.

Other pulled back the last bush, and together they stepped into the yard as if they had emerged from behind a curtain. The house looked not only empty but dead. The water pump had vanished in the dark, and night had dulled the flaking whitewash to gray. The house's wayward tilt, which

Helene once had thought made it look to be fleeing, now reminded her of mourning. All the lights were out—whatever her mother was doing, she didn't need a lamp. They stood for a moment at the edge of the yard, taking big gulps of black air.

"What is she doing in there?" Helene whispered. There was no flutter of curtains this time as she climbed to the porch with Other. The door opened directly with a creak and Queen Ester came out, a green scarf thrown over her head, patches of gray hair poking out from beneath it. Behind her the house was dark as a cavern. Spit ran down from her mother's lip and she clutched at the fabric of her housedress, pulling it up to her thigh.

She's sick, Helene thought, and I left her here by herself. "Mama?" she said, her arms out and reaching. "Mama?"

But Queen Ester did not move, stood firmly in the doorway. "Mama, let's go in the house and turn some lights on," Helene said, but Queen Ester continued to block the entrance.

"Listen."

"Mama, what do you hear?" Helene peered into the dark. "Wait, wait, I've got a tissue in my bag." She groped around inside her purse. "Here. Let me wipe your face." Pulling out a crinkled tissue, she gently wiped away the spit. "See? Isn't that better?"

"You think she left the radio on?" Queen Ester said.

"I don't know." Helene grabbed Queen Ester under the arm, surprised by her mother's feebleness. "Let's go inside and turn on a lamp. Remember that lamp you showed me? Does it work?"

"Maybe she left the radio on," Queen Ester suggested again.

"Mama, did you leave the radio on?"

"Naw, our radio quit working, I don't know when."

"Oh." Helene moved a bit closer. "Come on, let's go inside."

"You act like you don't hear all that."

"Hear what?"

"All that noise." She sounded younger suddenly, incredulous at Helene's deafness. "You sure you don't hear it?"

"No, Mama. No."

Queen Ester cackled loudly, and for a moment Helene thought perhaps all this time her mother had just been sleeping and had now woken up, mad as ever. "Well, look here." Queen Ester noticed Other, who stood silently next to Helene. "Yes, sir. Here come the messenger. Dropping off what's mine. You good at that, ain't you? Ain't that right?"

"Yeah," Other said.

"You get out of here! You hear me?"

"Sho nough." Other backed away.

"I want you off my porch!"

"Mama, please." Helene stretched out her hand to Other, but he moved beyond her reach, walking backward. More than nervous, he saw Queen Ester's face and remembered her rage years earlier in the dark of the hallway.

"See you soon, Helene," Other said. Without a word, Queen Ester pulled Helene into the house, followed by the moonlight.

"I don't know what you did, but I got to find them."

"What are you talking about now, Mama?" Helene spoke quickly, glancing in the direction of the stairs.

"You know what. Mama and him. They gone."

"Mama, I think we should get you——" The crash of glass

shattered the quiet in the room as Queen Ester knocked over a vase. "Mama?" Helene stumbled in the dark, her hands out in front of her, searching for a chair or a table to brace herself against. "Damn it, Mama. We need to get you——"

"Get me to where? I'm telling you they gone, just up and gone, and I can't find them nowhere." Her voice lifted, shrill and plaintive. "You hear all that racket? Helene, you hear it, don't you?" Helene moved toward the sound of her mother's voice.

"Gotcha!" Helene said with triumph. She clapped her hands on Queen Ester's shoulders. "Come on."

"Let go now," Queen Ester said evenly, not bothering to struggle under her daughter's heavy grip. Helene tried to pull her toward the pool of moonlight in the front hallway. "Helene, stop on that."

"Mama, damn it, I said come on!" She maintained her hold on her mother's shoulders.

"Helene, didn't I tell you to stop on that? Let your mama go, fore you hurt her." Her tone was pleasant, as if she had asked Helene to put away a toy or come down for dinner. "You done got yourself riled so, you liable to take off and hurt your mother, then it'll be too late."

"Don't turn all mama on me suddenly. Not now."

They stood shoulder to shoulder, equals. You still mine, I'm still Mama, Queen Ester thought, groping for the words to make Helene knuckle under her control. "I ain't never wanted you no place but here. It was Mama——"

Helene felt buttery and mean. "Goddammit, Mama, what were you all doing in this house?"

"Ain't nobody done a thing."

It was Queen Ester's innocence that triggered Helene's

fury. "Maybe. Maybe nobody else has done a thing, but I will, Mama. This, it's all got to end." What had always worked so well for her grandmother—unstoppable rage with a dash of mad planning—took hold of her, and with nothing but the moonlight she fished in her purse, pulling out her personal cache of old hurt. Letter after letter fluttered to the floor as the pages flew out of her purse like a deck of cards. I'll regret this, Helene thought. Later she would remember that she hadn't even trembled when she scratched the match to life. A tongue of fire lit up her mother's face and licked the side of the Valentine card, leaving a black scorch mark.

"You quit that! You got no right! No right!" Queen Ester's hand struck out at the burning letter, sending it to the floor. Instantly, the room flared into bright orange as the Valentine card latched its blaze to the other letters. Fire ate up the grocery lists written at Christmas, the one-sentence scraps, the heavy bond paper. Queen Ester crashed her foot down on the carpet, but the small fire leapt from under her house shoe, curling around the sole. The feeble kicking split the flame in two, and now one tongue snaked toward the couch while the other ran over the carpet and edged toward the curtains. "I'll get that bucket on the porch," Helene shouted.

She let go of her mother, raced out of the living room to the back of the house, and found the water hose, knotted behind the washer. Filling the bucket, she dragged the large copper basin through the kitchen. Helene smelled the blaze before she saw it. In the minute she had been gone, the flames had slid under the couch, caught at the netting, and were consuming the sofa stuffing. Fire engulfed the living room, the walls were burning up, fed by ancient dry wallpaper.

Blinded by a sudden sea of smoke, Helene called for Queen

Ester, but besides the chewing of fire she heard nothing. "Where the hell is Other?" she wailed, watching the fire suck at the plywood. For a moment it seemed as if it might sputter out of its own accord. The orange glow dimmed, and she saw black fingers spread across the length of the wall.

"Mama!" Helene yelled. "Mama, where are you?" She became frantic, unable to see Queen Ester, and ran back into the kitchen. As she called out again, she lifted the curtain to the pantry but found nothing. The back porch, Helene thought, she's probably outside waiting for me. She dashed to the door and pulled, stunned to find it locked. What the hell was going on? Her mother couldn't have locked the door from the inside and be outside at the same time. Helene's stomach lurched as she heard the hollow clatter of her sandals taking her into the hallway, her voice desperate.

"Come on, Mama! Mama!" The flame had poured down the length of the hallway, blocking the stairs from the front door. Now fire leapt from the first floor windows; the silvered blue curtains burned to ashes. Helene jumped through the fire to the front door, but this time she didn't try to open it; the large bolt told her it was locked. She heard Other banging furiously outside on the porch. "She locked the door!" Helene rattled the lock latch, her sweaty hands slipping on the latch. She tried to undo it, once, twice, the third time her hand steadied, and between Other pushing and her pulling, the door swung open. "Is Mama out there?"

"Naw." Other grabbed Helene's arms, pulling her off the porch into the swept yard, and together Helene and Other watched the house heave and shudder as the fire ate at its walls. Just before flames swallowed the roof, Helene thought she saw Queen Ester standing in the blackened doorway, her housedress unsinged. "There she is!" Helen was sure she saw her mother lift her hand and smile the way she had when she spoke about Liberty's walk. Then Queen Ester turned, vanishing in a cloud of smoke at the bottom of the stairs.

"She came out of the front door, her hair all wild—I don't know what happened to that green scarf she had on. All I could think was God I had to get her out of there. I just wanted to get her out of the house. She said that something was talking to her. You should have heard her.

"Thank you," Helene said, as Ed handed her his clean handkerchief. "I didn't know what to do. I couldn't hear a thing and Mama sounded so sure."

Ed kept his thoughts to himself, taking in his niece's hair that stood on end, her blackened clothes, the soot coating her skin. She looked just like her mother when Annie b had kicked her off their doorstep so many years ago. At any moment he expected Helene to race out the front door and hoot at the moon. All this havoc in just one day, and she wants to tell me the shape of her mother's hair. These women, Helene's family (and, yes, they were hers), could only act askance. The three of them—one dead, the next disappeared to who could say where, the last too young to know that with family no one ever escapes—all lived inside a bright fluttering innocence that allowed them to break souls in two without a thought in their heads. Ed bottled a weary sigh. Some lives should just be swallowed whole without being tasted.

"Maybe I would have been worse off, you know, if I really could have held their lives in my hands, known them all from end to end. Don't you think I'm better off, not having lived all that trouble?" Her uncle's face told her that he, and she, were unconvinced. She remembered, wrenching out of Other's grip, leaving him to stand alone in the yard and watch the flames eat the roof. Despite the woods and its darkness, she ran a clean line to her car while chanting, "Maybe I'm the better off. Maybe I'm the better off."

About the Author

APRIL REYNOLDS teaches literature and crea-
tive writing at Sarah Lawrence College. Her short
stories have appeared in numerous anthologies,
among them *Mending the World* and *The
Heretics Bible*. *Knee-Deep in Wonder*, her first
novel, received a Zora Neale Hurston/Richard
Wright Foundation Award for unpublished work.
April Reynolds lives in New York with her husband.